THE WORLD OF WILLIAM CLISSOLD

(Παντα ῥει).

II.

A

THE WORLD OF WILLIAM CLISSOLD

BOOK THE THIRD

The Story of the Clissolds—Essence of Dickon

BOOK THE FOURTH

The Story of the Clissolds—Tangle of Desires

London
ERNEST BENN LTD.
Bouverie House Fleet Street
1926

081

PRINTED IN GREAT BRITAIN

BOOK THE THIRD

THE STORY OF THE CLISSOLDS—ESSENCE OF DICKON

THE STORY OF THE CLISSOLDS—ESSENCE OF DICKON

THE SECTIONS

MY brother Dickon was physically very like my father, but he had a sturdier quality of mind. His imagination was as bold, but his self-restraint was steadier. Both of us indeed were honest to a greater degree; our consciences were livelier and more watchful, the sense of an obligation incurred gripped us more firmly and did not so readily slip its hold. Some ancestor of marked integrity must have been latent in my father. We were both mainly Clissold, but physically Dickon was nearer to my father than I. He was a better-looking youngster. He had my father's reddish hair and something of his physical swagger, while I mingled threads of my mother's darkness with streaks of paternal gold.

Dickon, I have told, professed individualism, but he has always been a very sociable individualist; I was an unsocial Socialist from the outset, with a greater disposition to go alone or with one companion. Clara once said that Dickon was canine and I was feline, and I think that expresses something very elemental between us. Dickon's pink skin freckles at a mere glimpse of the sun, and he has carried my father's sanguine amplitude of limb and body to a considerable massiveness. He is now, in fact, a very fine figure of a man indeed, a stout tweed-wearing man, " Nordic," they would say in America.

In the preceding Book I brought the account of Dickon and myself up to the later "eighties," when we were studying science very unevenly at the Kensington schools, and considering our attack upon the world. Then I went off on the trail of Marx and the economic history of the world. I left Dickon at loose ends.

He did not long remain at loose ends. It was at night in a show called the Inventions Exhibition, while we were sitting watching a crowd of promenaders and listening to a band, beneath festoons of fairy-lights—little oil lamps they were—and in front of a grass plot on which yet other fairy-lights, blue, red, and orange, made a flickering guttering enchantment, that Dickon's ends ceased to be loose and he unfolded to me his plan of campaign. It was to be his life's plan of campaign, but I believe that it had crystallised out in his mind only that afternoon.

That Inventions Exhibition was one of a series of annual shows; there was one called the Healtheries and another the Fisheries, and others, in what was then a great area of waste land in South Kensington. Now most of that land is filled up by the Imperial Institute and by Museum galleries and buildings belonging to London University, but in those days these exhibitions were able to spread from the Exhibition Road to the Albert Hall, the upper galleries of which building were somehow included in the spectacle. These grounds were put in order and laid out with beds of geraniums and calceolarias; they were illuminated in the evenings, and the Exhibition was favoured by a succession of fine summer nights.

It would be interesting now to disinter the plans and guide-books, if any copies survive, to that Inventions Exhibition. It was before the coming of the safety bicycle or the automobile; the gas-lamp still held its own quite hopefully against the dangerous uncertainties of the electric light, and gramophones, cinemas, wireless had hardly germinated in the womb of time. The germs existed, but nothing had come to exhibition pitch. I remember some very attractive omnibuses, driven by compressed air, wallowing to and fro in a confined space. They were the only anticipation of automobiles in the show, and I remember, too, how Dickon that afternoon doubted whether electric traction could ever be anything more than a scientific toy. It might be done, he said, but it could never be done to pay.

Yet what we had seen had stimulated our imaginations considerably, and while we listened to the band in the evening after a frugal supper, we were both much more prepared to expect great changes during our lifetimes than we had been when we pushed through the turnstiles in the early afternoon. Our talk had ebbed for a time and we were smoking unaccustomed cigarettes which Dickon had made with a machine for the occasion.

"It is no good inventing things if you do not get people to make use of them," said Dickon, coming up to the surface, so to speak, after a profound meditation.

"No," said I, not in the least aware of his drift.

"There's no money in anything until people have been told of it."

" The money?"

" No," contemptuously, " the anything."

I perceived that he was taking up his standing problem of " how to get it " again. " I suppose new things have to be sold," I said.

" Exactly. And you have to make people *want* them."

A pause.

" Advertisement," said Dickon. " Advertisement is only beginning. Billy!—I see it. That's where my money is. Advertising."

The distant band was playing a waltz tune just then, for I remember the rhythm of it. (Tra-la-la la pum pum, pum pum. Tra-la-la la pum pum, pum pum. Tra-la-la la pum, pum, pum pum. Tra-la-la-La pum pum, pum pum, it went. Am I filling in detail from my imagination or was it the Blue Danube waltz?) And the promenaders passed, keeping step to it; mysterious, romantic promenaders, for the fairy-lights were not enough to show their faces plainly.

With something of the manner of an explorer, the voice at my side began to talk of the dark and dismal advertisement of that time and to point out its defects and its possibilities. I understood now why he had been so silent and preoccupied throughout the afternoon. He had been reading all the advertisements in sight and thinking about them. He had been struck by their limitation of range; their crudity and formality; their inapplicability to the sale of new devices. A realisation of unworked opportunities close at hand had struck him dumb at first, and was now moving him to speech. He began to talk of advertisement, and to the best of my recollection he talked of advertisement for the next year or so.

That evening I had a lecture on the things advertisers did and the things they failed to do. It was delivered with the dogmatism proper to an elder brother, and with a note of reprehension as though I had in some way participated in the negligencies of the commercial world. I said little, and what I said was brushed aside or crushed. I did what I could to find excuses for backward and unskilful advertisers and was soundly scolded for their sins.

I recall the feeling rather than the substance of his outpourings. I remember that after a time we got up from our seats and walked about the grounds, and Dickon was still weighing pros and cons; we went into the more or less deserted exhibition galleries, and he held me remorselessly before silent exhibits and denounced the futility of their appeals. He was still at it as we made our way at the close of the exhibition, with other *jusqu'au-bout*-ists, along a tiled subway that echoed to our feet and led to the Metropolitan station.

"Look at that thing!" he would cry. "Look at that *silly* thing! What's the good of sticking that here?"

I recall distinctly my agonised protest. "Damn it! *I* didn't put it there!"

It restrained him not at all.

In the small hours he was sitting up in bed. "Advertisement, Billy," he said. "Advertisement! And the School of Mines may go and blast and burn and fuse

and run itself to Jericho. The Voice has reached me,
Billy! Come over and help us! The Hoardings call
to me, the Magazines are moaning, and I come. I
come."

"Oh, *shut* up, Dickon! Good-night!" I said, pulling the bed-clothes over my ears.

He dropped his work at the School of Mines almost
immediately; he made no pretence of finishing off his
term, and for some weeks he divided his waking time
almost equally between an intensive study of advertising
methods and brooding in Kensington Gardens upon
his course of action. His first definite step was to go,
after a very careful and elaborate preliminary exploration of the special field in question, to an advertising
watchmaker in Cornhill, to get an interview with him,
and tell him why his watches were not selling nearly
so well as they might do in the West-end, in various
suburbs, among the City clerks, in the East-end, and
what he thought might be done to stimulate their sale.
He had brought notes and sketches of almost all the
advertisements the firm was using, and very politely
and clearly he pointed out how stereotyped was their
appeal and how mechanical their distribution. He
convinced his hearer of advertisements going to waste
and reaching nobody here, and of areas neglected there,
and in the end he was allowed to make a scheme for
a more scientific campaign. Hitherto the work had
been done in an almost routine fashion from the office.
His scheme was accepted. It succeeded, and his path
in life was open before him.

§ 2

I DO not know whether it was luck or some mysterious flair that made Dickon pitch upon Milton for his first attempt, but I doubt if he could possibly have chosen better. Milton liked him from the outset; and with Milton, Dickon at the ripe age of one-and-twenty fixed up his first contract and began pushing Milton's Silver Guinea by the score, by the hundred, by the thousand, into the waistcoat pockets of the middle-class. Faster than Milton could assemble his watches Dickon assembled his customers. That was only a little while before the mass production of watches was fully under way. Milton's watches, I fancy, came in whole or in part from Switzerland. And when presently the Waltham watches came, ticking very loudly from across the Atlantic, Dickon made a brave and successful fight for Milton for some years, with "Milton's Silent Silver Guinea; each personally tested, numbered, and individually guaranteed."

In the end Milton left the field of popular sales and became a professor of quality. Milton's Limited now sell "watches that are beautiful and intimate," but Dickon still steers the bulk of the output along the path of assertive veracity to the grateful customer. Only last summer I discovered him in his smoking-room at Dorking meditating profoundly over Milton's current advertisement in *Punch,* a most gentlemanly affair.

"Do you remember Milton's in the old days, Billy?" he said, handing it to me.

"Rather."

"Changed since then. The money I've brought these people! Used to be cheap stuff."

I considered the page of *Punch*. I know of no other periodical whose advertisements so exactly catch the tone of the morning-room of a good West-end club.

"There are times," he reflected, "when I almost think of buying a Milton. . . . Beautiful and intimate. . . . They seem to be first-rate watches."

§ 3

MILTON'S was only Dickon's point of departure. A great light had come to him, and for a time he saw life wholly as a field of action in which he was to create appetites in people for commodities they had never in the least desired hitherto, or to direct their attention to the great superiority of common necessities when they are labelled distinctly with a proprietor's name.

Immense wealth lay in convincing people that an article could hardly be considered to exist unless it was vouched for by a respectable firm. In the days of our youth an enormous number of things were sold anonymously that are now sold under the brands of makers and packers. Our father had been one of the pioneers in this christening of goods with his Partington's Packet Teas. When I was a child every grocer had his own sorts of tea, his tea-chests with different qualities, and he weighed the tea out and packed it up for each customer. I can remember seeing that done. Almost everything he sold them—bacon, butter, lard, pickles, jams, biscuits—he sold from stocks of his own buying on his own individual reputation. He had pickled onions and cabbage in a great tub, as they still have them here in France. He used to display sugar-loaves in his window and chop them up in his shop; I would gaze fascinated at the sugar chopping in the Duxford grocer's. And the oilman sold his own lamp oil, and no one asked where he got it. Mustard used to be bought for Mowbray at the chemist's.

But even in our childhood there was already a number of vigorous firms reaching their hands over the retail tradesman's shoulder, so to speak, and offering their goods in their own name to the customer. As an infant I used to love a particularly fascinating Oriental who infested the back pages of magazines, pouring stuff into the mouth of a forked fish in the interests of Nabob Pickles. He seems to have vanished utterly. Colman's Mustard insisted already upon being the only English mustard. It just stuck up its name in bright letters—everywhere. I do not know if it ever became the only mustard, or if there are other mustards now. There was also a " Keen's Mustard." Is " Keen's " still with us? " English " mustard that is—there are all sorts of other mixings here in France. But I saw yesterday in the window of an *épicier* in Grasse neat little tins of Colman's, with the same vivid yellow ground and the lettering I remember spelling out from a train window in my childhood. If it is not the only English mustard everywhere, it is certainly that here.

Then there was soap. The great firm of Pears in those days had already thrust an individuality upon soap. *Pears' Soap* marks an epoch; I hope history will not neglect it. It was advertised with an unprecedented swagger; there were magazine and newspaper articles about how the firm did it; Pears bought Academy pictures by R.A.'s to reproduce in a sort of facsimile, gilt frame and all, and were among the first of all advertisers to be funny and laugh at themselves. Harry Furniss did a picture in *Punch* of a dirty tramp writing a soap testimonial : " Two years ago I tried Pears' Soap; since when I have used no other." They secured it and made a great thing of it.

These and a hundred other siren voices had called to me from wall and hoarding and printed page from my childhood up, but it was only now that Dickon was talking about them that I gave them more than a casual attention. I had never yet stirred up a restaurant by demanding Nabob Pickles and rejecting all inferior imitations, nor refused mustard until I was reassured by a sight of the Colman tin; but now I began, if not to clamour, at least to watch and discriminate under Dickon's critical guidance. He was grappling with a multitude of curious problems, and he insisted upon discussing them with me to the exclusion of every other subject.

" You see, Billy, you help me. The things you say— not much in themselves but they give me ideas."

Queer amusing problems some of them were. Cocoa had come into English life, and a number of firms were struggling to monopolise the market, among them

Van Houten, probably a Dutch firm, and Epps and Cadbury. I do not know if Rowntree's came then or later; I fancy they were never very deeply in the cocoa fight, but only came in later with chocolate, but I may be wrong about that. Dickon was making a careful comparison of their different methods. *"Epps' Cocoa, Grateful and Comforting,"* Dickon would repeat. "Wonderful words. Wonderful! Genius in them. . . . Billy, do you think *any* of these cocoas are the least bit different from the others?"

So earnest were our researches that we tried them to see. We sipped our cocoa and regarded each other with grave, inquiring faces.

These were purely English firms, I suspect. The battle of the cocoas, if it was fought in America at all, was probably fought under other names. I doubt if any commodity straddled the Atlantic in those days.

Another of our investigations was an attempt to discover why there was no advertising campaign for a salt or a pepper to put beside the omnipresent clamour about mustard. We never got to the bottom of the pepper problem. We decided that an opportunity was being lost there. "Harvester's Black Pepper Stimulates and Enlivens without Harmful Mechanical Irritation" we believed would have driven nameless pepper from the cruet. White pepper could have been denounced as an effeminate powder. There could have been bright attractive pictures of a stomach curly and vigorous rejoicing in its strength under the cheering influence of " Harvester," and of another, lax as a dead slug, debased by common white. Salt, common salt, we guessed, was deliquescent stuff to pack and handle; that was why no one touched it—except for Tidman's— was it Tidman's?—bath salt. Salt, for a proprietary sale, would have to be salt with a difference, we concluded, and we came very near to forestalling the dry table salts warranted not to cake into lumps, that presently appeared. "Cerebos," I think, was the leader.

I remember him sitting on the hard, wooden seat of a compartment in the dingy, dirty, sulphurous Underground Railway of those primitive times, with three or four magazines on the seat beside him, discoursing of the advertisements of a medicine called, if I remember rightly, "Owbridge's Lung Tonic." Always those advertisements were encircled by a monstrous O. "Now, why that O?" he demanded. "It individualises. It is also probably on the bottle. If there is any other lung tonic going, it serves to make the other fellow seem an undistinguished nobody. But does it make people want to take the stuff much? Does it do anything to catch the eye of consumptive people? Think of anyone with lung trouble and a cough. Suppose he had this advertisement on one side, and on the other side one that said quite quietly, 'Clissold's Lung Tonic soothes and gives peace. And in that peace you heal,' which would you want to try? Think of those words, Billy, not too big and noisy but put where they seem to catch the eye almost by accident! Just whisper it. *And in that peace you heal.*"

In that period there was a great clamour of pills and

proprietary medicines generally; I think they were far more vigorously pushed then than they are now. Hardly anything in domestic medicine that was not being dragged out of its anonymous phase in the prevalent research for big business in small things. It is natural that many people should experience a certain internal dullness on occasion, and require artificial animation. In the pre-Victorian days this was almost always supplied by homely remedies; castor oil which chastened and sweetened the soul, rhubarb pills and antibilious pills, Epsom salts, and, for the defenceless young, flowers of sulphur. One took these things and corrected oneself as a cat eats grass. But no philanthropist ever filled columns with the praises of these more immediate gifts from God. So they were thrust aside by Beecham's Pills, Worth a Guinea a Box (marvellous words, oh! marvellous words!), Eno's Fruit Salt, and a crowd of other highly named and vividly packed proprietary mixtures.

The age of the secret remedy, says Dickon, is drawing to an end. Advertisements of medicine decline. Not that people are giving up their resort to a tabloid or a cupful of something out of a bottle directly they feel out of condition, but they are more and more disposed to take known and specified drugs and preparations. This does not mean a return to the little chemist's scales and measures—in Britain the little chemist has been almost syndicated out of existence—but a development of the great-scale marketing of tabloids and capsules, made up to this or that prescription, by firms of manufacturing druggists. Dickon has been pressing manufacturing chemists to bolder and bolder advertisement for some time. He wants them to market attractive little medicine cases for dressing-bags. The ordinary citizen will then have his physic at hand, like a case of golf-clubs, to meet all occasions. He will play upon himself as a conductor plays upon his orchestra, summoning the drums, soothing the brass. Far more entertaining this will be than the tin-whistle solo of the old panacea. There will certainly be great changes of fashion in the contents of these cases, and the objective of the advertiser of the old-fashioned proprietary medicine will be more and more to get and keep a footing in the case; to ensure his position as a contributory instrumentalist, so to speak, in the internal symphony of the citizen. He will become like the advertiser of automobile accessories instead of a principal dealer.

But this is by the way. I was telling of the advertisements of London and the London press of forty years ago as I remember them. Even when they were not concerned with medicines they dealt largely with the comfort of the human interior. In addition to those things I have named, there was in my adolescence much propaganda of Cod Liver Oil; Elliman's Embrocation, always well advertised, flourished then as now; and the abolition of home-made beef-tea and mutton broth was beginning. Liebig's Extract of Meat was widely pushed, but I cannot now remember whether Bovril was already afloat; Oxo I am almost certain came later. We were to watch some pretty fighting presently over those meat extracts. The small tobacconist was still a single-shop adventurer, unaware of his approaching doom; he sold loose tobacco and cigars and matches and pipes and walking-sticks; the propaganda of cigarettes had scarcely dawned in those days. Cigarette smoking was a picturesque exotic habit that middle-aged people associated with Italy and Spain and the laxer morals of the south; one rolled a cigarette with a luxurious nonchalance and felt oneself a villain; the American machine-made cigarette was just creeping up by way of the shop-boy and art student. No one had heard yet of Russian cigarettes.

Besides these things I have named, and a few others at the same level which I have no doubt overlooked, there was really no very big and sustained advertisement going on at all. Big central drapery and provision stores had not yet learnt to advertise continually in the daily papers; many of them were still developing from moderate sized local shops in the footsteps of Nickleby's. Bicycles had not yet arrived, nor margarine, cereal foods, fountain pens, typewriters, kodaks, automobiles and all their accessories, and scores of other such things.

To compare one of the great American magazines, or even a modernised London weekly, with its equivalent of forty years ago, is an amazing revelation not only of the increased equipment of life nowadays, but of the continuous extension of strongly organised big businesses into what were then the trades and occupations of a great multitude of independent individuals. When I was young, England was far in front of America in the process, but American advertising has long since overtaken and outstripped anything we do on this side. France still follows us—now rather rapidly. Many of these big organisations seemed and still seem to be aiming at monopoly, but their sustained advertisement is the proof of their sustained sense of insecurity. Some have failed to achieve their object. Nobody has yet succeeded, for example, in replacing the small baker, though there have been various well-supported attempts; and cheese remains, like art, above all standardisation.

I suppose that, as far as provisions go, it helped greatly in the concentration of the distribution trade into big stores in England that so much of the food of the country was imported. The shipping of it necessarily accumulated it into bulk, and made bulky handling easy. And the fact that America and other new countries were exporting so much of their food production developed a collection at centres there, and so made concentration easy for them also.

It was after some rather unfruitful work for an advertising shoemaker that Dickon began to interest himself in the bicycle. Big-scale selling of boots and shoes, he said, would come a little later, when machine manufacturing was better developed, but the bicycle would not wait. The bicycle was here and now. So he jumped on to the bicycle and travelled some way on it. The more he inquired into this then fashionable toy, the more convinced he became of its future as a normal means of transport. First it would develop as a holiday amusement, and then it would cheapen down to the daily worker's needs. He attended early

shows and races and himself rode with some fury. He
was an early believer in the diamond frame which has
long since ousted all others. He was in bicycle advertising from the first, and he started one of the earliest
bicycling weeklies, the *Flying Wheel,* which he afterwards sold and which still survives in an incorporated
state. He made great efforts to organise the advertisement of wayside inns in cyclists' magazines. For a
time he was very keen indeed upon what he called consumers' magazines. The ordinary citizen, however,
refuses to accept the specialisation implied in a
specialised magazine. In the case of bicycles, motor-
bicycles, and automobiles, in the world of pet-fanciers
and photography, such publications have worked fairly
well, but they have never yet superseded advertising to
the general consumer.

Quite early in his novitiate as an advertiser, I remember Dickon pointing out to me the interesting conflict between the advertisements in what he called
Trade Papers and advertising to consumers. By Trade
Papers he did not mean the Trade Papers of such great
industries as iron and steel, but the Trade Papers of the
smaller distributor. These latter appeal to the retailer,
shop-keeper or hotel-keeper or whatever he may be,
and the goods advertised are often just those plausible
imitations against which the big advertiser is warning
his public. Often these less well-known goods are the
output of minor packers and manufacturers selling on
too small a scale for a public advertisement campaign,
but supplying a quite sound and honest article. These
typical Trade Paper advertisers want to sell their stuff

to the man behind the counter and not to the public; they are on his side against his big enemies, and they expect him to pit his personal recommendation against the pervading public advertisement. The retailers' Trade Paper was in fact, according to Dickon, not advertisement, properly speaking, at all, but anti-advertisement.

But for Dickon, I suppose, I should never have seen an inch below the superficial appearances of countryside commerce. But because of the education he has given me, I recognise still in every wayside advertisement, in every article in every shop, in the steep streets of Grasse here, and upon the highway through Magagnosc to Nice, in the patches of cultivation about me, and the inscriptions upon my wine bottle and mustard jar, the flying fragments, the living details of the great battle between small and big, between the standardising organisation and the huckstering individual, which is still a dominating aspect of human life to-day.

§ 4

ONE of Dickon's main discussions in those early days concerned what he called " media." A medium for him was anything you stuck your advertisement upon — a wall, a hoarding, a railway station, a landscape, a public conveyance, a book, a newspaper or other periodical. Or it might be an Exhibition or a Market Show. And then there was the house display, the shop-window, the imposing premises, the van. He invented for these primitive explorations

of what has since become, in America at least, the great
science of advertising, two beautiful terms, the *advertisand,* which was what you wanted to sell, and the
advertisee, who was the person you wanted to sell it to.
A good advertisement had to reach as many advertisees
as possible as inexpensively as possible; it had not only
to reach them but it had to create a buying desire for
the advertisand; it had not simply to do that, but it had
to make the route to the purchase clear and plain.
These were his criteria in his judgments on the advertisements we saw about us, and by this standard he
judged his "media."

He would weigh them against each other with
extreme gravity. Walls or hoardings lasted longer
than any daily or weekly periodical, and he went to
great pains to estimate the life of a poster; he would
even waylay and talk to bill-stickers. Enamelled metal
was already in use; sheets of that, he reflected, talked
for years. But they were difficult to place, and if there
was any need for a change of appeal they were hard to
recall. Also, they tired people by repetition.

"Imagine passing the same plaque every week-day
for a year! There's season-ticket holders have to.
Horrible, Billy!"

He was far in advance of the times in perceiving that
an advertisement should not bore; the advertisers of
those days sought strenuously to bore. He held also
that landscape should be respected; he believed that it
was very easy to arouse an antagonism to a commodity
by rude and blatant methods. He considered the advertisements he saw in stations and vehicles abominably

ill-done. They shouted where there was no need to shout. In those days railway advertisements were almost conscientiously ugly, and they vied with each other in the size of their letters. "No need for such an uproar, Billy—no need for it. You've got your people there—they're standing about and their minds are unoccupied. They're quiet and at your disposal. Ready to take an interest. Why bawl at them?"

He was the first to offer the public anything of length and interest to read upon a railway platform.

Yet he could be compact with the best of them when the medium required it. It was he who thought of advertisements on the risers of the staircases going up and down to railway stations, spaces hitherto neglected and mute. How well I remember the excitement of that novel idea, the weighing of considerations, the problem of who to take it to, the feverish hope of great developments. "It must be witty," said Dickon. "Short and witty. I won't have them just yapped at." To whom should he take it? For a time he hovered between a flea powder and a chewing gum.

It was in periodical publications that the greater future of advertising lay, he believed, and particularly in monthlies and weeklies. They were left about in the house and were turned over again and again by different people. "But advertisement must be fresh and different each time. This sort of thing——"

Yes, it was. I remember, that same conversation in the Underground Railway I am recalling, and he pointed to a standard announcement in the back pages of some monthly magazine.

"This sort of thing is as exasperating as hiccoughs. It comes up again and again and you can't control it."

He doubted whether the daily newspapers were very much good for proprietary articles. They were good for theatres and amusements of all sorts, but not for an advertisand that had to go on selling. He watched people reading papers in trams and buses. They showed a vulture's eye for the news they wanted and a wonderful capacity for sweeping disregardfully across the most tremendous displays of advertisement. He declared it was possible to print a newspaper advertisement so big that it was totally invisible. People would not read type that was visible three yards away. Their eyes went through the gaps.

"But any sort of stuff that has a quality of news— 'Salmon is exceptionally cheap to-day,' for example, with a reason for it, or 'Mackerel in the Channel and Oranges in the Bay,' would get them. *What* Bay? There you are! People would read that sort of thing like any other news."

He weighed that idea carefully. Fishmongering and fruit selling were still far from any syndication or he would have started a scheme for a "Fishmongers' Chalk Board" and a "Fruit Shop Bulletin" in some of the old dailies, a sort of eleventh hour announcement of goods to hand.

And as the grouping of shops into big centralised stores, which my father had done so much to promote, went on, Dickon became more and more keen on what he called bringing the shop window into the morning paper. In those days it was beneath the dignity of

the London *Times,* for example, to admit what are
called displayed advertisements or break its grave gray
expanses with pictures. The other papers in those
conservative days did not care to be very different from
The Times, and for a long time, indeed until the great
Americanisation of the press by Harmsworth and
Pearson, Dickon's idea remained an aspiration. Long
before it was done in England, the stores' advertisements
flared all over the American papers; there was an
interval of a quarter of a century or more before the
big London stores were brought into a similar intimate
relationship to the popular press.

How recent all this seems to a man of my age! I
remember when shop windows were made of little
oblong panes, and lit in the evenings by a few jets of
unassisted gas or an oil-lamp or so, and when the aim
of the window-dresser seemed to be rather to impress
the amount and nature of his stock upon the observer
than to interest and attract him. Then came plate-
glass and a depth and vastness of window-front hitherto
undreamt of, and gas-mantles and electric light. People
found a new interest in looking at the long array of
shop windows, and the enterprising heads behind them
realised by degrees—and there again my father with his
" Shopping and Social Centre of North London Life,"
was a pioneer—that it might be wise to allow people to
make a resort of the interior of their establishments
without being compelled, as they used to be compelled,
to make purchases forthwith or get out. But for a
long time the big stores were content with the local
crowds they assembled, and I believe it was Mr. Gordon

Selfridge, coming from America with the brightest and newest ideas, who at last realised my brother's anticipation and carried his shop window into the London daily paper.

My brother has a great admiration for Mr. Selfridge, and I have been privileged to meet him, an unobtrusive man with something of the shy quiet of a poet. My brother compares him to Mozart on account of his interest and variety. "He makes some of the older advertisers sound like the village idiot at a fair beating on a pan," said Dickon. "A great artist! Oh! a very great and subtle artist! Some day people will make collections of those Selfridge advertisements."

So it was Dickon developed. The lax and incidental student of pure science became the enthusiastic specialist in marketing, an active force in that change of scale in distributing methods which is one of the most striking aspects of my immediate world. He began as I have told, with watches and boots and the early bicycle. He extended his interests into the special journalism of the bicycle, and then into a great variety of magazine enterprises. He found helpers and confederates, associates with capital and partners. He has always had the gift of being liked, and, oddly enough, his name helped him. It gave people a shock to begin with, so that they always remembered it distinctly, and then as they got to know him they went about remarking upon the paradox of his sterling honesty. He always kept faith not only with what he said but with what he thought the other fellow understood by it. In a little time he was the essential partner of Clissold and Breakspear, and he had his active fingers in several of the most promising of the new popular magazine firms that were then appearing.

In six or seven years he was already very well off, able to marry and establish himself in a fine house in the Cromwell Road. Quite early he relinquished in my favour his share in the hundred and sixty pounds a year my mother allowed us, so that I could go and live in more comfortable apartments near to the Royal College and carry on as a research student there. He went eastward to a flat in Bloomsbury until his marriage brought him west again.

But of that marriage and of mine I must tell later.

§ 5

THERE drifts into my mind the substance of a silly little conversation that must have occurred somewhen in those old days before our divergent marriages had diminished our mutual familiarity. It was before my marriage anyhow, because I see Dickon in my only armchair as he talks, and there is a litter of notebooks and drawing material on the table.

He had been asking questions about the drift of my stuff and confessing himself baffled by it. " You're the brains of the family, Billy," he said a little ruefully. " Undoubtedly you are the brains of the family."

" Different brains," I said. " There is one glory of the sun and another of the moon and another of the stars."

"And another of the hoardings and magazine-covers," said Dickon—still a dozen years from sky-signs and twenty years from smoke-writing on the blue.

He fingered the pages of my first paper in the Philosophical Transactions, a tetter of formulæ, and then ran his eye over the rest of the contents.

"Blastopore of the snail," he objected. "Fancy poking about at the blastopore of the snail! It's—indelicate. And cryo-hydrates! This chap Oliver Lodge seems to be all over them. Wonder what they are! Well, this is your affair, Billy. It's up to you to display the name of Clissold properly in these Philosophical Transactions. If that is the end of life. Not my pitch. Not in the least my pitch. I wouldn't try to sell even a stethoscope through these Philosophical Transactions. No."

He ran his hand over the edges of the pages with a shuddering sound and reflected profoundly. A liveliness became apparent presently beneath his depression.

"But all the same, Billy, one of these days, mark my words, I'm going to cheer up this respectable and awe-inspiring periodical. Just to please myself. I know exactly what I'm going to do. I'm going round to the Secretary of the Royal Society, and I'm going to put such an innocent-looking contract past him that he won't see for a moment what I'm up to, and then I'm going to give these dull old Philosophical Transactions of yours a real, spirited Christmas number, a genuine advertisement display. I'm going to have everything —coloured inset leaflets, extra sheets in the cover, cosmetics, lip-salves, hair-dyes, wigs, corsets—*men's* corsets!—scents, sensational pictures of lingerie, toilet fittings in ivory and silver and gold, the Parisian note loud and clear, soaps recommended by Lillie Langtry and Sarah Bernhardt, and complexion stuff by Mary Anderson, ravishing portraits of these ladies in colour, super-colour, bath scenes by Alma Tadema, Lucullus bathrooms, smart restaurants, hotels, plages, Monte Carlo, Ascot week, Cowes, grey toppers, hatters to the Prince of Wales, manicure establishments, turf commission agents, dealers in real diamonds."

I said his advertisers wouldn't like that.

"The poor old dears! Temptation of St. Anthony wouldn't be in the same field with it!" said Dickon with the confidence of a man who knows what advertisers will stand. He did not worry about them. He was thinking of grave, earnest men in spectacles, aghast.

"Tonics," he said, as an afterthought. "Cures for debility. Ginger. Do you sing in your bath?"

Dickon never had a proper respect for the Royal Society. "They lead devoted lives," I said.

"Bah!" said Dickon. "I know 'em. I know their secret cravings. They'll eat those advertisements. Doctor Faustus asks for his youth again! Mephistopheles restores it—small bottles, one guinea. You bet."

"Confound it!" I remonstrated. "Dignified work! Vital work! Why *will* you always insult men of science?"

And then at the sight of my artless indignation he threw a great fit of chuckles. "Oh, Billy!" he cried. "Oh, Billy! I got you," and kicked his legs about. . . .

Always a great lout, my brother Dickon.

§ 6

WATCHING Dickon and watching the world through Dickon's eyes has been at times almost more instructive than watching it through my own. He embarked upon advertising at first, as I suppose most of the early advertisers did, in a cheerfully piratical spirit. It was to be his way of " getting it "—and that was all that mattered.

But as time went on and his interests spread and his wealth and power increased, he was obliged almost in spite of himself to recognise the part that he and his like were playing in the rephrasing of human life. They were assisting at a synthesis that was replacing the scattered autonomous various individualism of the past by a more and more intricate interdependent life. He began to think of advertising less and less as an adventure, and more and more as an integral social function, with obligations and standards of its own.

Temperamentally he had never liked falsehood; he had disliked even reserve if it misled; he always kept as clear as he could from the pill and patent medicine field, in which lying and bluff figure so largely, but he had never felt quite happy in his assertion that in the long run it was better to understate than overstate in an advertisement. It is largely true, but it has never been wholly true, that for the individual in business honesty is the best policy. For a trade as a whole it is certainly true, but not for the incidental adventurer. He can achieve his "get away," as the American criminals phrase it, leaving his trade discredited.

Dickon has been a prime mover in the organisation of advertisers into a professional organisation since the war. He has helped to found lectureships and establish examinations in advertisement. I believe he would like to see a special university degree, Bachelors and Doctors of Advertisement. Some day we may come to that. Even before the war he was thinking of schemes for making deliberate falsehood, either in an advertisement or in the news columns of a newspaper, a felony. "If it was felony for our father to issue a false balance-sheet which only caused people monetary loss, it is far more felony to tell some poor old woman in a cottage that the filth you want to sell cures the pain in her back, and so waste her last chance of proper treatment for kidney or cancer."

"Proper treatment!" said I. "Where?"

Dickon stuck to his own line of thought. "Here we have people making fortunes by keeping people ill, mis-informing them about their symptoms, inducing them to trust in misdescribed goods. Billy, it's a crime against the Empire. It fills the streets with uncomfortable people. Poor mothers, induced to give the children they cared for innutritious muck, so that they grow up disappointing weeds. All these weedy people in the streets, in the buses, everywhere—just because you let advertisers say their muck is flesh-forming and frame-building and bone-making when every competent authority knows that it isn't. The poor mother isn't a competent authority. How can she be? She finds it out too late. Can't help herself. And in the long run it's bad for advertising. *It's bad for advertising.* The advertising world has to sacrifice its black sheep. *Has* to! Advertisement, Billy, is too big a thing for lying—too big a thing. Much too big a thing. It's the web of modern life; it's the call of the flock. For most people, flat statement in advertisements is warranty, absolute warranty. And it ought to be. They take it as they take the news in the adjacent columns. The voice of print, Billy, is the voice of God. To them it is. And it's up to us to see that they get it divine and true."

I raised my eyebrows.

"Divine and true," said Dickon, raising his voice above me massively.

I said I supposed our legal theory was that if there was misdescription there could be an action for damages.

"But how can the poor mutts bring actions against a firm with scores of thousands to play with? How can they do it? No, I want the fellows handled by the Public Prosecutor at the instance of a properly constituted Advertisement Society, and sent to jail."

I was amused. It was down at Dorking, and in 1912 or 1913, that he discoursed in this fashion. We had been playing tennis and we were on the terrace above the court. Dickon was sitting in a deck-chair looking flushed and freckled and over-healthy and very, very earnest, drinking an inadvisable whisky and soda.

I raised the old issue between his individualism and

my Socialism. What was all this talk about? Where were his lifelong principles? He was preaching rank Socialism. Wasn't *caveat emptor* the sound principle for an individualist world?

"Individualist be blowed!" said Dickon. "*Caveat emptor* was all very well between two Latin peasants at a bargain in that little old parochial Roman world— as it *was,* Billy, as it was—but the odds have altered now. I'm thinking of those weedy children and the old woman with a pain in her side."

§ 7

THE Great War did much to develop Dickon's conception of his rôle in the world. He expanded mightily upon a diet of propaganda. There was a phase in the Reconstruction Period when it seemed to him that only an adequate advertisement campaign was needed to achieve the Millennium. I have given these vignettes of him in the eighties, in the later nineties, and in the pre-war days as he grew in strength and confidence. Let me anticipate for a section and complete his apotheosis of advertisement. I must recall what I can of a discourse of his towards the end of 1918. Then you will see how the imagination of Dickon the advertiser grew from that of the watch peddler he was forty years ago to its present dimensions.

If the Great War made nothing, it did at least appear for a time to have disorganised everything. The idea that society had been shattered and would need rebuilding was very prevalent in 1915. Everything was going to be rebuilt, fairer, sounder, juster, happier; that went without saying. That was the justification for a war that was otherwise inexplicable; it was a Phœnix flare. By 1916 this had become a standard promise for all the optimists who were engaged in whipping up the flagging enthusiasm of the nation. It crystallised into the word Reconstruction. All our English world talked Reconstruction, from the pro-war intellectuals, who dropped off from the war propaganda into silence or opposition after the collapse of the Stockholm Conference, to the deep *John Bull* bellowings of Horatio Bottomley, most popular of patriots and stimulators. " A world fit for heroes," said Lloyd George—phrase unforgettable. How tremendously that word Reconstruction was bandied about! It waved as gallantly, it vanished at last as abruptly, as a contested banner in a riot. Many of us can still feel uncomfortable if some thoughtless person chances to revive it.

There was much pitiful moral tragedy in that fiasco, but to begin with Reconstruction embodied some bold and righteous hopes. And it completed the evolution of Dickon. Under its spell he became temporarily a Utopian, more Utopian even than I in my Brompton days, and planned a world which never had been, but which, it seemed to him then, might very easily be. He had realised the tremendous possibilities of handling people in great masses revealed by this war advertising, in which he had played a conspicuous part; possibilities of teaching hygienic practices for example, suggesting new habits or routines, restating and changing general ideas, altering outlooks altogether. For a time these realisations possessed him completely.

His Utopianism was amateurish; he had all the crudity of a sudden convert. He wanted to see the energy that had been gathered into the great Ministry of Munitions turned directly to the material rearrangement of the country, the railways re-made, the countryside re-planned, slums swept away, old beauties restored, and much of our present towns and cities rebuilt. Then manifestly the war would not have been in vain. He saw himself directing the demobilising millions back to abundant work, and homes renewed and happy, through a vast advertisement organisation. "A land fit for heroes," he quoted continually—in his profession they call that sort of thing a "slogan"—and it seemed plain to him after the vision of large-scale human co-operation the war had given him, that the whole food supply of the world was capable of control, that population could be poured from district to district like water, instructed in the requirements of its new surroundings and held to its effort. He had some magnificent moments in that Utopian phase of his.

"The war's been a bloody mess, Billy, but at least it's taught us to handle things in the big way," he said : " the advertising way. We learnt it by selling mustard and motor-cars, but these were only the things we learnt upon."

And again : " Advertising; what is it? Education. Modern education, nothing more or less. The airs schoolmasters and college dons give themselves are extraordinary. They think they're the only people who teach. *We* teach ten times as much. Why! even the little chaps who write the attractions in the big weeklies and monthlies, Kipling, Jack London, Bennett, Galsworthy, Wodehouse, all that lot—teach more than the schoolmasters do.

" Schoolmasters! What do you mean by education? When you get down to hard tacks. *Just old-fashioned, primitive advertisement done by word of mouth in a room!* Why! a class-room schoolmaster teaching by shouts ought to be as out-of-date nowadays as a town-crier!

" The only use I've got for schools now is to fit people to read advertisements. After that, *we* take on. Yes, we—the advertisers. You may laugh, Billy; it's true. All new ideas come as a shock at first. Don't just laugh at it like that. Don't sit like an oaf and grin. Tell me what's wrong with it.

" And even *in* the schools we could put ten times better lessons over the heads of the masters now—with a properly organised cinema. Ten times better. But we leave the cinema to a lot of music-hall muckers and close-up chorus girls, as though it wasn't worth using."

He laid great stress upon the cinema, but I do not recall him saying anything about broadcasting in those Reconstruction days. But, of course! One forgets how fast the world moves. In 1919 there was no broadcasting. With broadcasting I can see Dickon reducing his poor schoolmasters to the last extremity of usherdom —mere conductors on his omnibus to knowledge. Before broadcasting he had at least to leave them an occasional use of their voices. Now they would just hum on the loud-speaker and stand about and mark registers. Gagged, perhaps, to prevent any personal intervention.

His denunciation of schoolmasters increased and intensified, of schoolmasters and the clergy, as his imagination of what might be done with the crowd developed. He would talk to me in his hectoring, elder-brother way, but always with a twinkle in his eye and a touch of burlesque in his tone and an evident readiness to jump overboard from his argument at any time with a sudden splash of laughter if it became too difficult to maintain; and his argument was always exaltation of the modern advertising method and always contempt for the refinements of the intellectual world.

" These fellows in caps and gowns think you can make things decent by being genteel in a corner and shuddering and sneering whenever you hear a noise. I ask you! You've got to *explain* your Millennium to people, Billy; you've got to make 'em want it, and you've got to tell 'em how to get it. Then they'll get it. Just as they get Lucas lamps and safety-razor blades or any other old thing. The advertisand is different, but the method is the same. Why, Billy! Look at things plainly. With all reverence——"

He adapted his ruddy face roughly and quickly to express all reverence. It was just an habitual concession unnecessary in my case.

" What were the twelve Apostles? Drummers, just drummers. Travelling in salvation. Introducing a new line. Why did Paul raise his voice at Athens? Because he hadn't a Megaphone. And the miracles

they did? Sample bottles. To this day it's advertisement. What is a wayside crucifix?—an advertisement
of the faith. What is Christianity?—an advertisement
campaign. Tell 'em. Tell 'em. Tell 'em all you
can. It's the method of social existence."

He turned to biology, to the poetry of life.

"The very flowers by the wayside, Billy, are advertisements for bees!"

My grin armed the fighting spirit in him.

"Vulgar you think it is?"

"Frightfully."

"If there's anything vulgar about modern advertisement, Billy, it's because it's been so concerned about
pills and soap and pickles. Just a passing phase. A
man or a class or a religion or—anything that will
not advertise isn't fit to exist in the world. It means
it doesn't really believe in itself. To want to exist and
not to dare to exist is something beneath vulgarity. . . .
That's why I have such a contempt for your rotten,
shy, sit-in-the-corner-and-ask-the-dear-Prince-of-Wales-to-
dinner-once-a-year Royal Society.

"If the soap-boilers did no more for soap than your
old Royal Society does for science," said Dickon,
"nobody would wash."

§ 8

BUT this post-war talk is, as I intimated, out of place. I will return to the Period of Reconstruction later. If nothing else was reconstructed then, we were, and our post-war interchanges form a distinct and separate chapter in our history. Before I go on to tell how the war shook up and released and stimulated our ideas about things in general, I must tell of his marriage and of a considerable divergence of our ways of living. When I was three-and-twenty things happened to make me break away from the life of pure research I had seemed destined to follow. I became an employee and later a director of Romer, Steinhart, Crest and Co., I left London to live at Downs-Peabody, and I became more and more involved in the huge industrial developments that have occupied the greater half of my life. They had little or no advertising side. They brought me into a world of associates quite apart from Dickon's; they carried me abroad for long spells and made me by comparison cosmopolitan.

He remained extremely English. He lived for some years after his marriage in the Cromwell Road, and then he bought Lambs Court near Dorking and became a substantial figure in the substantial suburbanism of Surrey. I, too, married a little while after he did, but marriage, which stabilised him, disorganised all my intentions about life. My marriage was a failure. I will tell of it in due course, but for some years a certain chagrin may have helped to make my visits to Dickon's home less frequent than they might otherwise have been. His marriage was heartily successful, ostentatiously successful; and for a while I suspected him, I think now unjustly, of feeling that I was to blame for the muddle I was in.

Ostentatiously successful I write, but whether it is to be regarded as a perfect marriage I do not know. I doubt if there is any such thing as a perfect marriage. It may happen—as an accident. To this day I find a certain lurking perplexity about my sister-in-law in my mind; I have never been able to exorcise it. There was something extraordinarily fine about her—and something cold and aloof. Nor do I yet see as a clear and consistent thing Dickon's relations to her. He was so incapable of aloofness. He was floridly and magnificently loyal to her and she was profoundly loyal to him, but I do not know, I cannot imagine what there was down there at the very bottom of things between them. Was it love, the tenderness and infinite consideration she had for him? It was love at first, no doubt. And mixed with his infinite respect for her, his pride and his rare overwhelming tenderness, there was something resentful. Did he always suppress that resentment in her presence? I do not know. I will tell as much as I know, what I saw, what I inferred, and leave it to the reader. Plainly there are things here outside the range of my feelings and experiences.

She was a very small person; she had fine exquisite features; she was not a short woman, not dwarfish in any way, but simply made upon a delicate scale; she looked much more fragile than she was, and when I

first encountered her she was a little strained and artificial in her manner because she was so valiantly resolved
not to be shy. I met her only a month or so before
the marriage, and when the marriage was already fixed.
Dickon had discovered her in Bloomsbury, and I had a
sense that she had been sprung upon me after a period
of uneasiness and concealment on Dickon's part. There
was a sort of tea-party in Dickon's sitting-room, and she
was there under the protection of a cousin, whom I
forget altogether, and I had the spectacle of Dickon,
my stern, dogmatic brother, almost dishevelled with
nervousness, proffering tea, handing cakes, asking me
—*me!*—if I took sugar, and watching my face for the
faintest intimations of a judgment.

She was little, not very well dressed, guarded. That
much I saw at the time. We talked about pictures,
about which none of us knew very much, and about
music. At Lambs Court there is still a photograph of
her in those early days. One had to sit quite still for
some seconds in those days in order to be photographed,
and so if one did not get blurred one looked like wax-
works. She had contrived to sit quite still. How unaccustomed now are our eyes to those later Victorian
costumes! She had a collar to her dress that reached
to her little ears and great puffed sleeves and a whale-
bone figure.

I forget most of the incidents of that meeting now,
but I remember Dickon afterwards parting from me at
Hyde Park Corner. " You don't see what there is in
her at first, old man," he said, for the third or fourth
time. Though I had never said a word to betray that

I did not think her the most obviously and instantly desirable of all possible sisters-in-law. I had hardly said anything. I did not know what to say.

On our way to Hyde Park Corner he had told me things about her. She was the daughter of a doctor in Bloomsbury, a very competent general practitioner. She was a connection of his early partner, Brakespear. She had passed some examinations—I forget what they were but they were difficult ones. She drew beautifully. She was clever at music and spoke French and German wonderfully well. She was an only child, which, I think, accounts for a sort of reserved inwardness in her manner; she was untrained in the exposures, criticisms, recriminations, and habitual intimacies of family life.

She read, I was to discover later, and she studied, but she was not accustomed to talk. There were moments when I was to watch her listening to Dickon's discourse and compare her in my mind with a passenger waiting for a ferry with the river in flood. Waiting as one waits on a fine agreeable day when waiting is no hardship. Waiting, moreover, with no intention of travelling on the stream. And—to begin with, she was, in a peculiar still way, in love with Dickon and devoted to him. He, too, was in love with her, but just the least bit disappointed, I felt, that she did not make a better show in front of me. Once or twice during those early encounters he tried to draw her out and exhibit her paces, but she had little, scarcely perceptible, ways of stopping that. It was amusing to see Dickon interested in an article that declined to be pushed. He would have been a terrible impresario for a showy woman.

I began to think her a little less undistinguished after a fourth or fifth meeting, and at the wedding I had a feeling that for some obscure reason she had hitherto been concealing from me and the world in general an ability to be, if she chose, conspicuously pretty.

But I still didn't see why it had been necessary for my bright and exuberant Dickon to marry her. I did not see why he of all people should be mated to incarnate restraint.

It was a thoroughly respectable wedding, and the household they set up in the Cromwell Road was in the highest degree respectable. A time was to come when I was to think a lot of Minnie's taste, but in the furnishing of that first house nothing of her sensitive fastidiousness appeared. Perhaps it was not yet fully awake. I suppose Dickon must have just carried her through the furniture shop with him and given her no time to meditate. The house was, my brief disturbing wife declared, when she paid her introductory visit, " utterly and hopelessly *banal*."

I was married, as I will tell later, about a year and a half after Dickon, and my marriage took him by surprise as much as his had taken me. I kept Clara an even closer secret from Dickon than he had kept Minnie from me. Perhaps I felt what his opinion would be of the Allbut ménage. I sprang her upon Dickon and Minnie within a few weeks of our marriage. I took her to call upon Minnie. I went in a faintly irritated mood because Clara had seen fit to supplement her wardrobe from an aunt's supplies, and had suddenly become much more a woman of the world and much less of a hard-up art girl than was seemly in the future wife of a struggling research student.

A natural antagonism flared up at the first encounter of Minnie and Clara. Clara was an effusive human being, and particularly so with strangers. She fell upon Minnie with cries and embraces. "What an exquisite *little* dear you are!" she said.

I was beginning to forget that Minnie was so very small; I saw her disentangling herself with an unobtrusive distaste from those swift familiarities. Clara praised her clothes loudly—they were in the current fashion of the time—insisted upon regarding them as the triumph of a special effort, and then, with an obscure perception of rebuff, turned her enthusiasm to the house and the furniture. "Jolly *good* things you have!" she exclaimed. "Where did you get them all?"

"Dickon and I went to Maple's," said Minnie, regarding her strictly later Victorian surroundings for a moment as though she had just seen them for the first time.

Clara looked round for some piece that might be exceptional. There was nothing exceptional. So she pounced on a book.

"*You* read George Meredith too!" she said.

"Here's Dickon!" said Minnie, relieved as the door opened. . . .

I became more acutely aware of the sketchy quality in Clara's smartness as Dickon came in. It was my turn now to watch for unspoken verdicts. Clara's way with men was sometimes a little over-confident. . . .

It was not a good call. Dickon, I could see, did not warm to Clara. Minnie seemed deliberately to be refrigerating the conversation, and we left with Clara in a splendid rage.

" So *that's* my prospective sister-in-law!" I remember her saying on the doorstep.

She paused. " *Watchful!*" she whispered. " She watches."

And then she embarked upon an exhaustive summary of Minnie's deficiencies. The burthen was that there was nothing in Minnie, but for all that it was clear that there was much to be said about her. Firstly, she was personally insignificant. Secondly, she was cold-blooded. Next, her style of dressing was provincial, timid, genteel. She was under-dressed. On such an occasion as this it was rude and offhand to under-dress. One was expected to dress a little. To meet a chosen sister-in-law was an important occasion and ought to be treated as such. One ought to make an effort.

The ashes of our controversy over the borrowed finery glowed again for a moment.

Minnie's furniture and her household management, insisted Clara, had the same limitations as her costume and the same uncivil negligence. The tea, for some reason, had greatly offended Clara. There had been a lack of variety in the tea; for the first visit of an imminent sister-in-law there ought to have been display; everybody nowadays gave little sandwiches, cucumber sandwiches, paste sandwiches. Amusing things. Light things one just took in one's hand. It looked skimpy not to do so. And dull. Buttered buns were ridiculous; hefty things like that ought to be relegated to the nursery. (At tea Clara had " adored " buttered buns, had received them with acclamation.)

And that furniture! That *heavy* furniture! Maple's! Carte blanche to them to furnish, no doubt. No individuality. No character. Where *could* my brother have met her? No doubt we should have to go to dinner there so soon as we were married. It would be our first dinner party together. Could we last two hours? What should we talk about? Even in that forty minutes' call the talk had caught and hung time after time.

" Well, anyhow," reflected Clara, " I shan't want much of a frock for *that!*"

I said very little to Clara's tirade, because it shocked and irritated me to hear my own secret judgments on Dickon's wife caricatured, made monstrous and preposterous, and expressed in terms of intense personal hostility. " She isn't so bad," I said. " And she makes Dickon happy."

" *Does* she make him happy?

" Your brother," said Clara, following up her own question, " would never own to a failure if he felt he could pull it through to look like a success. He's—stiff stuff. As stiff as you are. Obviously she's as flat as ditch-water. Uninteresting. Prosaic. She paralyses him. If she hadn't been there—he would have been different. . . . Sooner or later he'll be going round the corner. You mark my words, Billy. But he'll never own up."

I detested her for saying it, but there was something of a likeness to Dickon in that.

" And she won't either," jerked Clara, suddenly completing her impression.

" Won't what?"

" Own up."

§ 9

THERE with the help of Clara's vivid expressiveness, which sometimes succeeded in being on the whole unaccountably right with every detail wrong, you have a sketch of Minnie. She was neither flat nor prosaic; she was never uninteresting; but it is true that she never seemed to take hold of Dickon, and that she did not seem to take hold of life. He had taken hold of her, and she liked that; it warmed her as much as anything could warm her, but there was nothing about her holding on to him if presently he let go. She was, I had long realised, a creature of fine secondary shades and complicated shynesses and reserves, and I have never known anyone with a less voracious will to live.

I doubted from the first whether he appreciated her fine shades. His natural disposition was towards poster colourings more suitable for display. But gradually I came to see that it was not the delicacy nor the fine shades that he cared about. He had a profound unshakable belief in her honesty, loyalty and common

sense, and she justified his belief. Whatever else she
may or may not have been to him, she was, so to speak,
his treasury, his brake, his wary councillor. And
though she was never a brilliant talker in society, I
noted that when he quoted her sayings and cited her
opinions, there came out a shrewd individuality quite
different from his own.

They did not have children for a while. Then in
the course of four or five years came a couple of sons
and a daughter, and they went to the space and dignity
of Lambs Court and took a great flat in Queen Anne's
Mansions as their *pied-à-terre* in London. It was only
after her death and the marriage of young Richard that
Dickon left Queen Anne's Mansions for the chambers
in Bordon Street in which this book begins. There
were gaps sometimes of two or three years when I
would be abroad, or in the north, or in the Midlands,
and when I saw little of Dickon and Minnie, and so
my memories pass almost abruptly from that rather
commonplace, rather nervously self-conscious and
apologetic home in the Cromwell Road to a very prettily
furnished and well-ordered country house, with a small
but very well-dressed and maternal Minnie, keeping a
competent eye on her nursemaids and instructing an
entirely respectful gardener in the development of the
very beautiful terrace gardens she created. The two
figures do not merge so completely as they would have
done if our acquaintance had been continuous. In that
case I have no doubt the earlier, immature, more fragile
and shyer Minnie would have been replaced day by day
and bit by bit and effaced altogether from my memory.

In that second phase Minnie had far more confidence, far more grip upon the world, than in the first. There was a subtle difference in her relations with Dickon, but it would be hard to define what that difference was. Perhaps she had passed through phases of dismay and reassurance. I thought his attitude towards her was a little more effusive and formal than it had been, and more habitual. I thought that she seemed no longer to be observing him with the happy interest of their earlier time. It was as though she had got used to him and had accepted something that had not been present in the beginning, or resigned herself to the absence of something she had once thought there.

She had become a great gardener, which was rather wonderful after a girlhood in Bloomsbury, and she was also beginning to know quite a lot about furniture and pictures. Later on she was to become something of a buyer of pictures and etchings. She would help struggling artists, until she felt the touch of proprietorship to which the helped are prone. The children were happy and delightful then, in a perfect nursery and with an excellent, kindly nurse; but I do not remember ever seeing Minnie romp with them, and I doubt if in all her life she ever lost her temper with them. Yet she loved them. Flowers and furnishing, I think, she cared for more than living things; she could do so much more for them without provoking them to come back upon her clamorously. They did not climb upon her, they did not shout or hammer at her, as human beings might at any time do.

After a time I went no more to Lambs Court. I

stayed away for nearly seven years. While Dickon's marriage had turned out successfully, mine had ended in the uncomfortable tangle I will describe later. I was tied to Clara legally for the rest of my life, and unable to marry again. I was welcome at Lambs Court as a sort of bachelor brother, very welcome, even after I had been cited as a co-respondent in the Evans divorce case, but I felt a certain exemplariness in Dickon's attitude towards me and an implicit criticism in the immense discreet silences of Minnie. There were times when Dickon's gestures, pauses, acts seemed to say almost as plainly as though he spoke the words : " My dear fellow, why are you in this uneasy mess? It is so perfectly simple. All you have to do is to marry Minnie, make much of her, stick to her, stand up for her, stick to business—and keep strange women in their proper place. Out of the picture. And there you are, you know!"

Quite possibly my suspicions were unjust. At any rate he was habitually proud of her and as good and faithful a husband as most of the rich and rising business men of Surrey.

Then came my attempt to live with Mrs. Evans. That was in the turn of the century and people in England were still unprepared to tolerate a ménage, however stable, of two unmarried people. So long as I was a man of the world, carrying on a series of incidental intrigues almost openly, I was socially acceptable anywhere; but an attempt at illicit domesticity, with a still undivorced Clara, however disreputable, in existence, was too much for the standards of the time. If I could have divorced Clara and married Sirrie Evans, all would have been well. I wouldn't accept that verdict. I fought. I betrayed excessive resentment. I would not ask Minnie for any help in the matter, I made no attempt to bring her and Sirrie together, I said nothing to Dickon, but I felt acutely their failure to apprehend our situation. Minnie ignored it. She did not know this Mrs. Evans, and apparently she would not know this Mrs. Evans. She asked me to come to Lambs Court alone, and I never answered her invitation. I did not see her again or communicate directly with her until a year or more after Sirrie's death.

To this day that lack of initiative perplexes me. By the time of the Evans affair she and I had become very friendly. She did not know Sirrie, she may not have been prepared to take any very serious risks about her, but still she might have assumed that I should not have become attached to a woman without good qualities, and it would have been quite possible for her to have found out and met Sirrie in some roundabout way before committing herself. But she just did nothing. She was one of a number of people who just did nothing to help us. Something cold and distant there was in that. Or something profoundly timid? Or some aversion from relationships into which there entered a possible thread of passion?

Dickon knew Sirrie slightly. One might have imagined that he could have broken down that icy barrier by a word or so. But he did not, and perhaps he could not. The barrier may not have been solely for the benefit of Sirrie; I do not know. Sirrie may have symbolised many things for Minnie and Dickon that had little to do with me. I continued to meet Dickon in London. We had both become members of the Ermine Club, and we would lunch or dine and gossip together without any allusion to the complete separation of our households. Nothing was ever explained. We belonged to the same group of after-lunch talkers. We gibed at each other's opinions and went to one or two theatres together. But about the rest of his life during that estrangement I made no enquiry beyond such information as he volunteered. I continued to be aware of Minnie only in relation to him.

He varied towards her no doubt. Sometimes when I met him in London Minnie was as remote from him but as necessary to the world and as much taken for granted as the Atlantic or the Equator. At other times he was full of quotations from her and references to her. Then, oddly enough, I was not so sure of his serene and complete assurance about her. It has been the common habit of our two lives never to pry into the intimate proceedings of the other, but I have had a feeling that in these phases of allusion, these passages peppered with " My wife says this " and " Minnie does that," he perceived himself under a necessity to maintain her. Yet it would be difficult to define what it was he maintained her against.

Whatever imperfections and difficulties there were in his married life, whatever hidden relaxations there were of its outward integrity, none of them ever came to the surface as a visible infringement of Minnie's dignities. There were, I happen to know, what the French call

303

passades, but the heroines were obscure young ladies, amply compensated and silenced. He was, I repeat, as good and faithful a husband as most honourable, prosperous men.

One spring day in 1910 I found myself put down at a Romer lunch party next to Minnie. I was sure they would put me next to her as soon as I saw her in the drawing-room. She had altered very little; she was, perhaps, stronger and firmer and better dressed. She looked like very good porcelain amidst the metallic splendours of Lady Romer's assembly.

I put as good a face as I could upon the encounter. I asked after Lambs Court and the children.

"William the Second," she said, "is absurdly like you. He has a gift. He is going to draw—wonderfully. The two brothers together are like Dickon and you—even to the way they insult each other."

She said something about my coming down to see them.

Then in a pause she made a great effort. "Billy," she said very softly, "I was so sorry to hear of your loss."

I was too astonished to say anything.

"I wanted to write. I was stupid. . . . I often don't do—things I want to do."

She was feeling her way towards an apology, and she was flushed and sincere. It was a sort of confession—for one who could not confess. She became more incomprehensible to me than ever. I was quite unable to get her into relationship with that old and now healing sore. I dismissed the attempt.

"I would like to see something of William the Second," I said, after a clumsy interval. "I've neglected my godson."

"Next week-end?" she said as awkwardly. . . .

It was the most intimate moment we ever had together.

Thereafter our outward friendship—and I can imagine no friendship of Minnie's that except for the rarest moments was other than external—was resumed.

§ 10

BETWEEN that meeting and my later memories of Minnie, streams all the storm, tragedy, and illumination of the war. The war that has changed so much and yet at times seems to have changed nothing.

I never expected the war to happen until it was actually happening. Romer, Steinhart, Crest and Co. were naturally in touch with much pre-war armament business, and armament seemed to us—to me, at any rate, it seemed—a foolish way of using up good metal that fools had got to pay for as highly as possible. I still think the war need not have happened, and that the amount of good that has come out of it is incomparably smaller than the waste and evil. It is easy to be wise after the event and say how inevitable the catastrophe was, but I do not think it was inevitable even so late as July, 1914. More intelligent men in the Foreign Offices could, I think, have averted it even then. But few of us were intelligent and imaginative enough to realise the enormity of the disaster until it was upon us. We expected a quick war, possible humiliations, great changes of the map and far less strain, destruction, and uprooting. Most of our Governments and rulers were as little able to foresee and fear as so many mentally defective children with a box of matches in a powder magazine. At last a match was dropped. Then for a time the skies were darkened, the world was full of thunder, the torrents of disaster poured. There was a clatter of falling things, a flare of burning. Millions of young men suffered detestable things and died and passed. And at last when it had come to seem that no end would ever be possible, the storm was over and the skies cleared magically.

The tornado struck Lambs Court, seemed likely to extinguish the life of Lambs Court altogether, and left it at last—with scarcely a flower-bed ruffled. Dick and William, my nephews, both went into the war and survived it, William unscathed, Dick with a bullet wound and a six months' spell of prison in Germany after Gough's disaster in 1918. Indeed, Lambs Court came through it amazingly. Week-end parties were already resumed in 1919. And Dickon was made a baronet! Dickon was made a baronet and Minnie became Lady Clissold—to my infinite amazement and perplexity.

The war, I say, took me by surprise, but so soon as it was under way my rôle was marked out for me. I was too old for the earlier enlistments, and I doubt if in any case I should have volunteered. I gravitated naturally to technical work, and was presently involved in the new-formed Ministry of Munitions. I did four years of bitter contentious work, and I should suppose that Roderick and I between us saved the British taxpayer many, probably negligible, millions of pounds. My estimates of current honesty and current intelligence were considerably lowered by those experiences; I conceived a passionate contempt and distaste for the higher ranks of the British Army that I still have trouble in controlling, and I came to consider and treat the military, naval, and aerial expert, salaried adviser of the War Office to-day and highly salaried official of an armament group to-morrow, as the moral inferior of a Constantinople tourists' dragoman.

At the end I dodged the shower of honours with considerable difficulty. There were a number of people who were deeply concerned that I should get something and be generally soothed, pacified, implicated, and shut up. I transferred a particularly persistent suggestion of a K.B.E. to a useful subordinate who might have been passed over, the sort of man to appreciate it, and I tried to use whatever claim to attention I might have in hunting down one or two exceptionally scandalous cases. In that I failed completely. The Press would not touch my entirely convincing facts. Nobody would touch them. One of my worst offenders married his loot to American money and became a bright ornament for any London dinner party; another took the fancy of Royalty; another embarrassed me by appearing on the board of an allied steel firm with which we had the friendliest relations. After a while I realised that I was being unreasonable and self-righteous. I began to laugh at my own virtue. If there was to be a real inquisition into stolen goods, where should we end?

Dickon was more surprised by the war even than I was. He had never believed that these European armies were really in earnest, and he had been inclined to approve of German imperialism as of something pleasantly flamboyant and picturesque in an age inclined to be prosaic. It advertised amazingly. When the guns began to go off he was outraged beyond measure at the breach of faith. It was as though a large bill-stickers' hoarding had begun to kill and eat people. There seemed nothing for it at first but violence with an axe.

He was furiously indignant against the Germans. So indeed was I in the early months. So was all England. At this resurrection of war. The awakening of England in the autumn of 1914 may have been uncritical and foolish, but it was thoroughly honest, and so far at any rate as the million odd volunteers were concerned, heroic. By the end of the year Dickon had somehow contrived to get into khaki. He was fully fifty, and I do not know how he managed it, but he did. He had once in the early bicycle days spent some months in that now forgotten supplement to the military might of Britain, the Volunteers. He was keen then on cyclist riflemen. He may have exaggerated his former standing in that force. At any rate, he was taken on. I cherish a snapshot of his substantial figure with a lieutenant's star upon his collar, looking very earnest and unsuitable. Afterwards, for some reason of etiquette in connection with supplies, they jumped him up to be a temporary colonel, and at that he could stand beside the stoutest of them, stouter than any and taller than most. He was trained at Checkershill and then on Cumberbatch Moor, but that was as near as he travelled on the road to the trenches. He went to France, indeed, but by a different route. They found they wanted him on the commissariat.

A man who could advertise things for retail sale was naturally supposed by the military authorities to know how to buy and distribute anything. He did some thoroughly sound work for them, and afterwards he became a great factor in civil food-control organisation. He worked hard under Rhondda, an able, ailing, concentrated man who might be alive to-day, perhaps, if it had not been for the strain of that work, and after Rhondda died Dickon went on with Clynes, a Labour leader, who had joined the Government. Through Dickon I met Clynes on two or three occasions. He was a little intelligent-looking cockatoo of a man, who, like Brer Rabbit, kept on saying nuffing all the time, in the face of every conversational allurement. Perhaps, like one or two others of his colleagues, he needs a platform, a large hall and adequate interruption, before he can really express what is in him.

"Does he know anything?" I asked Dickon afterwards.

"He knows what he doesn't know," said Dickon. "He's perfectly satisfactory to work with."

A foretaste of the Labour Government of 1924.

Dick, my elder nephew, volunteered before his father

at the beginning; William was taken later, protesting, but without bitterness, that it wasn't his fight; Lambs Court was presently filled with convalescents and a trained staff, and my niece Winnie was sent up to London, out of sentimental range, to work with great energy at the manufacture of bandages, a little resentful because her mother would not allow her to drive a car for the Ministry of Munitions. Minnie presided capably at Lambs Court, and presently, after strains and endless petty hardships, scanty food, darkened homes, tiresome air-raids, gleams of leave for the boys, almost overwhelming anxiety over Dick's disappearance—he was " missing " for three weeks—and a sort of universal neurasthenia, the war came abruptly to its hysterical end. Down either side of Pall Mall hundreds of captured guns were displayed, the streets of London were alight again and swarming with a vast, wearily enthusiastic multitude which laughed and shouted because it did not want to howl and cry, and the war was over. And Dickon was talking with passionate conviction of a Britain born again out of these troubles and of a " reconstructed " world.

That was the background so to speak to the affair of his baronetcy.

I realised that he did not intend to refuse it, with an indignation that now strikes me as excessive. At the time it seemed extravagantly important to me that my brother should not accept this thing. I suppose I was overworked and worried, in a state of inflamed honesty, more indignant and less cynically patient than I have ever been before or since. I was in conflict with my business associates. Perhaps I should have been better employed in watching them. Brampsheet particularly— he had just got his peerage—was against all post-war scandals and enquiries, and my anger extended to the social world which was sheltering the men I wanted to expose. This had been the war that was to end all that sort of thing. These exasperations made me see Dickon's title as a sort of treason to the insurgent radicalism that had always been implicit between us.

"Dickon!" I protested. "That old livery! In an age of Reconstruction!"

"Historical, time-honoured."

"Everything we want to say good-bye to."

"All the same——"

"You mean to take it, Dickon?"

"Yes. Yes, I think I may take it."

"You'll have to kiss the king's hand?" I invented. Dickon pretended not to hear.

"You'll have to kiss his hand," I jeered.

"No more than kissing a book."

He went off at a tangent to answer unspoken objections of mine. "You live in a sort of dreamland, Billy," he said. "Science and the future and all that. Even now. In spite of your business and money. But I live in the present time. I'm here and now. I'm contemporary. A child of the age. This sort of thing is the fashion of our time. It's just a symbol of success and service. Very well. It may not be the best of media, but it's one way of saying 'I'm here!' That's how I look at it."

It was as if we were back in our Brompton diggings.

That, I remembered suddenly, had been his standing argument against my Socialism.

"It's bolstering up the old order. You take the honour, yes—but you give your adhesion."

He said I lacked *savoir-faire*. That if one went on those lines one would become a "lone wolf." One didn't bolster up the old order. On the contrary, it acknowledged itself subdued. It stood on one side to make way for one. Saluted. And besides—with a quick change of line—he wanted Minnie to be Lady Clissold.

"Have you asked her?"

"And the old man's name," said Dickon, with a second flash of deafness. "I've always had a feeling about the honour of the old man. Here it is at last— his name rather than mine. Sir Richard Clissold, Bart. After the way they let him down. After that last scene at the Old Bailey."

"Sir Richard Clissold Boop," said I.

"Eh?"

"Boop. The Boops and their Jubilee. Good God, man, you haven't forgotten the Boops, have you? All this, Dickon, strikes me as the most infernal Boopery. You'll have to wear a little Boopy sword. And silk legs! And the Boops will stand round in their little Boopy robes, dressing-gowns and tea-cosies and table-cloths and curtains and antimacassar wigs and news-paper hats, all very solemn and solemn, to welcome you. Don't you remember?"

He did. But he didn't want to do so. He embarked upon an insincere defence of royalty. "They" were so hard-working, so devoted. " Hardest-working couple in the Empire."

" To no purpose," said I, "except to stick on."

" So much to do," said Dickon. " Reconstruction everywhere. Why divide people by quarrelling with that?"

I told him that people of his sort defended the crown because they were too lazy to set about getting it out of their way. They only pretended to like it. It obstructed the traffic. It falsified realities.

" Bit too many royal visits and processions just now, I admit," said Dickon. " Still—they *are* the decentest!"

He shrugged his shoulders, and tried to look indulgent and reasonable and as much like *The Times* and *Punch* and a white top-hat in Ascot week as possible.

It was not only the traffic in the streets, I said. It was the traffic in men's minds. It put the common people wrong about the purposes of the State.

" They love it," said Dickon.

" That's just it," said I. "It's a lumbering perversion of human respect. A modern community can't afford to waste its respect like that!"

That consideration has been my unwavering objection to monarchy and has made me that rare being, an English republican. I am puzzled by the readiness of liberal-minded English people to acquiesce in and conform to the monarchy. The king is necessarily the head and centre of the old army system, of the diplomatic tradition, of hieratic privileges, of a sort of false England that veils the realities of English life. While he remains, the old army system remains, Society remains, the militant tradition remains. They are all bound up together, inseparably. The people cannot apprehend themselves in relation to the world while, at every turn and crisis of the collective life, the national king, the national uniforms, the national flags and bands, thrust blare and bunting across the realities. For millions these shows are naturally accepted as the realities. They personify and intensify and ensure the national distinction, the separation of the marching, fighting, grabbing Empire from the general business of mankind. How else can a monarchy work considering how monarchs are made and trained and flattered?

For a time Dickon and I wrangled over the issue between monarchy and republicanism. The United States, said Dickon, could be republican and intensely nationalist; France—this was in 1919—was republican and militarist. Americans, I said, were not nationalist, but were obsessed by an unavoidable sense of difference. As for France——

" King!" said Dickon, with a nimble change of front, " but after all what's the king got to do with my baronetcy? I shall scarcely see him long enough to make a face at him. He'll ask, ' Who's that fine man?' And forget when they tell him. It's L.G.'s affair. You're taking the whole of this business too seriously, Billy. You are indeed. You're putting it on too broad a basis. You're so fierce a republican I doubt if you'd read a book if you found it was printed on crown octavo."

He followed that up. " It isn't as though L.G.'s titles were so damned serious as all that. There's something like derision in most of his creations. They're just a flare up at the end. The last dance of the old costume ball. Before it is all swept away."

"In that case Lady Clissold becomes a comic title."

"If it was only for the pleasure it would give the servants at Lambs Court I'd take the title," said Dickon.

"You won't take it," I said.

"I'll do it—if only to annoy you."

I laughed.

"It's just like buying a fur coat for Minnie. It's a decoration. It's a way of putting her over the heads of a lot of showy, chattering bitches that aren't worth a tenth of her."

"There's no need to make Minnie a Lady by the King's grace," I said. "And as for putting her over those other—ladies, you're just putting her among them. And that reminds me: have you asked her about it?"

He had not. And I realised in a flash he was not quite sure what she would say about it. That was why he was trying over the proposal on me first of all, to get a review of the possible objections.

"She won't let you," I said. "She won't let you."

But she did let him. Dickon took his baronetcy.

§ 11

MINNIE died very suddenly in the early part of 1920. She died under an operation that no one had thought very dangerous. But though she told it to no one, she had a feeling of danger, and she did a thing that was to reveal to me as nothing else could have done, the real quality of her relations to Dickon and the world, their aloofness and their filmy tenderness.

Her presentiment of death was very strong. But I do not think she was very deeply troubled at the thought of dying. I suppose that people who live with delicacy rather than intensity can die without any great mental agony. She was troubled about Dickon much more than on her own account; she thought her possible death might be a shock for him, and she feared that shock. So she wrote him a letter—a letter that was only to reach his hands if she died. Otherwise it would just have vanished like many another thing she must have thought of and done in that reserved life of hers. I saw that letter. He was impelled to show it to someone, and he showed it to me.

I was at Dorking with him after the funeral, and he suddenly came into the library with it in his hand. It was already a little worn with much re-reading. He looked at me with eyes that were distressed and per-plexed.

" Billy," he said, " I want you to read this. I want you very much to read this. From her. After she died."

I was inclined to demur.

He pushed it into my hand. " Read it," he said, and again impatiently as he went out of the room, " *Read it.*"

A pencilled note, it was, but in a firm, clear hand. Written without haste. Punctuated, so that one seemed to hear Minnie's characteristic little pauses for deliberation. No outpourings. No abandonment to her impulses, no confidence in her impulses. A skilful letter written carefully for a definite purpose.

It was Minnie come back to life. It was Minnie quintessentially. Except for one or two phrases at the end that stuck in my memory, I cannot remember much of its exact wording. I read it only once. But it was, I think, the tenderest of all imaginable caresses that she reached across the grave to give him. Like Minnie, like all of Minnie, it was faintly aloof from complete participation in life. Because it was faintly aloof it was also faintly insincere. Insincere, I mean, in the sense that she did not seem to believe completely even in her own life and death. But not in any egoistic sense insincere. She was not posing. She did not seem to be thinking about herself at all. She said not a word of any unwillingness to be torn untimely from life. So far as she was concerned, I feel she was capable of saying: "Have I to go, then? Very well, I am ready," even with the faint shadow of a smile upon her lips.

But Dickon in distress, Dickon left alone, big Dickon with his capacity for vivid remorse hiding a heartache, and with no possibility of a word to cure it, was another matter. That had got through to her as a real and dreadful possibility, and she had done her best with it.

"If I have to leave this queer, wonderful existence," she said, "I want you to know how happy you have made me in it."

That was the text of it, that was all she wrote

about, the value he had given life for her. Nothing else.

I thought of many things between them. I saw for the first time as I read her letter with what comprehension she had understood his quality. I saw how well she knew him, and how she feared his easy and abundant remorse. She said nothing of any contentious things, harped upon no forgiving for the derelictions she must have known he had committed, but she said how happy and full she had found every hour with him, she reminded him of many kindnesses and generosities he had shown her, and of the great joint adventure of their worldly success. She recalled a score of little intimate delightful things, mostly from their early years, that she had treasured in her memory.

"The fun we have had, Dickon! The dear boys and Winnie! They were such fine and happy things to have launched into the world. And they get their brightness and courage, my dear, from you."

All things must end, she said, and if this was the end of this strange, lovely, difficult world for her—well, she was sorry to leave him, sorry indeed, but thankful for all she had had, and thankful to him.

"Dear Dickon, my own, be sorry—I know you will be sorry for the parting; but do not grieve, dear Dickon. Do not mind too much about things that never really mattered, do not mind about them. Think of the life that has been so good with you and not of the death at the end. Think of the work that lies before you and the big tasks you have to do. You are only beginning. I know there is endless work before you yet. I wish I could have watched you and stood beside you a little longer. Dickon, my *dear,* thank you and thank you and thank you. . . . And again, dear Dickon, thank you and God bless you, and, if it must be, good-bye."

In that manner, in such words, it ended.

Dickon stood before me again and I gave him back the letter.

"You've read it?"

I nodded.

"Well. . . . Tell me something. . . . Was she really happy, Billy? Did I really make her happy? As she says I did?"

"Certain, Dickon."

"Then why should she doubt?"

"Doubt what?"

"About what I should feel. If she didn't think that perhaps I had seen that she—she wasn't quite as hard and happy as she braved it out she was. There were times——"

"You're tormenting yourself."

"But isn't she just saying those things—— She may be just saying those things—— Thinking of me. . . . She did things like that. She couldn't bear—hurting. Anybody being hurt. She'd a kind of terror of anybody being hurt—or remorseful. . . .

"You don't know, Billy, at times when I've been a bit disposed perhaps to be heavy-handed with the boys —how she's stood in. . . .

"And the thought she had—for old servants. For people in trouble. . . . I could tell you things. . . . Noticing when an old housemaid wanted glasses. Feel-

ing when people were overworked or burthened.
Things like that. Always for going gently. . . ."

He stared at me. "A man lives with a woman all
his life, Billy. Eats with her, sleeps beside her. Happiness. Tears. Endless. . . . And he doesn't know
much about her. At the end, he doesn't know much
about her."

"She loved you all right, Dickon. More than you
deserved, old man. And you made her happy. I've
watched her. She was a happy woman, proud of you,
proud of the opportunities you gave her, proud of this
house and life here—and content."

"But you know, Billy, and I know—— I've been
like most men. . . ."

"So far above such things, Dickon," I said; "they
never touched her."

"But many a time I must have been—a bit of a
lump to her. . . . A man's so much rougher and
clumsier."

"She didn't feel it like that."

"Eh!" he said, and then for the first and last time in
my life I saw my brother weep.

Never in our childhood and boyhood had I seen his
tears, not even when our father died. But now he did
not conceal his distress. "Tears won't bring her back."
he said. "Not tears. Not wishing. Not repenting.
. . . Nothing will bring her back to me. . . . Not
for a word. Not for a moment—to tell her . . .
What could I tell her?"

He went to the window and stood there with his
back to me to hide his face.

"If I could be sure," he said. "If I could believe it! That I made her happy?"

He became quite still, an immense broad back against the park and the sky.

"Kindness," he whispered to the unresponsive heavens. "Kindness, tenderness, the years of it, from the beginning to the end. . . . That quiet kindness."

He turned and addressed me—how can I put it?—as though I wasn't there.

"Nobody knew her but me," said Dickon. "Nobody knew anything about her really but me. Nothing at all. Nobody thought enough of her. Nobody had any idea. I've been her husband for thirty-one years, Billy—I've never found her lying to me or herself. And courage—I've never known her flinch. A little thing she was and she could look pain in the face. Take it as something one had to take. And when Dick was missing—that April! Three weeks we had of it and never a flicker because she had to stand by me. I just saw one day how white her face was. Or else I might have thought she didn't feel. . . . But she felt. . . .

"What a time that was! . . . Loyal! Strong! And I've let her be in the background. I've let it seem as though she wasn't anything so very much . . . didn't matter. . . .

"Billy, I was silly to take that old title, but don't you see how desperately a man may feel that his wife ought to be honoured? Somehow. When she won't take any honour! So that he sticks tinsel on her—in desperation. She let me do it. She understood. . . .

My lady! Princess she was! Princess—with some-thing cool and sweet. Like moonlight. . . . Silver. . . . All my days ought to have been gratitude. . . .

"Oh, what *good* is it talking?"

He looked out of the window again and I could have imagined he was expecting a reply from the twilight.

"Silence," he said, at last.

§ 12

WAS she a cynic? I think the answer is Yes. On that basis I can explain her but on no other. Hers was a cynicism fine as carved ivory, but it was cynicism. It had neither aggression nor insult in it, but for her I do really think that Virtue, as the Ancient Cynics meant it, and Freedom, were the only good things. She was as completely disillusioned about the pomps and vanities, the received values and accepted gratifications of the life we live as I, but in addition she was disillusioned, as I have never been, about the power of the life within us. She was weak in effort and she knew it. So she would not thrust out to blunder. She accepted. She accepted good and avoided evil. She thought fighting evil was itself an evil. It made one hot and angry. So one went by on the other side. She could not understand the sort of drive that achieves, even if it achieves blunderingly. She could not understand the " dust and heat " of endeavour.

Because of that way of thinking she came a little to underrate Dickon, I suspect, after his first glamour had faded. His infidelities, his urgencies, his sudden changes of direction, his excessive admirations of questionable leaders—of Lloyd George, of Milner, of Northcliffe, for example—his storms of combative energy that had to find an outlet and so often found a wrong one, were incomprehensible to her. Yet as that last letter showed, she kept an infinite kindliness for him to the end.

Dickon, as people say, "adored" her, and yet he never seemed to me perfectly self-forgetful and at his ease with her. Even if she did not underrate him, his tender conscience made him feel she ought to do so. He was capable of a good deal of expressive coarseness in his conversation, but in her presence he was always rather carefully decent. He never talked before her of his sincere enthusiasm for his calling. The rising tides of Advertisement broke and recoiled from the gates of Lambs Court. The best conversations I had with him during her life were away from her, and it is since her death that he seems to me to have developed most interestingly and boldly. Dickon was incapable of amateurism, and not only his life, but his whole view of life, had to centre upon his occupation. Even more than in my own case, his activities had to be related to the beginnings of things and the utmost star. But he felt her gentle irony at the gravity of his prolusions, her scepticism of the values in his drama, her recognition of his egoism. She was terribly, because so unconsciously and inevitably, a delicate lady, and not an actress upon the stage of life.

This contrast between them intensified as the years went on. At first he carried her with him much more than he did in their later years. He talked most of his thoughts to her. When he talked to her he could persuade her. Then, I think, he became shy of something passive in her assents. She approved, but she never came to meet him. He felt that in her presence his ideas became huge and clumsy, sweaty and crude— as new things must be crude, and that he forced them on her. So he ceased to force them on her. There is a vein of self-distrust deep in Dickon's nature.

His ascendency over me was established so early and so firmly in our student days that it only dawns upon me now that at times Dickon must have been sensitive to my opinions. Innovation, experimenting, "giving the thing a try," were the quality of his life. He felt the risk in some of his views and acts. And she so manifestly favoured ripened and finished things, fine old furniture, works of art rather than works of science, polished conduct and acts as perfectly adjusted from their very inception as the muscles of a Persian kitten.

Dickon was greatly stirred by the war and by his own experiences of the war. As I have told, he was attaching very broad ideas to advertisement even before the war. Propaganda was an immensely stimulating discovery for him. And the idea of Reconstruction after the war seized upon him, interwove with those expanding ideas about advertising, and for a time possessed him altogether.

The Period of Reconstruction is still only five or six years behind us, and already it is difficult to revive its emotions and expectations. Even more difficult is it to recall the mental states of the war.

PERIOD OF RECONSTRUCTION

We began with heroism and sacrifice. I shall insist to the end of my days that the last months of 1914 were a tragically splendid phase in European experience, months of high, heroic, terrified living for a great multitude of people. I do not think that so far as we English were concerned the war degenerated greatly until the latter part of 1916. Then with conscription the mirage of greatness vanished. Like a mirage its disappearance was imperceptible. One became aware that it had gone. The war was discovered to be a daily tale of stupid and beastly destruction, moral even more than physical.

And then it was that the clamour for Reconstruction became strong. All this bloodshed and waste was the agony in which a new and fairer world was to be born; the war was to end war and social injustice. This slaughter was the seed-time sacrifice from which we should reap the brotherhood of man.

In the years immediately after the war, with the frightful squalor and sufferings, the fear, pain and stress, the atrocious wastage and tragic heroisms of the struggle fresh in our minds, it was a moral impossibility not to think that there must have been something more than mere destruction, mere warning, in this immense disaster; that somehow a price had been paid and a gain achieved. I suppose I am an exceptionally sceptical man, but I confess that was my conviction for some time. Only very slowly did I begin to accept the possibility that the abyss had swallowed up that enormous wealth of life, effort, and material accumulation, that it was gone for good, gone never to return, without recompense or consolation.

Now we can begin to face that monstrous verity. The war did no more for mankind than the Black Death or a forest fire. It solved nothing, inaugurated nothing. At best it swept away illusions. The Period of Reconstruction was the hectic death of one of the greatest of these; that good arises automatically out of suffering.

But while my resort to the consolation of the Reconstruction Period was at least temperate, Dickon's acquiescence in that idea of a comprehensive and forward movement in human conditions was passionate and complete. " A world fit for heroes," he reiterated. " Magnificent phrase, Billy! And it's alive. It will do things."

He did think it would do things. But what he thought it would do I still do not find very clear.

Across the seas came Woodrow Wilson, with that large, gaunt face of his, solemnly inscrutable, bringing his schoolboy essay in politics, his Fourteen Points. We knew nothing then of his vanity and narrowness nor of his limited authority. Nor did he. He seemed to promise the organisation of a world peace. Within the framework of security this ensured, there was to be a sort of voluntary collectivism. It was not to be Socialism we were assured—because a great number of influential people had declared they were not Socialists, and it would be embarrassing for them to contradict themselves—but it was to have the effect of Socialism. There were to be world-wide labour laws, health laws, protection of women and children, protection of races at a disadvantage, throughout all the planet. Just how it was to be done Dickon seemed to regard as an unimportant detail. He was too full of the spirit for any such particularisation. He would do his job of propaganda and preparation and the other fellows would do their jobs. In that magic word Reconstruction there was no really definite constructive idea at all, no taking apart and putting together again, but instead there was undeniably an enormous amount of what Americans call " uplift." Something was to be done, very large, very generous, very beneficial and splendid; and that was all it amounted to.

I write something was to be done, but now I come to consider it, I believe that what we really thought was that something was going to do itself. And we were to be its ministers and henchmen.

The Lytton Stracheys of 1990 or so may find in this Period of Reconstruction material for much amusing writing. My own failure to be thoroughly amused by it is due, I admit, to a want of humour. I am still too close to it and its immense, if irrational, disappointments. It was a movement of the extremest incoherence and inconsistency. Men full of undisciplined individualism were rushing about talking about collective effort and the subordination of every enterprise to social ends. Men of the rankest patriotism were rushing about talking of the League of Nations. Schemes for re-housing the people of London in great and admirable buildings in London jostled amicably with schemes for scattering the population of London over the countryside. Everywhere beautiful houses were promised for the populace, and nowhere did they appear.

Also there was to be a great exportation of the un-
employed to the Colonies. On scientific lines. And a
colonisation of England that would render emigration
unnecessary. There were to be wonderful new high-
roads. London was to have a railway clearing-house
and save incalculable acres of wasted building land.
Civil air transport, moreover, was to make both roads
and railways superfluous. Productivity at the touch of
the new spirit of collective organisation was to leap up
like a man who has sat on a wasp. Everything was
to fetch a good stimulating price, but then wages would
be enormous. Charing Cross bridge was to be rebuilt
very gloriously as a war monument, and everybody was
to go to school up to the age of sixteen. The output
of blue prints must have been enormous in those wonderful days. The projects were upon every scale and
with every amplitude of scope.

Entangled with a number of self-mobilised business
men and jarring upon them every moment was a mis-
cellany of young University " authorities," economists,
sociologists, professors of political science, very convinced
and guiding and empty; and there were temporary and
permanent Civil Servants in the movement, all mysteriously devious with the devious discretion of men who
have to think of their chiefs and their departments; and
journalists and novelists turned statesmen, making
generous vacant phrases for us in the utmost abundance;
and inventors of this, that, and the other implement for
altering human life completely; and so down to pure
faddists and founts of richly printed matter with which
one's letter-box was choked, beings who filled the souls

of men of affairs with terror and contempt, and drove them back in panic from their new viewpoints to their old business ways.

And the moral hotch-potch was just the same as the intellectual. Mixed up with the entirely honest types like Dickon were the complicated and half-honest; and about these again a considerable crowd of adventurers who were not honest at all, who canted reconstruction and presently canted de-control, and whose one clearly apprehended reality in the pother was an opportunity to snatch. Some of them snatched amazing handfuls. Though perhaps it is not for me to complain of that, seeing the derelict Government undertakings that have fallen back into the hands of Romer, Steinhart, Crest and Co. and their associated enterprises.

§ 13

THEN there came a chill. There is a book of Tarde's called *Fragment d'histoire future,* which Mr. Brereton has translated into English as *Underground Man.* It describes the unexpected extinction of the sun. A sudden extinction, like a gas-light being turned off. It is springtime in France, the almond blossom has come, the birds are nesting, people are going afield, when the catastrophe occurs. The sun rises already shorn of its radiance, cools to a red orb at midday, is dulled to a sullen coppery glow, and a snow-storm that grows thicker and thicker fills the air, driven before a cold and devastating wind. The young elder leaves, the almond petals whirl past and are forgotten.

329

Everyone is presently in flight for shelter and searching frantically under cover for fuel. The icicles gather along the eaves and fall clattering like broken glass before the freezing gale. The plants bud no more, the birds sing no more, a great darkness comes upon the world. Naturally those who have fuel cling to the fuel. The quicker-witted start for the coal-mines and begin to burrow down towards the central heat.

In much the same fashion did the hope of Reconstruction vanish from the sky. Peace conditions had returned and the phase of ready borrowing was at an end. The golden sun of credit veiled its countenance. A heavy ground swell in the European currencies gave place to a storm. The States had over-borrowed and mankind was collectively in debt.

Even during the war the belligerent States had rarely dared to take men's possessions outright. Lives and bodies they had taken freely and recklessly, handing over millions of men like cattle to their poor bluffing and blundering military chiefs to waste and torture as their fear and folly determined, but the property of men these Governments would not conscript. Because, you see, *human society is a labour-imposing, labour-shifting, property-money complex, and life, the more or less of it, only an unpremeditated by-product.* It ought not to be so, perhaps, but it is so. The human complex has grown in that fashion according to its nature, and it is not to be hastily and easily changed into some different play of relationships.

When they might have taken the warring Governments had bought, often at exorbitant prices, and they had borrowed to pay. The bills of these usuries were now being presented. Dickon and I and a number of others of us, business men first and money men afterwards, went to and fro in the year of the Versailles Conference, making a great noise about Reconstruction, putting heart, temporary heart, into a multitude of depressed people; and we no more realised what our real circumstances were than so many bumbles bees in a roomful of spiders' webs. But as the grey filaments wrapped round us and wrapped round us, the note of our buzzing and booming changed. Only those who have hard and vivid memories know how much it changed. But it would be interesting to take a newspaper of the year 1918, let us say, and another of 1924, and count how often the words " Reconstruction " and " Debts " are to be found in each.

The era of Reconstruction faded out, with practically nothing to show for its enthusiasms; it gave place to the era of Debt-collecting and what is apparently a strained and painful attempt to restore the comparatively stable state of affairs that had prevailed in the three or four decades before 1914. Finance and the manipulation of money became the burden of life. The voice of the " constructive " business man died away; nobody wanted to hear it any more; he himself did not wish to hear it any more; and all the world watched the quiet whispering goings to and fro of the bankers and finance ministers.

But though debt and debt-collecting now dominated our thoughts, I do not think that the rapid evaporation of human hope was entirely due to the entanglements of

331

finance. It was certainly not due to any plotting and scheming and foresight on the part of the financiers. No little, diabolically intelligent knot of men had waited at the centre of the threads and said, " Patience! Presently all these poor fools will be in our nets. Then we'll stop this nonsense of hope."

Finance is not a malignant conspiracy; it is only a malignant stupidity, a stupidity we all share actively or passively. It is a persistent, timid adherence to conventions and methods that cannot possibly work out beneficially for the mass of mankind. I have lived near and in business and finance for a large part of my life, and I here declare with the fullest deliberation that I do not believe there are any men of supreme intellectual quality, good men or bad men, now active in the world of finance. There are no doubt many very energetic and quick-witted men, but their acquisitive process is essentially auto-matic, arising out of the current methods of monetary issue and credit. Every human being alive is some-thing of a toil-shifter, and happier in getting than in yielding; most human beings have, in addition, a sneak-ing craving for power and precedence over their fellows, and the weaknesses of the system are found out by the pressure of these common tendencies, quite mechanically, just as the weaknesses of an embankment are found out by the weight of every particle of water it restrains.

Dickon, as he saw his dream of heroic Reconstruc-tion stained and crumpled and spoilt and defeated, was disposed to be very fierce about the Money Power. He would talk of the Money Power throttling the Pro-ductive Power, and assert that at last all great com-

binations of industrial plant fell into the uncreative grip
of the banks. He deplored his share in popularising
loans when he ought, he now declared, to have been
explaining and steadying the country under the " conscription of wealth." But I was never with him in that
direct antagonism between money and productive
organisation. Finance, I agreed, had sewn up the
world in a shroud of debts, but it did that almost as
innocently as a blow-fly lays eggs in a carcass. Without a carcass a blow-fly is a merely secondary nuisance
easily driven away. When you end litter you abolish
flies. Had there been sufficient constructive will and
knowledge in the world it would have made short work
of that web of debts, that enslavement of the world to
the counting-house.

It became very plain to me as things went on that
Dickon and I were impractically vague in our intentions. Yet we two were among the more clear-headed
and capable of the active hopes of the Reconstruction
movement. He had considerable prestige as a propagandist. I was a successful industrial organiser. Until
we came to this test we had neither of us realised that
in practical affairs we were mere fortunate amateurs
following the inertias of our early successes, and no
longer in the habit of solving novel problems. We
were two samples of a body of perhaps a few hundred,
or at most a few thousand, would-be Reconstructors.
All of us, individually and collectively, were entirely
inadequate to the task we imagined we were attempting. Opportunity gleamed upon us suddenly and
found us unprepared—and passed.

How shallow was our conception of Reconstruction!
—was every conception of Reconstruction I ever encountered! To most of the hopeful people of that time
Reconstruction meant simply—all they wanted—at once.
Labour, for example, demanded an immediate shorten-
ing of hours and a rise in wages, and was blind to any
necessity for intermediate phases or auxiliary constructive effort. In England, trade after trade struck vigorously, and got its advances, its eight hours' day, and
crowded off at once to see the cinemas and football
matches, leaving the working-out of the Millennium to
anyone else who chose to bother. Nobody chose to
bother.

I do not blame labour; it acted according to its
nature, just as the creditors and investors acted according to their nature; but the Reconstruction collapse was,
I think, brought to a crisis quite as much by the failure
of labour to understand as by any exactions and obstruc-
tions of finance. Neither the unhelpfulness of labour
nor of finance was the primary factor. The primary
factor was that the organising and administrative people
like Dickon and myself, men of concrete affairs as we
professed to be, men who ought to have known if
anyone did, how to set about reconstructing things,
were caught without a scheme of action—without the
ghost of a scheme of action. We had no sense
nor measure of what was happening to us and the
world. We ought to have known that labour would
be obdurate, and finance insist upon its pound of flesh
at any cost to the body politic. Labour always has been
and always will be unwilling, and creditors will cling to

their claims and have to be dispossessed as firmly if as gently as possible, to the very end of human existence.

We learnt our measure in those days. We were as planless as the Bolsheviks in Russia. We were planless for exactly the same reason—because there never had been any plan. There is no plan. There is no Capitalist plan; there is no Communist plan. There is no plan at all. We have traditions and usages on which we innovate timidly, and they have the claptrap of Marx and Lenin. Both capitalists in the West and the Bolsheviks in Russia extemporise and experiment—with an air of knowing all about what they are doing. We big business men had seemed to be running the economic system in Britain, but, put to the trial, we showed we had no power over it at all. Things had happened and we had happened in consequence.

I do not see that we Western Reconstructors have much excuse for looking down upon the Bolsheviks on the score of failure. They failed to reconstruct from the ground upward amidst the ruins of Russia, and they had a very bad famine and a series of foreign raids to complicate the job for them. We in a shattered and impoverished England failed just as much as they did. But since everything was smashed in Russia before they took on the attempt at reconstruction, their failure showed starkly. In the West nothing was smashed, although everything was strained, and the social and economic inertias carried us through. Our gestures and essays in reconstruction were swept aside by the virtual resumption of the old order, and there was no hitherto been open to criticism indeed, but good enough for him. He could still take a baronetcy in 1919. He is no longer like that.

The war was the beginning of this new birth, but like so many violent accidents, its real quality and consequences were masked by the immediate shock. Even now they are only beginning to come through.

It is curious how irrelevant the actual details of the war seem to be now, and how enormous the effects we begin to realise. I could tell a hundred stories of the war, of our special productions, of hunts for raw material, of ingenious substitutions, of our tragic explosion at Lembury, of our replacement of men by women workers, and how good the first lot were and how bad all the others, of the spies we suspected and the spies we had, of our poison-gas work, and of how we sank a hundred tons of that filth in the North Sea after the war was all over, because there was nothing else to do with it—stories interesting enough in themselves but of no wide significance in my world now, even to me.

Nor do the accounts of the air-raids we stood, the persistent attempts of the German raiders to localise our works and particularly the plant at Downs-Peabody, seem to matter very much now. One moonlit night of crashes and vast silences, in a wide empty street near Victoria, I came upon a man clinging to a railing and mooing like a cow, and his intestines protruded from his waistcoat; he had just been torn open by anti-aircraft shrapnel; I made up a bed for him with some cushions I borrowed and went off into the wilderness of Pimlico to find an ambulance, and when I got back he had disappeared and nobody knew what had become of him—or the cushions: I had to pay for the cushions; and I was dining not a hundred yards from Buckingham Palace with Stetson during an air-raid when a naval shell, which happily proved a dud, I suppose from some boat in the Thames, danced in from somewhere at the back, made a vast smash of falling brickwork and broken window-frames, and came to rest among the hats and umbrellas in the hall without injuring a soul; but these things are now like something seen in a show or dreamt or read about. They join on to nothing. They are like travel snap-shots or like the promiscuous collections of picture post-cards my nephew Dick used to make when he was a very little boy. They call for no more than a passing allusion here. What is of infinitely more moment is the revelation that they brought home to us of the undirected instability of the world's affairs, the realisation that we were not mere passengers but as much responsible navigators upon the ship of human destiny as anyone.

In the winter of 1920 Dickon and I had a long discussion. We had indeed several, we were much together at that time, but it will suit my purpose best to concentrate the substance of it all into one conversation. It crystallised out a number of ideas that I had had in solution for some time. That week or so of discussion marks the establishment of the new phase, the definitive phase, of our attitude to life. I find as I recall it, already well in evidence, the embryonic but recognisable form of that revolutionary project which it

Dickon reflected over his tray.

" And yet, for all that, there is a lot in this idea of Reconstruction," he said. " I've acquired that idea of Reconstruction for good. It's like being vaccinated."

Some sound of guarded assent from me.

" Bigger job than we thought it was," said Dickon, shaving delicately at the lemon peel with the razor Deland had brought for the purpose.

" We aren't going to make over this old muddle of a world yet for a bit," he said, and cut a translucent slice and rejected a pip fastidiously. " I shall leave you to put the sugar, Billy. . . . No. . . . But it's been a lesson."

He completed his duties as host.

He made a compelling gesture towards me with the open razor to hold my attention until he began. Then he composed himself to talk.

" I perceive, Billy, that this little old world of ours has been ready and asking for a revolution, a complete and thorough revolution, for three years. Three years. Since about the middle of 1918. The market was ready, the demand there—and no supply. What has been missing has been somebody to know what was wanted and able to produce it. The world had its mouth open. It was scared tame. Lord! Billy, how funny all this is really. The expectation! The result! That solemn goose of a Wilson laying his addled egg in Paris. Day by day, each day a little more of it out. Mankind awe-stricken. Go on, Great President! Go on! And the Bolsheviks—— Not even an egg——"

He sought for an image.

"Making a mess," I suggested hastily.

"Making a mess—a little weak mess—in the middle of the remains of Russia."

He shook his head at the fire. "Tremendous pause. Mankind puzzled. 'That is all, gentlemen. No, there is nothing more; nothing more at all!' And then presently the old things, the dreary things, the slow and pompous things, the shams, the vested interests and the ancient rights, the kings that mean nothing and the uniforms that mean nothing, come crawling out of their shelters and hiding-places, scarcely able to believe they are still alive. As they are, Billy. As they are!"

"Yet there *was* that pause," said Dickon. "There was a time when the door stood open."

He surveyed history at large. "I suppose there never has been much imaginative greatness in the handling of human affairs. The greatest of men is still an ape —what was it?—'imperfectly depiled.' Good phrase that! All damned nonsense about the dignity of history. Dignity hasn't begun yet. We've had great figures stuck up for us. Cæsar and Marcus Aurelius. Really no better than Winston or Wilson. It's always been this sort of thing really—or worse?"

Dickon returned to his main discovery. "These have been extraordinary years. If there had been a clear project ready and men to put it over, it could have been put over. It was the psychological moment for a great change. . . . I for one thought there was going to be a really great change. A new age. Here and now, Billy. . . . We seemed to see the promised land. And now, where is it?"

began a journalistic career with a jelly-graphed school magazine. The schoolmaster knew how to seize an aptitude and develop it, and he promoted Harmsworth's purple smudgings to the dignity of print and periodicity.

" I've seen some numbers," said Dickon. " It was pretty common stuff; cricket scores and school news and so forth. Northcliffe never wrote a distinguished line in his life. . . . Well—writing distinguished lines isn't—everything. Though, of course, it helps."

While still in his teens, young Harmsworth launched out with a weekly paper called *Answers*. Then came some awful things for errand boys and the cheapest public, *Comic Cuts,* that crying outrage. " Great money makers, I'm told," said Dickon.

The *Daily Mail* followed and was a brilliant success. The world became aware of a personality different from the ordinary newspaper personality, an influence and an energy. Then came opportunity, and this Harmsworth of *Comic Cuts* secured a controlling interest in *The Times* and became a power, presently a very considerable power. The peerages of himself and his brother were formal recognitions of his substantial success. Northcliffe and Rothermere became the golden flowers on the stem of Harmsworth Brothers. He pushed forward to something like a commanding position in the country among the uncertainties, hesitations, and novel occasions of the war.

" It makes our little rush up look quite a gentle ascent," said Dickon.

Dickon had become associated with Northcliffe during his propaganda activities. There was a real liking between them. "He's got imagination, real imagination, the quality that makes a great man, Billy; almost the only man he is with a touch of greatness in our public affairs. The only one."

"You don't think there's something great about such a type as Arthur Balfour?" said I.

"That damned Madonna lily!" said Dickon. "He grows where he's planted," and came back without further comment to Northcliffe.

"He knows that we are a new sort of men, and that this is an age of new things. He knows there is the possibility of great reconstructions in the air. He's not clear about it, but he feels it. He's alive to it. He's not afraid to change the world. That's what makes him signify, Billy."

Dickon gave me a little vignette of Northcliffe and himself sitting in a room in Crewe House, a fine town-house of the old régime that had been requisitioned for propaganda headquarters against the Austrians and Germans, an easy spacious town-house with a garden of its own up behind Shepherd's Market in the heart of the West-end, full of eighteenth-century dignity and eighteenth-century furniture. "They talk of revolutions," Northcliffe had remarked in that soft whispering voice of his. "Our being here *is* a revolution."

"That," said Dickon, "is Northcliffe near his top note. A bit exalted. None the worse for that. But seeing things. Seeing changes. Seeing forces."

He leant forward, poked the fire, and spread his amplitudes before the blaze. "In a sense," said Dickon, "it was true. In a sense—it was nonsense."

selves. And the power slipped away from them. It was like that moment when Wat Tyler, the Kentish rebel, was killed. The crowd stood irresolute. There was the Press, as the prince had been, mounted and in full view, capable of saying what it chose to say and take control. And there it was with nothing to say—exposed in that expectant silence.

"These men," he remarked, "came up by being new. If they stop being new, they fall back into a position of subordination to the old gang, and cease to matter. They amalgamate with the old crowd and are lost. . . . They don't know their opportunities. They are afraid of their opportunities. Too big for them. . . . Except possibly Northcliffe. I'm not so sure of Northcliffe."

Dickon made a gesture of despair and dismissal, with a glass that was fortunately nearly empty.

"They could say what they like," he said, "even now. The whole world still listens for an idea."

He went on to a general review, an irritated, exaggerated, influenza-touched review, of what he called the new forces in English affairs: "The men like us." Those new forces had never realised their quality and their outlook. That was our trouble. No mental synthesis, no clear understanding, was there.

I give Dickon's views as well as I can. They are not precisely my views, but they are the brothers of my views. He saw things from the angle of a great advertiser, he overvalued the conspicuous, and his choice of new men was very different from mine. But I do not remember that I argued with him that night. I let him cite his own cases.

Lloyd George, Dickon insisted, was one of the " new forces." In 1920, certainly, he was still a very big figure. " In politics he's just what I am in advertisement, and Northcliffe is in journalism, and you in metallurgy—a new sort of man with new scale methods." None of us could have existed in 1880, neither Lloyd George nor Northcliffe, nor ourselves, nor any of the prominent men of the day under sixty. Asquith and Balfour and Grey were by comparison just dignified statesmen in the Victorian tradition. They had learnt to be British statesmen at the Universities under the best tutors. They were incapable of freshness or adaptation. " Locums," said Dickon. They had been pushed aside for a time, and all their type and tradition could still be thrust aside. Thrust aside for good. An active figure like Lloyd George made them look like historical monuments.

But in Lloyd George also there was something that made for futility. " He's just a magnificent weed. In flower. Where one might have a great tree. He lives from hand to mouth. He's as clever as six foxes. Sane—too sane. Meanly sane. What's the matter with him? Just the opposite of Northcliffe. No end of cool, clear brains, but they don't seem to be in the right place or the right way up, or something. No length of vision. No imaginative warmth. There Northcliffe has the pull of him. And Lloyd George can't wait. You must have long views before you can wait. Temperamentally he can't wait. And less audible, less brilliant, slow and tenacious, the old gang of long-established property, of banking and rent, the implacable gold standard and the unwearying creditor, the old gang who want nothing more to happen for ever. He made an acute guess that found its confirmation in the General Election of 1924, when almost all the residue of his " new men," battling one against the other, were swept away or driven into secondary positions. The chill of the coming day when Mr. Asquith would become an earl and a Knight of the Garter, Lord Birkenhead a minister-journalist, and Lloyd George a comparative nobody was upon him. Though he foresaw the coming phase of reaction, he was not yet reconciled to its inevitability. He still clung doubtfully to his hero, Northcliffe, a loyalty that was so soon to be shattered by a pitiful death.

§ 15

THE fever and the whisky and the quinine that were working together in Dickon's blood that night seemed only to give his mind a wider sweep. He generalised with unusual freedom. He expanded his discourse upon British affairs, until it became an exposition of a world-wide struggle to re-make. He saw that struggle everywhere as a triangular conflict. First there were these " new men " of his, the Sons of Light, still uncertain in their quality; and next there were the " haves," the holders, the creditors, the financiers, the antagonists weaving the nets about these extraordinary Sons of Light he had chosen; and

354

thirdly there were the "have-nots," labour that would not labour, that did not want anything that anybody else wanted, but did not know what it wanted, the retrogressive obstruction, the massive veto, the eating, breeding crowd.

We two had grown up in an age of rapid progress, and we were too much disposed to take progressive change as the natural order of the world. We were only beginning to realise that the rush of progress had brought also a stimulation of the defensive, a strengthening of the resistances that protected established things. The forces that had been disturbing and enlarging the scale of human affairs for four or five generations might have exhausted themselves in the catastrophe of the Great War. "Crashed," said Dickon. It was an unpalatable line of thought for him, but he followed it manfully for some time. The owner was resuming his loosened grip everywhere; the creditor was recovering from his earlier dismay and confusion, and there was no residue of creative force to resist his return.

Perhaps we were in for a phase first of stagnation and then of retrogression. It was, yes, it was possible. It might last as long as the forward rush and undo much of its achievement. The conservative forces wanted, indeed, only to fix and retain; they were as unwilling to go back as to go forward, but you cannot fix and retain without stagnation, you cannot have stagnation without decay, and you cannot have decay without disorder. For a while Dickon was morbid. Life asserts itself in the unused organ as putrefaction or cancer. Decay meant conflict even more certainly than his destruction a loss to the world. And I agree, too, that he did embody forces that are still operating largely about us.

From his exposition of Northcliffe, Dickon began in a large febrile way to seek through all our world for what he called "creative far-reaching men." The world needed them; the world was ripe for them; these "new men" of to-day were only the precursors of the men who had to come. To him it seemed essential that they should appeal to a great multitude of hearers, be audible to the ends of the earth. Until a thing had been put through to the multitude and had taken hold of the multitude, it had not, from his point of view, been done. From the very nature of the case it was manifest that the primary thing in the career of these redeeming advertisers would be that we should know about them. And we did not know about them.

For a time he discussed the American publicity people and such great newspaper men as Hearst and the Pulitzers. From that he spread out upon a general comparison of English and American. "I've met Hearst," he said, "as often as I've met Rothermere; I've spent days with both the Pulitzers, and do I begin to know anything about them? No. I've not the faintest idea of what they are up to, or what they *think* they are up to. Billy, why are Americans, all Americans, Americans without exception, such mysteries to us? European race. More often than not *our* race. Our language. Conditions after all very like ours. A bigger country, of course. A different pace. Difference of phase. But while you seem to get Englishmen and Frenchmen all round and through and through, half an American is in a loud glare and the other half is darkness. It's like seeing things by the beam of a searchlight after you have been seeing them in a light that is soft and grey and generally diffused.

"That's it, perhaps, Billy. A profound difference in their publicity, using publicity in its widest sense. From the way that a child gets looked at and talked about, onward. They're lit up differently, inside and out. And what is life but a consequence of illumination? When you go to America and see headlines and interviews with a girl about her engagement, or with a professor about his resignation, you at first say, 'Good God. There's no privacy here at all!' And then you discover that outside that crude, cheap, hasty, flat, mis-leading lighting-up of salient objects and events, there's abysses of darkness, immense pits where much goes on and nothing is exposed—and people, rich people especially, unobserved in them and doing the most extraordinary things.

"In Europe a man may have a private life, yes, but in America he has a secret life, lit by sudden shouting judgments and flashes of journalistic lightning. In which you get an impression—vivid enough but wrong. Things about him that would be plain here are invisible there, even to himself. And other things come out with a kind of scream, all out of proportion by our standards. It's because of that, Billy, that to our Euro-pean senses Americans never seem quite real. The quality of the exposure, the method of illumination to

"This new reconstructed world, Billy, is like a big dragon-fly jerking itself bit by bit out of its larval skin. Jerking and then resting. It's wet and quiet just now, a little disposed to quiver, making no noise, but it's nearly here; it's almost out; it's coming on."

"And presently, all at once, it will spread out its wings and buzz," I said.

"And then we shall know about it."

He looked at me with that queer experimental expression of his, like a small boy who has given his little brother a dose and does not quite know how it will agree with him or he with it. I looked back at him and laughed. "You'd like to be sure."

"There is a lot in what your friends the Communists call the economic interpretation of history," said Dickon. "If material needs make political and social forms, then big business and international finance will presently develop a soul of its own, become really conscious of itself and make itself known to the world. The same experiences will beget the same ideas. There must be fellows not only in America but Germany and France who are getting, as we are getting, towards their idea of positively making a new world system—not letting it happen merely, but making it happen."

Dickon reflected. "China? Japan? India? It can't be all aimless mooning. Here two or three are talking, there someone is writing. Convergent thoughts perhaps. Surely convergent. Every day there must be someone pushing the new ideas just a little further, clearing up, rounding off, maturing, making possible and practicable. That is the real Reconstruction. But for the world in general they are still inaudible, smothering, unable to speak out yet within the swelling, uncomfortable old institutions. Then someone says something, definite effort is started, the trouble begins."

He paused, a little troubled by his growing and distending metaphor. He was always begetting these metaphors and finding them too much for him.

" Then is the time for the man-midwife," I suggested, " the propagandist, the advertiser, to set about his task, and bring the new order into the world."

As we talked we replenished our glasses with a reasonable moderation from the decanter and the kettle on the hob, and I think we talked on at last partly because the influenza made us feel as physically lazy as we were mentally flushed, and disinclined us for the little effort needed to get ourselves from the fireside to our waiting hot-water bottles. And it was interesting to have my brother spreading out his general ideas to me again after so many years. It was interesting to see how close he had come to certain speculations of my own.

At last the little clock upon the mantelshelf pinged one o'clock in the morning, and Deland, whom we had supposed asleep, coughed rather markedly in the passage. He would not go to bed before his precious charges were safely tucked away.

Dickon stood up, a great bulk, and stretched out his freckled fists.

" That whisky and the talk has done me good, Billy. Well, the Reconstruction of the world is going to be a long job—but it's going to be done. Even if *we* die— futile. The present muddle isn't going on for ever. . . .

Reconstructing the world. It's interesting. And besides, Lord! *what else is there to do with life?*"

He drooped and stood with his hands in his pockets staring at the fire.

" Minnie. And the children married and scattered. It's passed like a dream."

§ 16

SO, in effect, Dickon talked and thought four years ago—nearly five years now.

I think it was Dickon who first hit upon the image of Vishnu, Siva, and Brahma, the Indian triad of fundamental gods, to express the main forces in the world about us. We found that a very happy symbolism for our ideas. Neither of us can stand a dualism in politics or social life, a mere antagonism of the ins and the outs, the haves and the have-nots. Both of us have an instinctive hatred of eternal rhythms. Dickon, even more than I, insisted upon the triangularity of human affairs. The war of Vishnu, the stubborn conservative, against Siva, the democratic destroyer who ploughs up and inundates, would mean only a dreary alternation of dulness and catastrophe, if it were not for Brahma the inventor, the creative spirit, for whom politics has so rarely found expression. He is the innovating thing; he is always young and being born into the world, always struggling to become effective. That Hindu trinity is far nearer to political and social realities than the Persian dualism of light and darkness, the dualism of the good and the bad, that the party system suggests.

Like modernist theology, like all such applications of ancient and time-worn phrasings to new necessities, it fails a little under scrutiny. Dickon's treatment of Lord Northcliffe and Mr. Lloyd George as Sons of the Morning, lit by the spirit of Brahma, is decidedly unsatisfactory. Something has gone wrong there. I make identifications in quite another direction, but of those I will tell later. My identifications, too, are provisional and for want of any better. But I think they are nearer than Dickon's. Mr. Baldwin is better as Vishnu's Prime Minister, and there is much to be said for the view that the Duke of Northumberland is a modern incarnation of Vishnu. But the genteel Ramsay MacDonald and the inexpressive Clynes, man-of-the-world Thomas, and Catholic Communist Wheatley are not very good as—shall I say Sivatheria? Siva keeps his temple, if he keep a temple anywhere, in Moscow. Does Siva tolerate temples? One thing I know, that in the heart of every youngster forced at the very dawn of adolescence to accept a destiny of obedience, inferiority, and uncongenial toil there is a potential altar to Siva with the red fire waiting to be lit.

Perhaps it would be better to stress the eternal intermingling of the triad. The spirit of Vishnu—that is to say, the stiff, fierce cowardice of established advantage, the spirit of Siva, the wild resentment of exclusion and imposed inferiority, the spirit of Brahma, the urge of curiosity and creative experiment; all these in varying degrees work everywhere and in all of us. Wherever there is ownership and government Vishnu installs himself; wherever there are dispossessed masses Siva reigns. Brahma, who makes all new things, dominates neither ruler nor crowd, but moves throughout the universe, progress eternal. . . .

If Vishnu rules among the creditors and conservatives and Siva is the god of debtors and the parties of the left, does it follow that Brahma is to be identified with liberalism?

This is a matter for discussion not so much for me as for the bright young gentlemen, often now quite middle-aged, who spend their vacations reviving the Liberal Party in conferences and summer schools. I admit that liberalism has always attracted me, and even in my socialist days as a student I called myself also a liberal, I still call myself a liberal and my views liberalism, but the repulsion of the Liberal Party has been as strong as the attraction of its name. When I dabbled in politics in that rather excited and uncritical reconstruction period after the war, I joined the Labour Party—I do not now recall exactly why. Possibly because of the little bunch of intellectuals who gave it a delusively constructive air. Under democratic conditions all parties are the same stuff and all politicians are alike; the game they play is the same for all of them, and every team must be made up of much the same sort of men. But nevertheless—though Mr. Vivian Phillipps, Chief Whip I understand of the surviving fragments, would not own me—I am a liberal. And so is Brahma the Creator. Though I do not think he would own Mr. Vivian Phillipps.

Of all kinds of men who have ever been active in affairs, I suppose the English Whig of the eighteenth century is most after my heart. Yet I doubt if the real Lord Brahma is very like an eighteenth-century English Whig. . . .

Since Dickon took to monetary reform as his special and comprehensive task, he has, I remark, restricted Vishnu more and more to the creditor spirit and the power of gold. And if he were pressed for some evidence of the existence of Brahma, he would find it in the projects for a regulated currency as they have been sketched by Mr. Maynard Keynes. But where he will find the spirit of Brahma expressed in the public affairs of America I do not know. I hesitate between Mr. Henry Ford and ——. But why should I be thus specific about men so far away from my continual observation? Let me keep my personal allusions for the lands I know. Here in France they are quite sure that the one God of America is Vishnu, the Trans-atlantic Brahma is as inaudible to them as he is obscure to us, and Siva, they gather, is either detained at Ellis Island or safely in gaol.

A golden incarnation of Vishnu rules America, as they see it from these broken European countries, rules America absolutely, sitting upon a Treasury full of gold. Indeed, the American Vishnu sits, in this vision, like a golden weight upon all the world, smiling gold stoppings at the figure of Hope. But I am an Anglo-Saxon myself and I know that I do not know America. More may be hidden in a market-place than can be hidden in a desert. America seems to be leading the world now, and seems likely to go on leading the world for some time, in the reconstruction of economic life upon this new scale, the scale of the great modern business combinations. It cannot do this, I hold, without producing, in addition to a vast encumbrance of merely wealthy common persons, a great number of energetic and capable directive men and women of a definable type, people who will ultimately be bored and irritated by existing political institutions and current ways of living, and who will set themselves, more and more intelligently and co-operatively, to the entire reconstruction of human affairs.

At present such types are still ineffective in America, because, among other difficulties, they have to struggle towards understanding through thickets of mind-destroying slang and swamps of verbose cant. You do not hew your way across a great continent in three generations and carry your vocabulary intact. America has partly lost the ancient gift of rational speech. American thought is more hampered than we realise by the necessity of expressing itself in a language that is habitually depraved. It is kept at a low level by the universal resort to the common school, with its badly trained teachers and poor equipment, and by those peculiarities of illumination upon which Dickon expatiated, which sacrifice clearness so ruthlessly to vividness, and precision of dealing to harshly dramatic effect.

§ 17

ONE other aspect I want to give of Dickon before his picture is completed, a glimpse of something very deep in him. What I have to tell may seem extraordinarily nothing to the reader, but to me it is the very heart of Dickon. It was one day, at most two years ago, after my very first discovery of Provence and before he went off to Brussels, that this incident occurred. I was sleeping that night at Bordon Street, and when he came in I was reading by the fire.

It was late. He was a little flushed and crumpled, in dinner dress and with his decorations. I did not know at the time where he had been; I learned that afterwards.

There had been a great dinner of Advertisers—I rather think it was one of the organisations he had created—and he had spoken and let himself go. A little warmed by champagne and professional fraternity, he had spread out his dream of the Advertiser as prophet and teacher to a pleased but incredulous gathering. Someone had laughed, and he had sounded a prophetic note in reply. " We are the masters of the newspapers and they know it," he had said. " We and we alone have the ear of the world. We can dictate what shall be known and what shall not be known, what shall exist and what shall not. We can educate the people or degrade the people, exalt right things and humble base things. We can be the guide, philosopher, and friend of the common man—working together (renewed laughter). Why should we not rise to the full height of our possibilities?"

Then he had paused and come to something like an anticlimax.

"Are we never to reach beyond motor-cars and medicines, cigarettes and pickles?"

He lowered impressively for a second or so and then sat down.

The Organised Advertisers cheered and hammered the tables, but also they looked curiously at one another and glanced at Dickon, flushed and already doubtful of the wisdom of what he had said. They had heard some of this before from him, but not so much nor so plainly.

"There was moderation in all things," commented a subsequent speaker. "Our energetic and masterful friend to whose organising fervour our profession owed so much," was, he thought, a little prone to exaggerate. It was not perhaps altogether a fault in an advertiser (laughter) within limits (renewed laughter). But though it might be good business to exaggerate, it was not wise to threaten (hear, hear). We had our share, a great share, he would indeed go so far as to say a vital share, in stimulating and in sustaining the currents of trade, the prosperity of our mighty empire, but it was a share — in subordination. It had its place and its limits. There was such a thing as taking one's bit too seriously. . . .

Possibly through sheer clumsiness he had circled about and repeated this thought three or four times. But he was encouraged by " Hear and hear " and some gentle rapping on the table. What had been intended as a friendly reproof became an attack upon Dickon, and at the end what they call a trouncing.

Dickon was a respected and popular figure in the advertisement world, but his was the reluctant popularity accorded to success. His associates liked him but they felt at times, I think, that he did a little to compel them to like him. This talk of their high responsibilities after dinner had not so much flattered them as made them feel uncomfortable, and the gathering fell back very readily into a sympathetic deprecation of "exaggeration" and "lack of humour." They applauded warmly; they nodded their approval. Later speakers showed an increasing disposition to echo and even exceed the trouncer, and a funny man saw his opportunity, and the applause and laughter grew.

The arrow still chafed in Dickon's hide. He stood before the fire and brooded immensely before his explosion.

"This damned sense of humour!" he cried suddenly and violently.

"Eh?" said I, looking up from my book.

"You might do a decent thing that would make you look a bit high-falutin'. And so you do a shabby, lazy, second-rate thing instead, and grin and say, 'Thank God I've got a sense of humour.' That's what it amounts to."

"Is this me, Dickon, you're talking to?"

"Oh no, Billy! I never talk to you. I was thinking. Man I heard speak to-night. Took me up—for blowing a bit too strongly about advertisement. . . .

"Perhaps I said too much. . . . Perhaps I did."
He went on as if he addressed some third person.

"But *Modesty!* Knowing your place in the world!
Rot it all is! Rot I tell you. Cringing, shamming,
shirking muck they bully into boys in public schools.
And from an Advertising Man of all people! An
Advertiser! Think of it! Modesty! Not going all
out for the things that have to be done! Let a child
drown under your eyes! Thank God *you* don't pro-
fess to be a swimmer. *You* don't take upon yourself
to rescue all the drowning kids in Christendom. If
some presumptuous silly ass who can hardly swim at
all chooses to go into the water and gets himself into a
mess, *you* aren't going to do anything but smile. Flick
a pebble at his head as he comes up for the third time.
You're a quiet smiler, you are!"

I leant back in my chair to appreciate my brother
better. There was nothing else to do. I was still at
a loss to know what it was all about. He was just the
slightest bit drunk, but mostly this was, I perceived, a
rational passion.

"Sense of humour!" said Dickon. "There isn't
much of that poison in Advertisement, anyhow. . . ."

He seemed to recall my presence.

"You may laugh, Billy! But that blamby-pamby
idiot to-night has got my goat. I've been a hot man
to-night in a world of quiet smiles. Fuming. He let
me up to seeing what all this gentlemanly grinning and
smirking and enjoying the fun of it quietly and un-
assumingly really means. Why should a man be guyed
for taking himself seriously? What else *is* there to

take seriously? Those chaps who won't take themselves seriously ought to have been headed off by birth control and never begun. All this half-doing things! All this living with the guts out! . . . A joke's a joke in its place, but most of this not taking yourself too seriously is a dirty sin against heaven."

And suddenly Dickon soared above me. He became a pulpit and my admirable armchair a pew. His voice mingled expostulation and passionate assertion in the most extraordinary way.

" Because one sets out to do big things, Billy, because there are big things to be done, because one works until one gets ragged and sore, it doesn't follow one is presumptuous. We two are successes, Billy; life has pampered us, petted us, put its best carpets under our feet. Have we a right to be anything but serious men? *Damned* serious men! It's no want of modesty to attempt everything one can; to play as big a game as one can; it's a sense of obligation. What we *are*. . . . That's another question.

" Don't we know each other through and through, Billy? Do we pretend? Do we put on airs? Don't I know what asses we are, I who can't leave a scrap on my plate and you who brighten at the swish of a girl's skirt? But you *do,* Billy! Everyone sees it. Don't we know how we blunder, how we lose our little tempers, the endless *silly* things we do? Yes, and all the same, with all our weaknesses upon us, we've got to be in deadly earnest and do our biggest job.

" If we don't, who will? Look here, Billy. . . . Is there a race of Gods among mankind, that you and I can slack? Which will do things if we don't? If we stand aside, smirking in our elegant modesty, who is there to take hold of things? A sense of humour, I tell you, Billy, is no fit possession for a decent man. Let the failures have their damned sense of humour! Cuddle it and nurse it. They need it. Let them snigger and sneak and steal, and make funny faces behind the backs of the men in earnest. That's *their* road, the low road. But for us—things have been put before us, Billy, and we have to take hold of them. We may not be aristocrats; our luck may be all chance; but for good or evil, God has put us among the masters in the affairs of men. And a master I mean to be. Oh, I'd rather——"

He paused to assemble it.

" I'd rather be a skunk and set myself to outstink this drain into which I have fallen, stink and stink hard, instead of making for fresh air, than be one of these damned sense-of-humour business men."

Queer how Dickon could be stung at times!

He was quiet for a moment. "I know I'm a fat ass," he said in an altered voice. "Oh, I know I'm a fat ass and deserve to be grinned at. Don't I *know* it!"

He went on talking to himself in broken sentences. " Take the second plateful. . . . Go to the club. How can one help eating too much at the Ermine? Sleepy afternoon. . . . Half one's efficiency gone. . . . Things like that. Temper over a tight collar. . . . The times I've shocked Minnie! Such a poor *comic* thing! . . ."

374

The muttering died away into an incoherent rumbling that was presently ended in a nod and a " Yes."

Then he stood quite still. And suddenly whispered something that gripped me strangely. He whispered it quite forgetful of me, as one whispers a phrase that one has thought out and chosen long ago and repeated many times. I perceived at once that it had been his ultimate consideration on many such occasions of trouble.

" *Weak as we are,*" said Dickon, " *those others are weaker.*"

I stared at him. I had known Dickon all my life, and suddenly it dawned upon me that in some things I hardly knew him at all.

He woke up again.

"Pity I got in a temper!" he said. "Oh!—a damned pity!

"I could have murdered that fool. . . .

"I showed it and they grinned at me. . . . I'm glad I had you to blow off to, old man. . . .

"I shouldn't have slept all night. Sometimes cursing him and sometimes cursing myself. No one knows the nights we spend, some of us, Billy. . . .

"You see, Billy, what I said wasn't exactly what I meant to say. I overdid it. What I said was right, but somehow I overdid it. I gave him a loophole. I don't say things exactly. It's too beastly hard to say things exactly.

"But they got what I was after all right. . . . Damned sight too much for them. . . .

"They like being funny little nibbling beasts. They *like* it. . . ."

I forget what else he said. I was not listening any longer. I was turning over his astonishing aphorism in my mind. "*Weak as we are, those others are weaker.*"

That, I think, is the quintessence of Dickon.

§ 18

IT is curious how the social uses of Lambs Court have dissolved away since the death of Minnie. Richard Clissold Junior has married now, and Winnie has gone to live with her husband in Italy, and young William, my godson, is something of a rebel and a painter (but, I begin to think after my last visit to his studio, a very good painter), and until my great-nephews and great-nieces repopulate it Lambs Court above stairs is an empty place, left more and more to the routines of old and trusted and conservative servants.

Dickon's life, for all our early divergence, reverts to the pattern of mine—the life of a man who has come through the ordinary drama of the world with the sense of a part played out, who is yet full of vitality and anxious to get things done, who still has strong and deep desires, but who is no longer swayed by that intensity of personal reference that narrowed his life before. In that period of renewed intimacy that followed Minnie's death we discussed almost as if we were students again what we were doing with the years that still remained to us. Both of us were at loose ends. Both of us were becoming acutely aware of our dwindling handful of life, and both of us were asking ourselves, as it soaked away between our fingers: "What am I doing with it? What is the best that I can do with it?"

We were pulling ourselves together for the last lap of coherent living. We were entirely vague then about our objectives. I had been so for some years; but with Dickon the phase was more acute. And more decisive. Since then Dickon, with characteristic concentration, has settled down to a task of his own, a task that will need all that is left of him to accomplish, and I, for more complicated reasons, am no longer under the same cloud of feeling that then made me unhappy. But for a while it was as if something long forgotten—anxiety of youth, anxiety about the purposes of life—had come back to us out of those far-off adolescent days.

I find myself wondering how many of our contemporaries have experienced such a fresh start, such a phase of doubt and resumption in their middle years. I question if many intelligent people escape that sort of trouble in adolescence. It is so universal that I would call it distinctively "anxiety of youth." Then for most of us comes immediate necessity, the pressure of events; we are caught up and hustled along and excited and distracted and amused, and many of us, perhaps most human beings, never reach those open and interrogative silences again before death ends the storm of experience. Unless there is a space of leisure, a release from the thickets of need, I do not see how that trouble can return. And some happy souls hear no more of these interrogations, because, like Sir Rupert York, they have answered them once for all. It is well I have already given a picture of him in this book, because there at least you have one man who has said, simply and completely : " This work is good enough for me." He will go on unhurryingly, with his bones and his other specimens and the subtle and satisfying problems that concern him, until at last one morning he will not get up, but lie, peaceful and done.

He is one of a number of men of science whom I know to be men serene in their souls and happy in the essence of their lives. But scientific work is a world apart, a magic island cut off from futility. Music, too, may be another magic island, cut off not only from futility but from reality. There is a protective isolation about most of the arts. But Science has most of this precious detachment. And is yet profoundly real. Scientific workers work to the end, though at last they may go gently like a boat coming home as the wind falls in the evening. I was once upon that island of enduring work. Had I kept upon it I should not have been writing this book now and making these half-envious, half-admiring reflections.

Even when there is a space of leisure I doubt if that phase of middle-aged unrest happens very generally. It is natural for me now to find the quality of middle-aged people's lives particularly interesting. I am impressed by the present proliferation of the middle-aged. They form a larger proportion of mankind than was ever the case in the world before. And I am more aware of them.

Quite as important in human affairs as that change

of scale upon which I have been dwelling in recent sections is the prolongation of life now in progress. I do not think I am being led away by my own circumstances to exaggerate its importance. The average age of the English, for example, has risen steadily for the last century. For that, at any rate, we have fairly trustworthy figures. In Elizabethan times one was mature at thirty and old at forty; Shakespeare was already a worn-out, unproductive old man in retirement at fifty. Everything was earlier and younger then; Romeo had the years of a raw undergraduate, and Juliet was a child. One loved and loved again and married and had children, and by the time they were of age the game was done. The ordinary man of fifty was fat or grey or bald and his teeth had gone beyond repair. There was no repair.

Young people died freely at all ages; more children died than lived to maturity. There was a fever, therefore, to get to the crises of life before the chance was snatched away.

> " What is love? 'tis not hereafter;
> Present mirth hath present laughter;
> What's to come is still unsure :
> In delay there lies no plenty :
> Then come kiss me, sweet and twenty,
> Youth's a stuff will not endure."

That was the note of it. To be old and hale was remarkable. It was to be distinguished and isolated. The aged of fifty and upward formed a dwindling chorus to the song of youth. They sat and looked on at the dance—a little outstaying their welcome. The literatures of the world still preserve the spirit of that more transitory time, and its tradition dominates us to-day.

In all classes now, but particularly in the prosperous classes, people do not die as once they did. More and more hold on. And they are cared for and mended; it is not merely life that is prolonged, but vigour. Vigour and the desire for living. An accession is developing to the human life cycle; a stage after the family life, which itself grows less and less prolific and uses up the available energy less and less completely. And this elder stratum has no traditions as yet to shape its activities. Literature has not prepared us for it, and we come through to it with a sort of surprise. As soon as they have done with loving and getting, the novels, the plays dismiss us with a phrase. We are supposed to be enfeebled, sated, and done. We discover we are not so easily dismissed. We have not finished. We are not enfeebled. We demand a better rôle than to act as chorus to the next generation and offer it out-of-date advice. Here I declare on the edge of sixty is living still to be done, in a new mood and for a new end.

I believe that as civilisation develops this elder stratum is going to play a determining rôle in human development. In the first part of this book I told of a talk I had with Dr. Jung of Zurich. Among other things that I brought away from that evening was the fruitful idea that the prevalent states of mind of quite grown-up people in past ages are preserved as phases in the development of the immature to-day, and that a new, more fully adult phase is spreading from the fifties and forties downward in human experience. This proportionate increase in the elder stratum will contribute greatly to the intensification and extension of this new adult phase. It will ultimately make life more disinterested and more deliberate and less romantic. It will make novels and plays that set out to present life aspects of history instead of stories of mating. But that will only be when this stratum has developed a consciousness of its distinctive quality and rôle. Then it will impose its standards upon the younger generation and assist it sooner and sooner to maturity. At present things are still the other way about, and the elder stratum is dominated by the over-emphasised standards of the younger generation. At present it has still to realise itself. It is like a new actor thrust upon the scene before a part has been found for him. For a time it is a conspicuous encumbrance even to itself.

What an extraordinary spectacle of waste do the lives of the great majority of us middle-aged and older pros-perous people present to-day!

An immense proportion of the property and spending power of the world is now in the hands of old folks, who would in every previous time have died and left things to their heirs. The heirs remain allowanced and functionless, going about the world in a state of arrested reality. They are amateurs of everything, provisionally active, waiting for a call that lingers.

About here in Provence, and especially along this coast from Saint Raphaël to far beyond Genoa, there is gathered an abundant assemblage of this old, pros-perous multitude for my astonished observation. Under eighteenth-century conditions not one per cent. of these people would be alive. Now their still peculiar sham youthfulness sets all the fashions of living. The amount of altogether futile vitality upon these hills and coasts is incredible, until one has gone to and fro through it and mixed with it and watched it.

There is, first of all, a very considerable resident population here of oldish wealthy people. They build, they own or lease beautiful villas with great gardens and lovely prospects. There must be hundreds of thousands of such people along these coasts; from England and America alone they must number scores of thousands; and they must represent an aggregate income of hundreds of millions of pounds. They employ the lives of hundreds of thousands of servants, they spread their gardens over great areas of land, they send up the cost of living for everyone, and they crowd the pulmonary refugees out of the sunshine. They are often men and women who play a vigorous game of tennis, stand the fatigues of whole days of motoring, they come and go among themselves, lunching, dining, assembling, dispersing, and I cannot find a soul among them that is doing anything of large importance in the world or stretching its energies to the full, in any direction whatever. They declare they have played their parts in the world and finished. There are women who have borne and brought up one or two or even three children, and women who have produced none. I could assemble a score of men within an hour's motoring of this *mas,* younger men than I, who say they have " retired." Under that phrase they contentedly rule themselves dead for all effectual ends. They are just playing about, the little innocents, until Nurse Angel-of-Death comes to put them to bed.

Close to me here is a fairly representative sample of these Riviera residents; she is the widow of old Sir Ralph Steinhart, and she was a niece of the original Romer; she inherits an interest in the activities of Romer, Steinhart, Crest and Co. and their subsidiaries from both sides. Every time I have done a hands-turn for any of our concerns I have made her richer. Here she is, within half an hour's drive of me, silver-haired—the natural grey made an even white by skilful bleaching—high-coloured and bright-eyed. She is a little bent and restlessly active. Her gardens are very spacious and fine. We pass them usually when we go to Nice. She has, I observe, obstructed a number of the peasants' paths to make her domain more secluded; she threatens them on boards with *pièges à loup,* and they must go round by a longer way outside her fences to do their business. Inside one rarely sees anything moving among the olive terraces and the frequent stone jars; it is still and deserted except that sometimes in the cool of the evening a manservant is visible taking a pet dog for its sanitary stroll. Nearer the house there are great hedges of agave and cactus, groves of palm and glimpses of glorious colour which, save for herself and a few guests, delight only God and her gardeners. She has bought and evacuated half a dozen peasant houses, she told me one day, to assure the amenities of her view—which, on the whole, is not so good as mine.

I am obliged almost in spite of myself to know some-

thing of her house and her life. When she is here—
for two-thirds of the year she is not here and the house
stands empty except for a caretaker or so and a casual
priest or so, a luxurious blank on the face of the earth—
when she is here, she makes continual efforts to cultivate my acquaintance. It is not that she likes me or
that I even pretend to like her, but because she is
inordinately curious about my relations to Clementina,
and because generally I perplex her and because, more
than anything else, she has nothing better to do. She
persists in raiding me with parties of high-coloured,
bright-eyed, observant Romer and Steinhart nieces and
in-laws. Or with a literary party of those beastly little
cigarette dealers who write novels for the English
county families, and their crumpled and dishevelled
womenfolk. Or with a scratch lot from the dramatic
world. Or even with one of her selected collections
from the aristocratic Catholic circles of Paris. But
these last are rarer. That is the side of her life she
turns away from me. Her car does its best and sticks
inside my pillars, and up they all come on foot, either
quietly agog and staring about them, or else with an
impelled reluctant look, according to their race and
breeding.

As soon as the car is observed below, Jeanne flies
upstairs to put on what is known with us as a Lady
Steinhart apron, and while I entertain the party upon
the terrace with a taciturn amiability, tea is served in
cups of coarse Provençal ware. The party is made to
spread a peculiarly fluid and difficult cherry jam on
toasted crusts with large holes in them, through which

384

the red stuff drips on anything below it, and I converse about the Provençal climate—which has recently developed Anglomania—and intimate my readiness to hear the purport of the visit. If Clementina is present she is silently polite, and regards the visitors in a way that serves at least to embarrass their scrutiny of the books, newspapers, and other oddments scattered about the terrace. Her dog goes a little way off and yaps protestingly and usefully, in a tone that shows that the whole affair is to be considered unusual. After a time something seems to break, and her ladyship and party gravitate down the hill again. I never ask her to repeat the visit, and she always does.

She cannot understand why I should live here for so much of my time in a house that I rent for three thousand depreciated francs a year, wearing dirty old flannels and employing a solitary servant. She knows that I pay ten thousand pounds a year or so in super-tax and income-tax, and this way of living seems to her like a wicked waste of God's bounty. She cannot understand why I sit for so many hours in this upper room to which her way is always barred. And, above all, she cannot understand why Clementina sometimes isn't here and sometimes is; why she has so many meals here, and why she sits dangling her long legs over the wall of my terrace and smoking my cigarettes with an air of complete domestication, while I am upstairs writing. As I never explain Clementina to anyone, as I shall probably not explain her completely even in this book, it is natural that to Lady Steinhart she remains unexplained.

Consequently Lady Steinhart never quite knows whether she really knows Clementina and whether she may, or possibly even ought to, invite Clementina to lunch, and what would happen if she did. And all that is excellent exercise for Lady Steinhart's mind.

Visits like this seem to take up a large part of her time. She and a multitude of other people are always rushing about this country seeing each other; and I will confess I cannot imagine a less interesting series of sights. Like all Romers and Steinharts, she is addicted to discovering and dropping young musicians, and for these special parties have to be assembled. And also she gets through a considerable amount of time altering her house and garden. She is always digging something up or laying something down, or planting out something or opening out a vista, and if she can manage it she takes you to the spot affected and asks your advice. And while you are giving your advice she is thinking of the next thing she will bother you about. She pursues and buys old furniture, pictures, pottery, and jewellery remorselessly and voraciously. It's a clever little fifteenth-century pot that gets away from her once she is on its trail. And when she has bought a thing she glories in it for a little while, and shows it to her friends and makes them guess what she gave for it, and puts it in her already very congested house, where it presently sinks down out of sight among the other stuff; and when she has forgotten all about it, as she must do, I hope her tremendous and implacable major-domo steals it and sells it to someone to sell to her all over again. Then there is also much to be done about her clothes and her dresses and her hair. So her days are always emptily busy and the net result of them is exactly nothing at all.

But you must not think that Lady Steinhart's life is wholly consumed by these activities. She is a very moral woman; there is no talk of a lover for her although she is still short of sixty, and she does not dance more than two or three times a week. But the gap thus left is filled in by a rather distinguished serious side. This serious side she does not let me see as much of as I should like to do. It is the one thing she does not press upon me, and it is the one thing about her that interests me. She is a little bashful with me about it; I do not know why. It reaches high and far. You might imagine that a born Romer, who is a Steinhart by marriage, would be a Jewess, but this is not the case with her. She is hostile to Jews. She is a Catholic. She is substantially one of the old noblesse. She is a Catholic and a reactionary, and it is alleged that she made even Sir Ralph a Catholic after he became speechless before his death. She is involved in French politics at an angle proper to an aristocratic and pious woman. Priests, bishops, monsignori are to be found at her house, moving about quietly, speaking in undertones, forming little black clumps in the bright flower-gardens, obscurely active, mysteriously wary. She has done much for the Church, and she may do more.

And the Church which has always had a weakness for pious women of property makes her a great concession. She has a private chapel of her own to play with; it is her dearest interest. She buys it petticoats and lace and ornaments and jewels and metal pots and pans to put on and take off. It is in the house some-where, and often when one goes in, one is reminded of her serious side by a whiff of incense from some recent function. She can go there alone and meditate, and I suppose she can regale herself with special services, but what she thinks of God when she meditates is as hidden from my imagination as what God can think of her. There is usually a subdued-looking priest or so at her table. Not excessively pampered. The Romer blood is in her veins, and you feel, and you can feel they feel, that they have been paid for.

That private chapel is the crown of her life. It is a great privilege, and she must have sought it for many years. It is the consummation of her bric-à-brac. No doubt the Church weighed the matter and decided that it was worth while to respect her spiritual possibilities to that extent. Perhaps the Church does not know the Romers quite so well as I know them. Anyhow, she has it. The chapel is her distinction. Take that away and substitute a lover, or bridge, or the higher amateurishness in art or criticism, or a specialised col-lecting mania, or a cherished illness, or just blank inter-ludes, and you have the life of quite a large number of these great ladies of the Riviera. And the men, the " retired " men, the resident sort, cultivate their gardens also, play tennis, make love in a vague, furtive way, indulge in wistful reminiscence of the days when they were alive, and are on the whole much less animated than the women. Some are vicious in an elderly, elaborate, Roman way, and their establishments are barred and secret, and their rather too smart men-servants go about visibly clad in light and becoming blackmail. French journalists are modest upon such questions, and the Riviera has no Suetonius. There are not many married couples in constant association among our residents. The prevalent thing is a single personality engaged, with the widest, most dignified, and expensive of details, in futility.

But the residential side of the Côte d'Azur is not, after all, its most typical aspect. Where the big hotels cluster, the multitude grows dense. Sooner or later everyone in the Western world who has more than three thousand pounds a year must come to the Riviera. An invisible necessity seems to bring us here just as the souls in the Swedenborgian books go un-driven to their ultimate destinies. I am here, and, after all, I am rather pretending not to belong to it than honestly detached. For so many of us there is nowhere else to go—quite remarkably there is not. To the north are murderous climates and to the south murderous discomforts. A few come once or twice and then not again, but most who have come continue to come. A middle-aged hunger for the sun is an active, physical cause. The transients come and go tremendously. Many of them still function in some reduced or inattentive way elsewhere; some of the younger set between forty-five and sixty are frankly recuperating; but most have altogether discontinued any contribution to the world's affairs. In the hotels we sit and watch them, guessing ages. The average is astonishingly high. Golden lads of sixty step it briskly with gay girls of forty-five. The grey heads bob to the black music. The other day we found an incessant couple in a Cannes hotel, who golfed all the forenoon and danced together until one in the morning, and both were over seventy. The only young people here seem to be subsidiaries. I make no objection to all this activity on the part of old people. I would rejoice to see them dancing and generally active at ninety and a hundred, but my perplexity is their universal disregard of anything else in the world but amusement taken in a quasi-juvenile form.

For a large proportion of this multitude the belated juvenility finds more questionable expression than golfing and dancing, Darby and Joan. Since they have yet to discover that there is any graver business in life than getting, they must gamble, though they are rich and easy; and since they know of no livelier desires they still want most desperately to go on with the adolescent modes of love. With a little care and effort much may still be effected in that matter. One can still be jealous and vindictive, still charm here and break-off there, be cold and cruel and fitful and make the yearning lover realise the wretchedness of an insecure allowance. When one is no longer over-anxious to steal away with one's dear mistress, one can still be seen about with her. Which accounts for the prevalence here of a large number of really very beautiful and brilliant and highly decorated young women between the ages of fifteen and forty, and a large variety of utterly detestable young gentlemen. A mistress must look the part and have a lavish and pampered air. And for some of those who have had a hard struggle to win to this Paradise of ease and power, there seems to be a peculiar charm in gilt-edged passions; Russian exiles, often with quite genuine titles, nobility from almost everywhere, countesses, duchesses, princesses divorcing or divorced, royal bastards (in profusion and with every degree of authenticity), ex-royalties, and even precariously current royalties are here, and only too ready to oblige. The Americans, they say, are particularly generous and abject paymasters to such people. That is probably a libel on the Americans; there are merely more of them with money.

And, thirdly, there is the sport, the mechanical gratification of shooting pigeons, the assembling to look on at racing, polo, flying, fencing, tennis. The worship of tennis becomes more amazing every year. The papers that come here, even the *Manchester Guardian* and the *Nation* discuss it earnestly, deeply. Photographs of its heroic figures fill the illustrated weeklies. The women have a sort of wadded look about the feet and ankles; the men's faces, in the absence of a ball to hit, are alertly empty. We study the characters, the mannerisms, of these gifted beings. Minniver, it seems, is amusingly short-tempered; he insults his partner and swears. You can hear it all over the court; you can hear about it all over the world. Judkins has a peculiar penetrating sniff. It is, I understand, to be broadcasted.

In relation to all these things cluster the shop-folk and all sorts of dealers, the professionals, the teachers of dancing, the manicurists and complexion specialists, the hoteliers, restaurateurs, and so forth, with their own sympathetically imitative tennis and sport and private vices out of business hours.

It is still full season down there on the beaches, for I got my *lit-salon* reservation for next week from Cannes at only eight days' notice—I have to run to London for some business and leave this writing for a few weeks. But presently this widespread crowd of aimless property will begin to pour home like a sluice along the roads and in the expresses *de luxe,* and so to Paris and more especially to England in May and June, to the Paris dressmakers and body-makers and face-makers and on to the jostling splendours of the London Court, and the culmination of all things at Henley and Ascot— especially Ascot. Grave men will wear grey top-hats with the serious elation befitting such an act, and every sort of dress except the old and shabby will be displayed. The King and Queen, those perfect symbols of the will and purpose of the British Empire, will be gravely presiding over the parade amidst the clicking cameras. Wherever there is a foreground there also will be the Countess of Oxford and Asquith, and no doubt some oaf of a Labour member will be well in evidence in a white bowler hat and a loyal grin—just to make it clear that there is nothing different about Labour. And if you study the photographs and pictures of this immense inane gathering you will see they represent mature and oldish people in an enormous majority, deliberately and gravely assembled, dressed with extraordinary attention, and doing nothing, nothing whatever except being precisely and carefully there.

In the wane of the season here, to replace our first-class assembly, there will come a char-à-banc crowd of the merely prosperous, also middle-aged and getting on with it, filling the Monte Carlo Casino at reduced entrance fees, gambling at five francs a go, and learning how to be rich from the margin. They will envy, they will emulate, they will peep over the villa walls and up the Casino staircases to the private rooms. Some may even go up those staircases. Adventurously. The wives will return to Sheffield or Main Street or Pernambuco marvellously changed about the hair and the skirts and the souls. These are the reserves of the great spending class. They are learning. They spread the stratum wide and deep into the general life. Tons of illustrated papers go out weekly to them to keep them in touch; books and plays of a special sort are made to satisfy their cravings. They have no God, and Michael Arlen is their prophet.

I have written of the " elder stratum," but when I think over my occasional glimpses of life at Monaco and Monte Carlo and Nice I am doubtful whether " elder fester " would not be the better expression. When one traces it away from here to Paris, London, Vienna, New York, California, to Biskra and Egypt, to High Savoy, to Biarritz, Palm Beach, and endless other places, to race meetings and summer resorts, to Scotland and New England, and so to its town houses and country-houses and its places of origin, one realises something of its scale and significance in our Atlantic world. It is all that pays super-tax; it is the surplus of the world's resources. Yet extensive and impressive as it is,

393

it is nevertheless, so far as its present characteristics go, almost as new as the great growth of advertisement in Dickon's lifetime. Its precursors in the town and Court life of the eighteenth and seventeenth centuries were relatively younger, more actively self-assertive and more assured, and incomparably less abundant and diffused. They were a little intimate community, and this is an auriferous flood. I do not believe that its present development is anything more than one distinctive feature of a transitory phase in the great unfolding of human society that is now in progress. This way of living is no more permanent than the way of living one finds recorded—in caricature indeed, but in illuminating and convincing caricature—by Petronius in his *Satyricon*. It is an overspill of gathering human energy like the spots on an adolescent face. No state of human affairs that releases so vast a splash of futile expenditure can be anywhere near equilibrium. It must be, it manifestly is, undergoing rapid changes. Intelligent people, even the intelligent people in the rich elder stratum itself, will rebel against this mode of life, as Dickon and I have rebelled. And all those who are outside of it have only to learn of it to desire to end it, because it is so plainly a vast waste of spending power by essentially powerless people.

Circumstances may have made Dickon and me rather tougher and more refractory stuff than most of our class, less afraid to lie awake at night and look what used to be called the Eternities in the face. But none of these people can be of a very different clay from Dickon and myself, and what has happened to us must happen with slight differences in quality and quantity to most of them. There is a great dread of lying awake at night manifest everywhere. The activity to escape mental solitude is remarkable. Most of the rushing about in motor-cars is plainly due to that. The rich, ageing Americans in particular seem constantly in flight across the Atlantic from something that is always, nevertheless, waiting for them on the other side, whichever side it happens to be. There would not be all this vehement going to and fro if they were not afraid of something that sought them in the quiet places. And what else can that something be but just these questions that have confronted us. "There is only a little handful of water left now. What do you mean to do with it? What under the stars is the meaning of your life?"

"Oh, hell!" they say at the first intimation of that whisper, "where are we going to-morrow?"

Below and behind and all about the petty glittering activities of the elder fester a sane and real next adult phase must surely be preparing even now, the realisation that life can be lived indeed to the very end, and that learning and making need never cease until the last hour has come. Surely there dawns the immense undying interest of social development, of the establishment of a creative order, of the steady growth of human knowledge and power upon the blank outlook of the present. Can these poor, raddled, raffish, self-indulgent, aimless, wealthy types of to-day go on existing as that grows clearer? There is no need of any great convulsion to chase them from existence; they will fade out of the spectacle. Some will learn, some will be expropriated;

many types among them will be made impossible by less speculative methods of production. In that direction things must be moving now.

If I could return to this countryside in only a hundred years' time, I am sure I should find the villas, hostels, roads, promenades of all these places, and all the life that fills them, changed profoundly. The buildings will be for the most part rebuilt and less miscellaneous in their quality. Villa Cocotte in its louder variations may have gone; the gaudy casinos and dancing restaurants will have been cleared away; the gardens will be more beautiful and less strenuously exclusive. The present fences of wire, the *pièges à loup,* and fierce little intimations against trespassing will have been abolished noiselessly by a general amelioration of manners. The peasants' homes will have got bathrooms, and their cultivations will be less laborious and more skilful.

These bathrooms may be already close at hand. Jeanne tells me that one reason given for the cutting down of olive-trees here is that the olive harvest comes in winter and that picking olives swells and stains and chaps the hands. Enough labour cannot be got for the picking. People will not lend their hands to such work. A new phase of civilisation is near when the human hand has won to this much respect.

Swift, silent cars will run about this fairer land on smoother roads, less numerously perhaps, and with a greater appearance of purpose. The advertisement boards, like a clamour of touts that ruin so much of the roadside scenery, will be banished altogether. This Provence is too kind and lovable not to remain the resort of great multitudes of people, but they will no longer be living days of busy inconsecutiveness and pursuing the shadows of unseasonable pleasures.

Perhaps my hopes run away with me, but it seems to me that even in so short a time as a hundred years there may be a far larger proportion of true adults amidst the retarded adolescents of our elder stratum, and that their tone of thought and their quality of conduct will have soaked far into the whole social body. Youth is eager and passionate, but youth is not naturally frivolous, and at present an artificial and meretricious frivolity is forced upon the young by the greedy urgency of their aimless seniors. Youth also may be something graver and stronger a hundred years from now.

However evident its approach, it is certain that the coming adult phase is not yet in the ascendant. And since it has still to come as a general thing, and since its essential quality is a merger of one's romantic, adventurous, individual life into the deathless life of the being of the species, manifestly it is not to be attained in its fulness by a few isolated pioneers. The men of science of this time are as a class more nearly able to be adult-minded than any of the rest of us—so far, that is, as their science goes. They are more in touch with an enduring reality; they have their side of the world comparatively organised, and they are joined up into a kind of collectivism. The rest of us are rather people who have heard of this way of living and are seeking it than who are actually living in the new stage.

Meanwhile all the available forms and conveniences necessarily remain those of our stratum. We must wear

the clothes the fashions prescribe unless we want to have
our lives eaten up by minor troubles and explanations.
We must live in the usual way, for how else can we
live? If we want to travel we must travel by trains-de-
luxe or go slow and dirty, catch colds, and be crowded,
stifled, and disgusted; we must go to the hotels that
quiver to the strains of jazz, for there are no others at
present to go to; and eat either in restaurants amidst
processions of mannequins or with dancers jogging our
elbows, or perplex our poor stomachs with questionable
fare. And if we want air and exercise, is anything so
convenient as tennis? Which demands all sorts of con-
formities.

So we two Clissolds go about the world looking like
any other fairly rich spenders—crypto-adults at the best.
If I live upon the hills here, and very simply for a part
of the year, it is only because I have hit upon a remarkable young woman who has seen fit to make it possible
for me. And Heaven knows how long that will last!
It is only here that I can live like this—it is a little
abnormal adventure of my own—and for the rest of my
existence there waits a setting of hotel managers and
porters and maidservants and valets and all that is
comme-il-faut.

Yet we appear to be much emptier worldlings
than we are. We are both, after our fashion, refusing
to accept the fundamental stigma of the elder stratum—
which is the cessation of all serious work. We have no
blank enjoyments and we work as long hours as ever we
did. Longer perhaps. Dickon grapples now day and
night with the mysteries of what he calls the Money

Power. To release our dear Lady of Business from the paralysing grip of the Creditor is the final quest of his life. He is thrusting in a sullen, persistent way through a dark jungle of finance round about her in search of something vulnerable. He believes there is a concrete dragon somewhere in that darkness to be slain, and if so he will slay it. Wherever there is a promise of light upon these obscurities Dickon goes. Last November he was in Detroit in earnest conference with Henry Ford, who possessed, he thought, a peculiar point of view and special experiences about the evil thing. He crossed the Atlantic in winter for that. And he is developing an angry, industrious patience with currency and credit theorists. When he catches me in England he makes me talk about them. He wrangles with me and will not be denied. He talks now about money just as he used to talk once about advertisement—continually, with his heart as deeply in it.

I am quite unable to estimate what his activities amount to, whether he is just hammering at a door which isn't a door but a rock, or whether he is getting through to some working generalisations. In the past Dickon had a way of getting out results, but this is an immense business.

Apparently he cannot wring anything fundamental out of the bankers. I have heard him in his wrath denouncing them as " beastly little Abacuses; rotten little roulette wheels, bagging the odd zero chance." He clings to it that they are automata and have not the least idea of their rôle in the general economic life of the world. He compares them with the Freemasons, who

" had some sort of a secret once and have forgotten it."
He talks of " going into banking " to find out. A
pretty manager he'd make for a local branch! The
district would wake up.

I cannot write down his opinion of various Chan-
cellors of the Exchequer. The Treasury he sometimes
reviles and sometimes only bemoans. " Some of these
chaps seem to think," he says. " Seem to be able to
think. But being officials by nature—they won't let
on. They control it. Or they might hit on something
important and upset their nice little lives." He wants
to have the Treasury " dug up and replanted." It is
" pot bound "—which is, I believe, some sort of horti-
cultural metaphor. (I am no party to these criticisms.)
Certainly he has hit upon nothing definite yet, or we
should have had him at once setting about to " put it
over." Just as once he " put over " Milton's Silent
Silver Guinea.

May he do so before I die! I dream at times of my
dear old Dickon, so amazingly stout and still so amazingly active, engaged upon his last and greatest campaign, leading a band of big manufacturers and
engineers, Titans of industry, mammoth distributors
and cosmic shippers, piling Pelion on Ossa, newspapers
on hoardings, and cinematographs on wireless, shaking
all the markets and shocking all the mints in the world,
in a stupendous effort to scale and storm the Olympus
of Wall Street and the City and dethrone the golden
usurer who reigns there.

As for me, I work along a different line. I doubt
if this simple treatment of the Money Power as the One

True Devil gets to the bottom of things. We need a true sound money, yes; but that is only to be got with quite a number of other developments that belong together. I have failed to find any place in politics, which is just as well for me; I have satisfied myself that I was in a state of dangerous fog about economics and education, and at last I have come to this quiet and seclusion in the sunshine—I said last year, to think things out, and now as I get them thought out, I say, to write my mind clear and try my creed over by making this book.

BOOK THE FOURTH

THE STORY OF THE CLISSOLDS—TANGLE OF DESIRES

THE STORY OF THE CLISSOLDS—TANGLE OF DESIRES

THE SECTIONS

BUT now I must come to my own personal history, which perhaps I have kept back unduly. I must tell of my own marriage and my lapse from scientific work to industrial chemistry, and how I also like Dickon became a rich man, as perplexingly aware as he of creative power almost in reach and yet evading us. To tell the story fairly I must go right back again to our student days.

It is part of the romantic travesty of reality that youth is a happy trivial time. Childhood can be made happy and is made happy nowadays for an increasing number of children, but I doubt if very many human adolescences can be truthfully called happy. For the enormous majority of human beings since ever humanity began to develop social life, adolescence has been anxious and perplexed. The creature is still at bottom the child of the Old Man of the rough Stone Age, half-man, half-ape, and wholly egoist; its adaptation is imperfect, and as adolescence comes on there is a struggle between the necessities that keep it tame and social and the deep-seated urgencies of its past. As the instinctive obedience and trustfulness of childhood fades, the natural man, the natural boy or girl, is discovered to be reserving a personality, becoming self-assertive, difficult, recalcitrant, and interrogative. " *Why* should I?" is the note of youth, and usually it is consciously a resentful note, a plea in opposition.

The parents and schoolmasters of our simpler past made no concealment about the matter. They understood the reality of original sin, and they did not spoil the child by sparing the rod. Youth was a sobbing, snivelling, howling time, jackets were dusted thoroughly and great girls trounced and spanked, and withal the Old Adam was never very thoroughly beaten out. To this day, smacks, blows, shakings, bangings, confinement, privations, and threats are the normal fare of ninety-nine out of a hundred young people. So soon as they come out of the gentle shelter of parental affection—and even that is sometimes very free with hand and slipper—the storm begins.

People so intelligent as to read a book like this are also probably intelligent enough not to have many children, and to provide those they have with a skilful, kindly, healthy upbringing, and it may seem to them that this is a too distressful view of human existence. But let them think not of their own clean nurseries, but of all the world from China to South Africa and Peru and of all classes of people. We are too apt to think about life in terms of cultivated homes in hygienic Atlantic countries. Taking the whole world over, almost half the children born into it are dead before they reach twenty-one, and most of the survivors have suffered great hardships. It is a quite unnecessary state of affairs now, but so it is. The process of getting dead before you are twenty-one cannot, I maintain, be a very jolly and amusing one—all the optimists and kindly smiling humourists of the world notwithstanding.

By the time they are eleven or twelve most of the

young people alive in the world—less than two-thirds of the children born, that is, for more than a third are already dead—are put out to toil. By toil I mean uncongenial exertions that are imposed upon their free activity, exertions we would all shirk if we could. A few advanced countries hold off the curse of Adam until thirteen or fourteen, and some are making a serious effort to retain young people at educational work, and to make that attractive and even joyous, until they are sixteen. The rest of mankind is neither consulted nor persuaded in this matter of toil; hardly any have a choice between this toil or that; they are put to it and there is an end to the matter. And they hate it, and if their lives are not altogether unhappy it is not because they do not suffer humiliations, frustration, physical deprivation, and futile desires and hopes in abundance, but because they are submissive and forget.

They can forget and they can hope and they can forget their hopes and still hope again. And at length as energy ebbs comes resignation.

The common human life is a tissue of expectations that are never realised and anticipations that are never fulfilled, of toil for unsatisfying ends and pursuing anxieties, of outrageous, tormenting desires, of fever and fatigue, anger and repentance, malaise, and death.

I state these facts as brutally as possible because I think they are excessively disregarded in the art, literature, and general thought of prosperous, cultivated people. Perhaps in the past it was necessary to dis-

regard them because there was little power to alter
them. But now there is power to alter them, and
literature may venture to make a step from poetry
towards sincerity. We can face the fact that a very
large proportion of human beings are still fobbed off
with the mere offals and broken meats of life, because
now we are beginning to realise that there is a possible
salvation for them. It is no longer necessary to pretend that youth and everyday life overflow with excitement, fun, and happiness.

In the past I cannot imagine how the ancestral ape
could have been carved into our present poise of tormented association and dawning collective power without the sufferings of billions of lives. That struggle
was a necessary thing—so far as I can apprehend any
necessity in things. It was in effect an immense surgery.
It was not indeed an immense cruelty, for the sufferings
of a million people are no greater than the sufferings of
a single soul; such things do not aggregate because there
exists no central brain to aggregate them; nevertheless,
the operation was immense. The chloroform of a
thousand illusions and distractions was unavoidable, but
now those fumes pass off—and may pass. The price
of power has been mainly paid. Where once the ape
lurked in the thicket there are fields and houses and the
lowly multitudinous rich material for a secure, powerful, and generous society.

It is possible now so to launch human lives and so
to care for them that they may be balanced and serene,
full and creative, eventful and happy, from beginning
to end. And, moreover, these human lives we set

going can be so directed that death will no longer appear as defeat; they will rather broaden out and flow on into the general stream of perception and effort than end, in any tragic and conclusive sense, at all. We are living in a cardinal change of phase in the history of conscious and wilful being. For the first occasion, it may be, in the whole process of space and time, a star of conscious and immortal resolution has been born out of the dreaming inconsecutive sufferings of animal life into the night of matter.

But we are still begotten carelessly, and we are still foolishly prepared for life.

When I go back among my memories I find the partially effaced evidences of profound conflicts. These are largely effaced, because that is the self-protective habit of the mind. But infancy and childhood are normally distressful for human beings. They are not necessarily such happy phases as they seem to be in the case of a kitten or a puppy. Much of my subsequent life, though it has been full of activities and satisfactions and the liveliest interest, has often been far from happy. There were long phases of sustained strain and dissatisfaction. And yet I have been one of the fortunate few. I have had physical vigour, I have had worldly success, I am comparatively rich, and have won through to freedom and monetary power, and it is this that gives me the measure of the common lot. What has distressed me must have distressed and distresses most people more than it has done me. My difference is only in my luck and in my escape to consolations and security. If life has not been wholly happy for me, if it has been troubled and vexed, then much more so must it be for most of the people about me.

When I probe among these faded and suppressed recollections of the unpleasant side of my past, I find among the early scars the traces of a queer instinctive struggle against instruction and direction. As a little child I had already a lively and curious mind. I wanted to learn, but I wanted to learn in my own way and for my own ends. But this I was not allowed to do. So that from an early stage I seem to have been protecting my personality against invasion almost as strenuously as I was attempting to add to its powers. Instinctively I disbelieved in the good faith of my teachers.

I believe most children have a similar instinctive disbelief. At the bottom of my heart I realised that the teachers did not particularly want to teach me; that they found the job irksome, got through it as easily as possible, and cared scarcely at all whether they distorted me by their reluctant and insufficient direction and the pressure of their compulsions. They hated me as the keystone of a hated but unavoidable job, and subconsciously they sought to injure me. They, too, had personalities in defensive revolt.

My lesson-times with my governesses and tutors were full of petty malignant conflicts of will. It was so with most of my schoolmasters. Their work, I knew, was jaded and insincere. Gilkes at Dulwich I came to believe in, Wallas, and one or two others, but even under these exemplary teachers I was jealous of direction.

The same self-protective conflict went on against the

customs and procedure of out-of-school life. Why did they shove all these good manners on me? My recalcitrant soul objected obscurely but perceptibly. Why should they be so insistent that it was for *my* good that I had to keep these observances? And new clothes? Things that altered one's feeling of oneself and made the mirror unfamiliar. Were these changes really for me or for the sake of some hostile subjugating outer power? There was always a fuss, persuasions, resistance, slappings, and scolding, and when I had new clothes, until I was ten or twelve, and even after that I was darkly suspicious about them for some years.

At first I was horribly frightened about religion. Then, long before I had come to clear-headed scepticism, I became incredulous and began to detest the people who were trying to put this dismaying obsession upon me. I cannot remember a time in my boyhood when I really believed that a clergyman went about his business in good faith. It was his business, and a jolly rotten business I thought it was.

And as I grew up I began to apprehend the confused dangerousness of life and to perceive that I was being driven into the scrimmage anyhow, that though my mother and stepfather made large, copious gestures of concern, yet at the bottom of their hearts they did not care very much what kicks and shames, what subjugations, servitudes, and frustrations awaited me in the struggle.

Aided by Dickon, encouraged by one or two teachers, helped by my astounding luck, I found myself doing intensely congenial work before I was nineteen, but I went through enough conflict, anger, and anxiety to realise what must be the obscure inner tragedy of a lad who, without any special gift or advantage, is sent to drudge in a shop or office or mine, just when his intelligence is awakening to the interests of life at large. That is the common lot. That is what happens to ninety-nine out of a hundred youngsters in a modern civilised community. They are pushed into work they do not want to do, and it cramps and cripples them. It is the meanest cant to pretend that we people who succeed are in some way different from the general run, that "they" don't feel it as we did, that "they" are really interested by subjections and routines and duties that would bore us of the finer strain to death. Going to work is a misery and a tragedy for the great multitude of boys and girls who have to face it. Suddenly they see their lives plainly defined as limited and inferior. It is a humiliation so great that they cannot even express the hidden bitterness of their souls.

But it is there. It betrays itself in derision. I do not believe that it would be possible for contemporary economic life to go on if it were not for the consolations of derision. I suppose nearly all servants and employed people find it necessary to ridicule their employers and directors. They find it necessary to divest these superiors of their superiority, give them undignified nicknames, detect their subtler frustrations, and then with a gasp of relief, ha, ha! life becomes tolerable again.

The root of all laughter lies in that whim of Fate which in the course of a brief million years or so made of the fiercest and loneliest species of animals the most socially involved of all living things. The adaptations are complex and clumsy and lie heavily upon us. We live under the tension of an imposed respect for our fellow-creatures. When that tension snaps, when the compelling orator sits down on his hat, or when the neatly dressed dandy struts defying our depreciation, all unconscious of the flypaper he picked up from his last chair, we shout with joy at the release. And none of us likes to be laughed at, because we feel that thereby our protection from our fellow-creatures is stripped from us. Our claim upon their respect is torn and flung back at us. There is sublimated rebellion and menace in all laughter.

Dickon and I in the days of our youth were both great laughers. We showed our teeth at the toils of existence about us, at the religious fears we struggled to escape, at the dull pomp and circumstance of monarchy and law, at the vast solid arrogance of well-off people. I have told of our standing jests of Mr. G. and the Boops. I have told how for days we hardly spoke to each other except to talk facetious nonsense. Almost all our reading beyond the bright circle of our special interests was in funny books, and all we really cared for in public entertainments was the comic part. We read Mark Twain and Max Adler; Jerome K. Jerome rose upon us and seemed to us a star of the first magnitude; Dickon and I were both married men and very busy when W. W. Jacobs began to write, but my discovery of him was a matter to tell Dickon with haste and enthusiasm. More laughter we sought, and yet more. We had, and I believe the whole human race in bondage has, an unappeasable craving for laughter. Nearly all our world could be made digestible with mockery, and it was intolerable to us in any other mode. But there was one thing we two could not laugh about, could not talk about, and which, indeed, we never tried to talk about, and that was the immense urgency of sex.

So far I have been able to tell of the forms and quality of my world without very much more than a passing allusion to sexual things. But now I must begin to deal with that vivid and disconcerting reality. From my late days at school onward I was tormented by sexual desire. It was not desire for any particular person; it was plain unassigned lust, and the tension grew with every year of my life. And interwoven with it, a thing springing up with it in me, and not, I am certain, derived to any considerable extent from teaching or other outer influence, was a feeling of intense shame and an impulse to conceal this burning appetite.

I do not know how far I was abnormal, or how far it is the common lot to be thus obsessed throughout adolescence. I can only tell my own story. I think perhaps Dickon and I were both rather more reserved and restrained than the average; our circumstances reinforced our natural character and developed our distrust of our fellow-creatures very early. I did not betray this red secret, I know, to any living being, nor did I attach my desires to any living being. I do not remember that I ever looked to any human being for their gratification except in the most transitory fashion. I kissed the servant at my lodgings once in a sudden tumultuous fashion, and was instantly disgusted with myself and

416

ashamed. She was, poor girl, so manifestly a substitute for something else, with her untidy hair and soiled apron. My desires were developed in relation to nude pictures and statuary, they were stimulated by monstrous dreams, they were directed by glowing imaginations that arose unbidden. And since I was convinced that they were essentially enervating desires, I kept myself, except for the most incidental lapses, under a rigorous restraint.

That sexual desire arises of itself in young people in their early teens, that it is something quite distinct from personal love, and that it may never become closely associated with personal love, are facts that run altogether counter to the romantic travesty of life upon which most current moral judgments are based. Edwin, in a state of spotless purity, encounters the lovely and if possible even blanker Angelina. Innocent toyings lead to the naïve discovery of passion. Which burns, without heat or smoke, with an instinctive moderation, and Edwin and Angelina are happy ever after. So it is supposed to happen, and generation has followed generation with the strangest, richest, most terrifying, distressing, and debasing tumult in their blood and in their moods and dreams, and a bright pretence of never having heard of the business in their general deportment.

I doubt if there was anything in my behaviour during those strained years before my marriage to betray, except to a skilled observer, the tormenting distraction within. My work suffered from phases of inattention, and I had moods of sullen and sometimes frantic anger. At times the drive in my nerves would summon up alluring visions of sweet, lovely, and abandoned women, and I would count the scanty money I had available and leave my work and prowl about the dim London roads and streets looking for a prostitute, and when I approached one her poor painted charms and cheap advances would seem so repulsive that I would quicken my pace and hurry past her in a commotion between desire and disgust. I would wander for hours in that fashion, and return fatigued and footsore and still incapable of restful sleep.

I do not know if this sort of thing happened to Dickon. I can only guess. We never betrayed our sexual life to one another. We were too close together and unable to escape from each other to risk even the beginning of confidences. To this day Dickon and I have never talked about sex.

I want to insist upon the fact that this wolfish impulse, with its disposition to carry me out with it and prowl in the twilight with me, did not lead me to fall in love with anyone and was on the whole a barrier to my falling in love with anyone. It was something much deeper, more animal, more elemental in my being, prehuman, something a tom-cat could understand. There were women students at the college, some very clever and attractive; there were friendly girl students in the Art College near by; they seemed aloof from passion and preoccupied with minor interests; I did not associate them with my hot desires. They had an inordinate liking for walking about the Museum and making tea and conversing in groups after the tea was made. Such entertainment offered small solace to my feverish cravings. I can guess now that they were not so serene as they seemed. And no doubt I seemed to them also cool and detached, a very self-controlled young man reputed to be good at molecular physics.

Since those days fiction and conversation in England have grown much more outspoken, but I doubt if that increasing frankness has done so much as people pretend to assuage this part of the stress of youth. That was an age of repression and concealment, yes; and to bring a thing into the light is the first step to dealing with it sanely; but mere frankness and exposure alone will no more cure these troubles than they will heal a broken leg. So far as I can judge, humanity suffers from periodic waves of putting too much clothing on and then of taking too much off. From round about the end of the century up to the present time we have been flinging aside everything, from top-hats and collars and neck-wraps and boots and shoes, down at last to the fig-leaves. And the breadth and freedom of our conversation, and particularly the conversation of some of our clever young ladies, leaves nothing unspoken and everything to be desired. But the questing beast does not fly from the sight of itself; lust does not evaporate under the influence of chatter. Lust remains lust and is going to be a monstrously troublesome thing to human beings, whether we hide everything and never speak of it, never name it, never think of it, or whether we decorate our nurseries and elementary schools with nothing but un-draped marble and wax models, and treat all conversa-tion that is not directly sexual as improper. I have studied these affairs, not always theoretically, through nearly forty of my fifty-nine years of life, and I am inclined to think that between the utmost frankness and the severest concealment there is very little practical difference. It is a matter of usage.

Some there are, going a little further than the frank exposure school—moral homœopathists—who would allay by gratification. There is something to be said for that doctrine; it abolishes most of the morbid repressions and shifts the stresses from the deeper to the more superficial strata of the mind, but it does not end the trouble. I am for moderation, for moderate gratification, but it is not always easy to arrange or define moderation. It is in the nature of sexual desire to be inordinate. That is the crux of this perennial perplexity of our species. That is the justification of decency and restraint.

This is a thing that I now see I realised instinctively in my youth, and which is present and very important in all adolescents. Sexual enterprise grows with success. It clamours for more. Give it an inch and it takes an ell. Permit the song of Pan to be sung and presently it will be demanded with variations. Nothing complicates so easily and rapidly. Nothing is so steadfastly aggressive. Nothing is so ready to enhance itself with insane fantasies. Nothing under check or defeat is so apt to invade and pervert other fields of interest and take substitutes and imitations rather than accept complete denial. I can quite understand the disposition of most churches and religions to fight sexual desire from the beginning, to kill it at the door rather than fight it when it is already half in possession of the house.

A point that I think is very important if one is to see this business clearly is that I never really identified my lust with myself in these early phases. So far as I can ascertain how matters stand with other young people, that is the normal case. I can best express my state of mind by saying that I felt it to be a damned thing that had come in me. It did not seem to be myself as my passionate desire to carry on research in crystallography and molecular physics was myself, or as my care for my future or my affection for my brother and my few friends was myself. St. Austin has drawn the most interesting theological deductions from this autonomous detachment of carnal desire from the essential personality, and it is plain how easily it must have led to a belief in diabolical possession.

If anything was needed to clinch our belief in the naturalists' explanations of man's origins, it would be this extravagance of our sexual side. No designing mind, no mind, at any rate, with a glimmering of human reason, would have produced a sort of life so dominated and swamped by sexual desire as we are, nor have permitted that desire to escape so easily from fruition to quite fruitless gratifications. But a mechanical process whose variations of method were subjected to no other criterion but survival would plainly have produced just such a state of affairs as exists. Only such a process could have made an unconditional clinging to life, hunger, and an insensate direction of every accumulation of energy into the reproductive channel, even when that channel led almost certainly to nothingness, the crude elements of existence. The billion futile pollen-grains of the cedar-trees are no more astonishing than the futile cravings, love-makings, couplings, and sexual tumult of human beings. "What matter the waste," says old Nature, "if there is a chance of one pollen-grain reaching an ovum? What else do you think you are for? Why should I economise? What is economy? I neither need you nor hate you. Take your chance. More of you. More of you to live or more of you to die. What does it matter to me?"

So it is that for the begetting and bearing of three or four children, a matter of a few minutes in the life of a man and of a few months in the life of a woman, the sexual shape is imposed upon almost all their activities. No other shape has any appeal to Nature. We are driven by imaginations, feverish wishes, rivalries, hostilities, hates, resentments, all arising out of sex; we dress for sex, we disport ourselves for sex, it drenches our art, our music, our dreams. For that much practical outcome our whole lives are obsessed. And if it were not for that obsession, for its hopes and excitements and collateral developments, I do not know where the great majority of lives would find the driving force to continue.

§ 2

SO I remember my adolescence and my young manhood as a period of hidden struggle and sustained anxiety, mitigated by ridicule and laughter. Careless youth indeed! Within was this ever-recurrent, alluring, and terrifying attack of sex upon my freedom and activities; without was the dangerous world, the hostility of the tradition of the Old Man to youth, the social obstacles and imperatives, the powers of direction and the powers of denial and restraint that manifestly meant to trip up and capture and subjugate the vast majority of my generation to lives of subservience, self-effacement, frustration, and toil.

I had an objective clearly before me, which I believed to be the realisation of my essential self; I wanted to saturate myself with immediate experimental knowledge of molecular science and to give all my energies to its prosecution, and I knew that I had to win and hold, against a mass of adverse influences, the necessary position and opportunity. Research in those days was even more scantily endowed and permitted than it is to-day. But I had got my foot in the door, so to speak, and I think I could have won through to an assured place if I had kept myself steadfast and concentrated. But I could not do so. Sex caught me unawares one day and wrenched away the mastery of my life from science. I fell into a passion of desire and I married. It was as if the walls of my laboratory collapsed, and my instruments and notebooks were overturned and scattered by a rush and invasion of stormy, common-place, ill-conceived purposes. I married for the sake of a kiss, and I made a great entanglement for myself in life.

I do not know whether even now I have emerged from the developments and consequences of that great entanglement. It diverted me altogether from the narrow scientific trail I had intended to pursue. It turned me into the paths I have followed. I fought my way through it to this very different sort of freedom that I now enjoy. It is, perhaps, a broader freedom. But it is an encumbered freedom; it is not aloof and serene like the freedom of science. All the problems and cares of life seemed enmeshed with it.

I dislike having to tell this story of my marriage. I perceive I have delayed it as long as possible; that I have, for example, told almost everything I have to tell about my brother first, very largely because of this reluctance. There is no sound reason now why I should not face the facts of this the most remote phase of my past—for it seems really much remoter than my childhood—but I have suppressed it so long that the habit of suppression has been established in me. I find it difficult to recover the facts in their order, and about many of my moods I must needs be as speculative now as though I told of the acts of someone quite outside myself.

After Dickon went to Bloomsbury I was very lonely for a time in Brompton, and then the gaps of time his departure left me began to be filled by other people. The social life of the South Kensington student in those days was hardly organised at all; there was no Students' Union as yet and no tennis clubs nor suchlike facilities for meeting. There was not even a students' refresh-ment-room. There was a small debating society very much in the hands of a little gang of biological and geological students, from whom I got my first ideas of socialism. I scraped acquaintance with a youngster of my own age named Crewe, who was also doing advanced work in physics, and with him I began to walk and gossip in the park and gardens, and I became fairly intimate with one or two of the debating society men. Crewe had a brother in the art school, and introduced me through him to that more picturesque side of South Kensington life.

The London art student in those days was still only very imitatively Bohemian; he was very new to the art of being an art student; but there were Morris dresses and florid ties and velvet jackets and casual meals in studios and a research for conversational brilliance. Presently I found myself rather shyly a visitor at the Crewes' house.

The Crewes occupied a large, ramshackle, grey, semi-detached house in a road that branched out of the Fulham Road; though I went there scores of times, I cannot now remember either the name of the road or the number of the house. They had gatherings there every Sunday afternoon and evening; open house and a cold supper with sandwiches and salad and stewed fruit. The paternal Crewe was a very old, mooning gentleman with a long, thin beard, who seemed always to be standing about with his hands in his pockets, wishing he was somewhere else. He had kept a private school and retired. The presiding spirit was Mrs. Crewe. She was much younger than he, very pink and very ample, with a shapely wrist, a harp, strange, elegant gestures, and a remote allusive style of conversation acquired from the novels of Mr. George Meredith. She was a woman of letters; she wrote charming little love stories and children's stories in the magazines, and poems and criticism. She did not get much money for these things, she made you understand; so far she was among the elect. She loved youth and youthful hopes; she had a devouring sympathy and a great craving for confidences. She was constantly trying to " draw one out," as the phrase went, but as there was very little in the depths of my mind except quartz fibres, certain little riddles about the relations of various triclinic crystals to their monoclinic cousins, and an impatient but very formless rage with nature and the social order, it was very difficult for me to respond as freely as I wished to her kindness.

She wrung from me that I had scientific ambitions, and that for her meant that I wanted to be "like" Professor Huxley or Lord Kelvin. That I could possibly want to know things without dramatising myself as a copy of some eminent savant never entered her head. And she was restlessly eager to find out that I had some-one, a girl necessarily, who "inspired" my ambitions, although I should have thought that feminine inspiration was biological rather than molecular. I evaded her probings—sometimes, I fear, a little ungraciously—and it is only now in the retrospect that I realise how sedulously she must have restrained her appetite for confidences in the matter of my father and mother. And it was also an alleviation of her inquiries that the influence of Meredith robbed them of any brutal directness.

She irritated me, she embarrassed me, and I liked her—I don't know why—very much. She liked me too. I would find her very bright little brown eyes seeking me across the room, and her funny round face, under the tremendous cap she wore, bobbing and nodding to

me, with an effect of encouragement and reassurance—
I cannot imagine what about.

She would even beam deep understandings at me
while she was plucking her harp strings and exhibiting
her Victorian wrist. Always every Sunday she played
the harp for a while and all the talk was hushed. And
one of us would always be caught to sit on the little
stool close beside the harpist. But usually this fell to
some unwary newcomer who had not discovered the
imminence of harping. He had to look rapt.

"Young Sir Philosopher still brooding over his
crucibles," she would cry across the room to me.

"Beware the witch's warning!" And she would
shake her finger. "There are cauldrons as well as
crucibles, Sir Alchemist."

I would pretend to understand what she meant.

"Not only the stars can twinkle," she would throw
at me and turn for some other victim.

I had never before encountered such perplexing
brilliance.

All sorts of people came to these Sundays of hers.
One or two were quite well-known literary and dramatic
people, people whose names you saw on programmes or
at the bottom of signed articles, but mostly the company
consisted of beginners, some of them manifestly late
starters, but as portly and important and whiskered as
the well-known. There were early Fabians and
eccentric thinkers. A modestly resolute man in a drab
kilt with wildernesses of hairy knee was frequent; he
was Erse or Gaelic or one of those things, and he
explained to me on one occasion that properly he ought

to be wearing a broadsword. He felt "incomplete," he said, without it. One evening Mrs. Crewe's conversation was exceptionally delirious; "red hair from green meals," she said, "warbling his Dublin wood-notes wild. That delicious accent!" and I became aware of Mr. Bernard Shaw in his celebrated Jaeger costume talking in a corner. At that time he was a lean young music critic with an odd novel or so to his credit, giving few intimations as yet of the dramatic career that is now culminating so magnificently—if even now it is culminating—in "Saint Joan."

But the larger element was undistinguished youth. There were three Crewe girls, each with a large circle of intimates, and both the sons also brought in their friends. And often youth prevailed to such an extent that the pretence of a conversazione was abandoned and we played juvenile games. We would play dumb-crambo or charades, and in these charades a certain inventiveness I have, and a certain capacity to act preposterously and gravely, gave me a kind of leadership. Dumb-crambo is an inferior entertainment to fully developed charades, and after a time the latter banished the former from the Crewe household and grew into a kind of consecutiveness. We contrived to make many of them into quaint little three, four, and five act plays. Those were the absurd days of the British theatre; Barrie and Shaw had yet to dawn upon us; even the mockery of Wilde's *Importance of Being Earnest* had not relieved the pressure of the well-made play, and two leaden masters, Henry Arthur Jones and Pinero, to whom no Dunciad has ever done justice, produced large, slow, pretentious three-act affairs that were rather costume shows than dramas, with scenery like the advertisements of fashionable resorts, the reallest furniture and the unreallest passions and morals it is possible to conceive. This sort of thing lent itself to joyous burlesque. I remember we spent one very happy evening in the big ramshackle drawing-room with the folding doors upstairs, reading and rehearsing a play called *Michael and His Lost Angel,* by one or other of those twin glories of that departed age. I was Michael, very dark and high and gloomy, as far as possible in the manner of Mr. George Alexander, and there was misconduct " off stage " in a lighthouse or down the barrel of a big gun or in some such bed of roses.

The Crewe gatherings went on until the schools broke up in the summer, and in May and June they flowed out into the garden, a town-stained garden of gravel and plane trees, which owed whatever magic it possessed to twilight and darkness, assisted by perhaps a dozen Japanese lanterns.

And it was in that garden one moonlight night that Clara was suddenly transfigured to beauty and mystery, and that we whispered very close to one another and hesitated and kissed. For the first time in my life I knew what it was to hold a sweet and living body in my arms and drink the passion of a kiss.

In that moment all the diffused disturbance of my life became concentrated upon one desire, to possess Clara. I held her to me, but abruptly her responsive passion ceased, and she wriggled out of my embrace.

The door had opened and someone was coming out

tell is a mere framework of facts, a skeleton robbed of all living substance and significance.

Apparently at this time there were in my mind two sets of motives so entirely inconsistent and incompatible that I sit and ask myself whether I am not seeing all this phase of my past through some distorting medium. There was my passion for research which called for all my best energies and my most lucid and energetic hours, and there was this new passion for Clara, which also was bound to develop into a whole-time job, and yet for more than a year at least I do not seem to have realised any contradiction in these matters. I seem to have gone right on with both, and to have been sincerely perplexed and astonished when at last their divergence took so practical a form that it was no longer possible for me to ignore it.

In some way surely I must have sought to reconcile them. I doubt if I could have adopted Mrs. Crewe's idea that the desire for the constant companionship, kissing, fondling, and embracing of a young woman constituted an " inspiration," that it disposed and empowered me to speculate deeply and subtly upon the constitution of atoms and the nature of electrical charges. But I may have had a persuasion that these love exercises gave pride and energy and peace of mind.

I do not remember that I ever talked very much to Clara of the work I was doing. I recall her on one occasion when we were at Deal, praising the beauty of a lighthouse, and saying that with its steady light, its smooth and certain rotation, its beautifully adjusted mirrors, it was " like science." I was extraordinarily pleased at her saying that. I was so pleased that it is plain she did not often say things like that. But generally our nearest approach to my scientific concerns was the canvassing of the characters of Professor Guthrie and Dr. Boys and others of the Royal College workers in those days, and speculations about the fortune of Lord Kelvin, and the possibility of making artificial precious stones, and so forth. The thought that I might make diamonds dazzled her. On the side of my socialism we were better able to meet. She, too, called herself a socialist, but she approached it rather as a campaign of benevolence towards the " slums "—supplemented by a general preference for wool garments, red ties, art fabrics, and archaic oak furniture.

If I can remember no moods of actual lovingness between us, I can at least say that we were greatly interested in and desirous of each other. We must have gone for walks together, walks and talks, from first to last, for many hundreds of miles. She had read much more widely than I had in the literature of the time, and she instructed me in the study of Meredith and Hardy and Walter Besant and Swinburne and the Pre-Raphaelites. She introduced me to the writings of William Morris and the early Bernard Shaw, the Shaw of the *Star* days. She was keen on pictures, keen on music, keen about the theatre. She was keen about the movements and characters of public people; keen about fashions and social events. So keen she was upon so many things that at times her whirling conversation seemed to whistle like a blade through the air about me. She made me feel thick and slow and under-

433

My reading of my part was entirely different. I was,
I conceived it, the masterful male, recipient of Clara's
furtive but extremely effective endearments, conqueror
of her heart and instincts, aspiring to be her kindly
owner and ruler with the privilege of soothing and
entertaining myself with her easy delightfulness whenever I chose. Her physical docility, her lively attention, was the cause of an enormous pride in me. She
ruffled my hair and called me "Flosopher-lost" when
my demon-patience was particularly disastrous; she
seemed unable to keep her quick hands off me, and all
four of them evidently found my ineptitude a very
promising and endearing trait.

I remember that first afternoon very vividly; the
rather dark room, the circular table from which the
cloth had been removed, the bare arms, the soft glowing faces close to mine, Clara's hair sometimes brushing
my cheek as she reached across me with a card. Doris,
the third sister, was the quickest of all. "Stop-Out!
no you *don't!*" she would cry, return some belated
card to its player, and cut short the pelting struggle.

Later on I stole an evening or so from my work to
study this demon-patience. I was not used to cards,
but I perceived that it was absurd for a fairly good
mathematician to be unready with the groupings and
variations of four sets of thirteen cards. I drilled
myself a little, thought out a few principles of action,
and afterwards made up in science what I lacked in
speed. Until at last I could truncate a hand with
"Stop-Out!" as often as Doris and win a hundred up
against her.

I was rewarded for these infidelities to my work by Clara's brightly expressed approval. Doris was amazed and dismayed at certain tactical inventions of mine; she would scream and lose her head as I slapped down an accumulated series of cards, humming distractingly as I did so, and Clara would slacken her play and come near to applause. It was evident her sisters had pronounced me stupid after my first début, and that it pleased her to see me vindicate myself.

For more than a year Clara filled all my waking thoughts that were not given to my work, and she dominated my dreams and reveries. All my vague and dispersed sex fantasies gave place to the thought of her. She was a very exciting girl by nature, bold in her thoughts and for that very remote and decorous time very bold in her talk and acts. We found a thousand opportunities in that ill-lit old Kensington for kisses and embraces, and she taught me everything that there was to be known in the fine art of caressing. For that she had a natural genius. It is wonderful what lurking places and kindly shelters there are to be found in streets and parks and house-porches and passages and gardens that seem quite open and exposed to unimpassioned eyes. Since no other girl now existed for me I could not imagine that any other man existed for her. And she volunteered the information time after time that none did.

After a time I defied the possible disapproval of my landlady, and Clara ventured with books and parcels and messages to my lodgings for bouts of philandering. I can see again the little circle of light upon my scat-

tered notes under my shaded lamp as we stand body
to body in the shadow.

"*Shall we turn the key in the door?*" she whispers.

And in the summer she went with her mother and
sisters to St. Margaret's Bay, and I went to Deal so
that I could walk over and discover them by accident
and share their bathing tent and join them in the sea.
Clara and her sisters were good swimmers, and we
would float side by side or bask on the beach in the
sun together, and in the night I would lie in bed and
bite my wrists and arms black and blue with the
violence of my desire for that wet body in its closely
clinging dress. She had a project which was never
realised of a great swim by moonlight. It stirred my
imagination greatly, and in my reveries we struck out
into the unknown, into the darkness further and further
from shore—and, at last, faint with effort and delight,
turned with our arms wide open towards each other.
And sank.

But there were various other youths and men about,
and they made it very difficult for Clara and me to get
at each other alone. A certain Billy Parker was particularly obnoxious. His elder brother was affianced
to Marjorie, the elder sister, and he had a stupid proprietary way with Clara, hovering about her, joining
in her conversations. She assured me he bored her to
death, and that when they were alone together she said
the most humiliating things to him and praised me
continually. Clara, not to lose a moment of me, would
walk part of the way with me back to Deal, and Billy
would always insist on coming with us, so that she

should not return to St. Margaret's Bay alone. She would take my arm up to the parting and do most of the talking to me, and then as she and he went off back she would take his arm, no doubt to hold him the more firmly while she drove the barbed humiliations home. And there was a Mr. Crashaw staying at St. Margaret's Bay, quite a middle-aged man, a friend of her father's, she said, but evidently focussed upon her. He had twice asked her to marry him, she told me.

"I'd send him packing altogether," said Clara, " if it wasn't for his kindness to mother. You see, he's got no end of money."

Until that seaside holiday I had not been jealous of Clara nor even very urgent to be finally engaged to her. Now an irrational jealousy infected me, and also an extreme impatience to possess her wholly. But she would not be engaged to me until there was an immediate prospect of marriage. "You can't doubt I love you," she said, "but life *is* life. Marjorie marries Fred Parker this September, and then mother will be at me to get out of Doris's way. Night and day she'll be at me."

"But you don't mean——!" I was breathless.

"It's tragic, Billy. It's horrible. How can I love an old man like that? How can I endure him? After your kisses. And babies! Little old babies they'd be! Oh! don't let me think of it, Billy! Don't make me cry! Let us be happy while we can."

My soul went cold and white within me. I thought no more of stresses in crystals for a time. I was filled

those methods of examining by reflected light the rup-
tured faces of crystallised alloys that later stood me in
such good stead with Romer, Steinhart, Crest and Co.
It would have been imperceptible to anyone else; for
some time it was imperceptible to me that the mental
exaltation of the work had vanished.

I had grown up, I had become fully adult, I had
consummated my life; I had bought my young woman
and held her exultant in my arms. We made an
excellent festival of each other. And presently we
emerged from our mutual preoccupation a little
habituated to these excitements with most of the
problems of life still before us.

As I have told, we called upon Minnie and Dickon.

I suppose it was—if one may use a preposterous
metaphor—the intention of old Mother Nature that we
should now produce a number of children, and that
while Clara bore them and cherished them I should
go hunting for more and more food and comfort.
That also was the tradition of human society. Some
of the children would live and some would die, and by
the time the task was done, our jokes exhausted and
our tears dried, we should be ready to depart. In
those days it was not the custom to correlate the large
developments of human affairs with the things of the
individual life, and so it was only vaguely and personally
that we apprehended that children were no longer
wanted in such abundance as heretofore and that a new
sanitation, new methods of education, were lifting the
burthen of complete reproductive specialisation from
womankind—and putting very little in its place. For

442

a time upon quite personal grounds we were resolved to have no children. We had insufficient money; we had insufficient room; and Clara, with her all-round intelligent amateurishness, was left very much at loose ends. I, too, with my ill-paid, pure research was far away from the traditions of the normal breadwinner. I needed time. I was always in want of more hours, hours for thought, hours for calculation and experiment. Clara on the other hand had nothing to do with her time. She was quick and clever with her little home, and through with its monotonies in an hour or so. Between our séances of love-making, therefore, I was hurried and driven, and she was slack and bored.

Though neither of us was nearly as avid of life as young people seem to be nowadays, we were still sufficiently impatient to develop the discordances of our position into very great distresses. The once wonderful house in Edenbridge Square with a green door and a brass knocker, brightly furnished with money that Dickon had lent me, which had seemed at first the most delightful of love-nests, became a lair from which we both absented ourselves more and more. I would steal an increasing proportion of our waking hours for the laboratory, and she would be driven abroad, almost penniless, in her cheap but clever clothes, to find some amusement, some excitement, for her vacant hours. For a time she came to the laboratory to help and work with me, but her nimble hands were more often than not in the wrong places and her quick inaccurate wits were extraordinarily fertile in faintly irritating misconceptions. And after a while she found laboratory assistance, without complete intellectual participation, boring, and took offence at my frequent disinclination to knock off and make love to her in my private room. It seemed to Clara the primary use to which a private room ought to be put.

She thought she would act; she thought she would develop her gift for painting and drawing. Philip Weston, who afterwards as Dickon's prize artist was to do so much to make the London poster artistic, was very ready to give her lessons. She made considerable progress and attained to everything except originality and intensity. She rejoined the Fabian Society, which she had left before her marriage, and various other societies that promised drawing-room meetings. But most of these things were things of the evening, when time and the exigencies of life were not so heavy on her hands. Art in a convenient studio is on the other hand naturally an affair of the afternoon.

Across the interval of a third of a century I can look back at the strains between these two young people, one of whom has become myself, and I can see that neither she nor I can justly be blamed for our disaster. Like all human beings we were borne upon the great flood of change, and it chanced that we were caught in an eddy. She did not know the forces in her and without her that had taken hold of her and were spinning her so giddily, and I had as little self-knowledge. I wanted to drive on with my work and drive on with my work. In such time as I could spare she could minister to my love and pride in her. For the rest of her days I had no care except that she did nothing to infringe my lordship over her. And being anxious not to distress me unduly, when presently under the urgency of her need for entertainment she began to infringe upon my lordship, she saved my pride and temper by some very excellent lying.

What a vivid silly creature she was, and how inevitable was her drift to that exciting exploitation of her physical personality which was her instinctive gift! It needs all that third of a century for me to record with detachment that while I was sitting over my petrographical microscope, getting nearer and nearer to the interference colour scale that enabled me to determine the proportion of the bases in the micas and felspars, she and Philip Weston, having discovered they were perfect physical types, were obliging each other as models for a series of drawings from the nude. In the atmosphere of æsthetic gravity thus created, what the world in general calls misbehaviour became an almost negligent extension of their interesting studies. And I admit she was a pretty thing, well worth drawing and deserving to be drawn, and for the moment less mischievous when posed than active.

I did not know of such little adventures in liberality at the time, but I felt them in the air. I became curious about her movements. I was horrified to find myself suspicious and jealous. I did not think of Weston at first, but I was startled to find that Billy Parker had turned up again with a touching disposition to take her out to rather expensive lunches. Billy was her sister's brother-in-law, a privileged relationship; and she talked of him so frequently and needlessly that a wiser

445

husband would have perceived that he was not at any rate the central figure of the situation. But after a time I began to see all sorts of things about Billy down the petrographical microscope.

Now it was against all my conceptions of our relationship that I should question her, much less make any objection, about her use of her leisure. We had had many very liberal and far-reaching talks about the relationship of men and women before we had married, and it had been agreed between us that we should not be "tied" by that antiquated ceremonial. We were both to keep a "perfect freedom."

I suppose young people of high and advanced pretensions have talked in that way for generations. It pervaded the brief life of Shelley, and in his letters and recorded conversation the phrases of a noble sexual generosity have already a used and customary quality. I suspect the revolt against marriage, and against the fierceness of marriage, has been growing with changing social conditions, with increased social ease and security, with the decline in the necessity for the lair-home, for a long time. It can be remarked in the social life of Imperial Rome; it peeped out in a score of usages during the days of chivalry; the last two centuries are full of it; half our novels are about it. I doubt if an animal can become so rapidly economically social as man has done in the last million years without becoming also sexually social; a solitary beast is a pairing beast, but man is almost the only gregarious beast that attempts to pair. But at the time I did not philosophise so broadly as that. I did not realise that half

446

the trouble in the little houses round such squares
as Edenbridge Square and all the similar and kindred
squares and roads and suburbs of London and Paris
and New York—and I suppose Pekin and Bombay—is
a struggle between the dispositions of the lair and the
dispositions of the herd. I happened to be on the
liberal side, by chance as much as by anything; I
preached the tolerations of the herd with the exclusive
passion of the lair rich in my blood. I controlled my
instinctive impulse to dominate and monopolise. But
the tension of these suppressions found an outlet in
other directions. The things I would not allow myself
to say about Clara's morals I said about her meals. I
became abruptly aware of a galling disregard for my
comfort in our little home. I became acutely sensitive
to Clara's domestic casualness, to the indiscipline of her
one servant, to her absence from home if by any chance
I came back at an unusual hour. I began to nag, I
became irritable and objectionable. We quarrelled, we
sulked, we made it up without explanations under the
compulsion of our vigorous young appetites. Presently
we found ourselves in money difficulties. She had
supplemented her pocket-money by diverting various
sums due on our tradesmen's bills. On our first year
of housekeeping together we were nearly a hundred
and seventy pounds in debt and with nothing in hand.

And just at this inopportune time she became extraordinarily preoccupied with the idea of a child. She
declared she wanted a child passionately, that it was
dishonourable for us to go childless, that it was our
duty to balance our peculiar gifts against the rapid

multiplication of the unfit. And she was going to waste. She was demoralised through her thwarted instinct of maternity. She was no good without a child. Anything might happen to her unless she had a child to steady her. She expressed herself with extreme impatience. I objected. While we were entangled and short of money a child wouldn't have a fair chance with us. Couldn't we wait a year or so?

"While I muddle about," she said. "Billy! I'm going to have that child."

"Not yet," I said.

She spoke slowly and with her utmost emphasis. "Billy, you don't understand. I'm going to have a child."

"But, good God!" said I. "How is that possible?"

She made no answer. Suddenly I took her by the shoulders and looked into her face.

"How is that possible?" I said.

She explained garrulously and unsoundly. One was never sure. In a dozen ways it might be possible.

But my doubt of her had been a very transitory one. My solicitudes as a reluctant breadwinner came across my mind to shield her from my scrutiny. And as yet I did not distrust her to the extent of that doubt.

"Well, we'll have to face it," I said, singularly free from the joys and exaltations of fatherhood. "Will you be ill, do you think? So far you've carried it well. You'll carry it off all right. You're a very perfect female animal, you know, made for the business. And we must squeeze some sort of a nursery into the house. . . . I wonder what it will cost us. . . . We'll manage. . . .

But it will be a tight job for us. You're a devil, Clara, at getting your own way—in spite of science and art."

She seemed, I thought, to flinch.

"Nothing to be afraid of," said I. "You're one of Nature's daughters."

There was something already at the back of my mind which had been there, indeed, since I realised the deficit on our first annual budget. But I did not tell Clara of it, because I hated to think of the alacrity she would have displayed in grasping all the possibilities it opened to us. I knew that I could carry off all this trouble quite easily by a simple transfer of my activities from the laboratories of the Royal College of Science to the laboratories of the great metallurgical and chemical firm of Romer, Steinhart, Crest and Co. They had heard of me, they wanted me badly, although they did not nearly know all I might be able to do for them. But at any rate they wanted me to the extent of eight hundred pounds a year, rising by increments of fifty pounds to twelve hundred, and that seemed to offer an immediate surcease of all my present anxieties. The heavy work of the elementary course of the college was over for the year; it had finished in February, and there would be little difficulty about my resignation.

A year before I should have told Clara of this possibility and discussed it with her, but now I kept it to myself. Even in that moment of acceptance of the new situation I wasn't quite sure of myself. I thought it over for three or four days still before I went to Romer, Steinhart's. I seem to remember that I was on the whole amused, bitterly amused by what had happened to me. I realised quite clearly that I was bidding a long farewell to the living realities of research. In all probability it would be a lifelong farewell to the service of pure knowledge. For the rest of my life, as I saw it then, I should be nosing out artful ways for underselling magnesium or making aluminium cheap. Fine fun! I was to be a scientific truffle-hunting dog for predacious business. Which was predacious by instinct and did nothing worth doing with the money. I remember recalling one day how old Mrs. Crewe had said to me, " Ah, now—you will be human!" and laughing aloud in the street. This was being human.

I did not pay very much attention to Clara during these days, but afterwards I perceived that she, too, had been greatly preoccupied. She was manifestly dismayed at the prospect of bearing a child in our diminutive house, and though I could have relieved her of that apprehension in half a dozen words, I did not find it in my heart to do so. At times she would express an effusive penitence for the trouble she had been the means of bringing upon me; at times she would be extraordinarily thoughtful and aloof. One of the chance things I had said to her stuck in her mind. " I'm one of Nature's daughters," she said. " And she's got me."

I wonder if I felt tenderly for her. I do not recall any tenderness at all.

I had an interview with old Romer, and then with him and three other of the directors, and after that we clinched our arrangements. I informed the Royal College people of their approaching loss, and still I forebore to tell Clara of her improved prospects.

Perhaps I wanted it to be a pleasant scene, and I feared that her joy and relief would provoke my resentment and make me say something bitter.

Then one day at breakfast I saw she was looking unhappy. I had never seen real unhappiness in her face before. Hers was a very animated face, and I knew a thousand of its expressions—angry, bored, and forgetful —but this was something different. She thought I was reading my paper; she had forgotten I was there, and she was sitting quite still and staring in front of her— as though hope had suddenly gone out of her being. "Cheer up, Clara!" said I, and she became aware of me with a violent start. She looked at me with a question in her eyes.

"I'm all right, Billy," she said.

I glanced at the clock. "It's nothing to be afraid of," I said, getting up and gathering together some papers for my despatch-case. I took her in my arms and kissed her. She kissed me back, but how forced was her kiss and how dead she had become to my touch!

I had to hurry away or I would have told her of the Romer-Steinhart arrangement there and then. But her expression of wretchedness went with me. It troubled me all day. She showed deep feeling so rarely that the idea of her being miserable came with a special painfulness. I felt I had been too hard with her over a misadventure that was as much mine as hers. And generally lately I had been hard upon her. She was in for much the worst side of the trouble before us. I wasn't playing the game by her; I was being a vexatious and unhelpful partner. I was making her suffer for my disappointments, disappointments she could not possibly understand.

I was so concerned to relieve her worries that I came home early. But she was out; she did not come in until past six. When she came in she was no longer wretched looking; she was flushed and grave-faced, but extra-ordinarily alive. I had been sitting in the little drawing-room and living-room that was also my study, poring rather inattentively over a file of notes upon some work I was closing down, and waiting for her to come in. I stood up as she entered.

" Back early? " she said.

" Before five."

" Your fire's out."

" I didn't watch it."

" Ellen got you some tea? "

" She was out. I got it myself."

She stared at the things on the table, with her mind far away. " Billy," she said, " I want to talk to you."

" At your service," I said.

" It's—serious stuff."

I stared at her, unable to guess what was coming. She did not look at me. Her eyes looked past me at the blank fireplace behind me.

" It's got to be said," she remarked. " Sooner or later it has to be said."

Her voice quickened. " It's better to have it out—than to go away with nothing explained. It's better to have things said. Better to be plain. It's something I've had in mind for weeks. Now it has come to a head.

I don't know if you remember all we used to talk about before we married, about either of us giving the other their freedom if they wanted it. I don't know how much you meant about that sort of thing, or whether you mean to stand by it now. But all these months while we have been so unhappy together I have been thinking of what we used to say. I've been thinking of how we used to declare that no law, no marriage, ought to hold a man and a woman together if they did not love. And all the while you have been growing colder and harder to me and making life more difficult for me. I have been asking myself, Billy, more and more if you and I are really lovers any longer, if you and I can even pretend any longer to be in love."

"Quite recently," I remarked, "the pretence has—worked."

"Oh! Proximity! Habit! How can one save oneself? But is it love, Billy? Is it truly love? For that matter, has it ever been love?"

I realised that I was facing something absolutely strange to me. This was a new, a different Clara who stood before me. I remember vividly the picture she made in our darkling room and the effect of discovery her words produced. And I noted for the first time that she was already physically changed. Her pretty shoulders seemed a little broader and lower, her neck softer and whiter. Her eyes; there was something changed in her eyes. I observed, but I do not remember what I thought nor what I said in reply to her words. I observed that she was declaring that we had never loved, and I apprehended, with a kind of astonishment

453

at not having had it clear before, that that was true. Why had it not been clear before?

This opening comes back to me very plainly, but much of the talk that followed must have slipped out of my memory altogether. I cannot remember in what phrases she made me aware that she meant to leave me nor by what transitions my mind adapted itself to the new situation. Then in harsh relief against that fog of forgetfulness I see her with her hands gripping each other and a sort of swallowing movement in her throat before she blurted out: "I'm not going away alone. You don't understand, Billy. You don't understand what I am trying to tell you. I'm going away with Philip Weston. I have been at his studio all this afternoon."

In a flash I saw everything plainly. I recall a gleam of sympathy for the wincing courage with which she faced me. A dozen different mental processes seemed to be going on in my mind, quite independently of one another. I remember quite distinctly that I thought I ought to kill her, and that it would be extremely agreeable and exciting to take her pretty neck, which I had kissed with delight a thousand times, and squeeze it, squeeze it in my hands. I was dangerous, and she knew I was dangerous. And yet at the same time, in the same brain was a leap of relief that I was quit of her. And then a pang of exasperation because my agreement with Romer, Steinhart was signed and fixed and my successor at the Royal College already appointed. For a time I didn't think much about Weston. Clara in the foreground blotted him out.

I stood still on the hearthrug, and the moment for murder passed.

"So that, in all probability, is where the baby comes from?" I said.

She moistened her lips with her tongue and nodded, with her eyes still warily on mine.

"And Weston—is in a state to believe that?"

"He loves me, Billy."

She felt she was over the worst.

"He doesn't know you yet. All this—puts one out to a certain extent. I didn't see it coming. Where, for example, do you propose to sleep to-night, Clara? Here? We might fall victims to—what did you call it? Proximity. Habit. And then I might strangle you. And that would surprise and annoy Weston."

She did not seem to have thought that out yet. She decided to take a few things and go back to Weston. He would be waiting in the studio. He would be sure to be waiting.

"I ought to be strangled," she said, with that idea still lingering in her mind. I perceived that she would have liked a little strangling—and then perhaps tears. But I was immeasurably remote from tears.

It came to me as I stood on the hearthrug before her that I was gathering and expanding and spreading out a sort of peacock's tail of derisive hate. I had no feeling for her then but derisive hate. It was as if I had never done anything but hate her. I was teeming with insulting phrases like a thundercloud ready to burst, and saying nothing. At the same time I realised that this was not how a civilised man of advanced views ought to react to our amazing situation. It was before me, but I did not grasp it yet.

"I don't know what to say to you," I confessed. "Get your things together. Tell Ellen some old lie. Tell her your mother is ill and you want to be with her. And go. Get out. I shall go out—now. And just walk about and try and figure out what has happened. I shan't come back for an hour or so. I promise you that. You'll have plenty of time to pack and get off. . . . It's sudden. And yet I suppose I ought to have seen it coming. . . ."

I considered. "What else is there to say?" She appeared at the door of the sitting-room as I was going out of the house. An idea had dawned upon her. She spoke with a note of perplexity.

"Billy," she said, "this may be our good-bye!"

I stared at this new aspect. She wanted an emotional parting! She wanted a scene in which I was to play the part of poor old Billy. She felt a certain remorse and pity was due to me. She conceived the situation as cheaply as that. She had no sense of the murderous fury that filled me.

"Well," I answered, after a pause, in a brutal voice; "what the hell else do you suppose it to be?"

"*Billy!*" she whispered, aghast, and gripped her hands together. "Oh, Billy!"

I did not slam the door wilfully, but it seemed to slam itself.

§ 5

IT is a difficult undertaking to reach across the interval of thirty-odd years and reconstruct the state of mind of that dismayed and angry human animal who walked about Hyde Park while his wife, dismayed likewise, and as troubled, perhaps, at herself and him and the universe as he was, packed for her departure from the poor little home that had contained their passions and dissensions for a year and a half. There was no tenderness, no pity in my mood; it was almost entirely a state of rage. And I do not think that even then it was directed against Clara. What I raged against had the shape of Clara, wore her delightful body, but it was really the passion and desire in myself for the glories, thrills, and gratifications she could give me that maddened me. She had become a consuming necessity in my life, and I had lost her.

I do not remember that in all the storm there entered anything at all that one could speak of as love. In most —in ninety-nine per cent. of love affairs, there is, I am convinced, hardly any love at all. There was hate. Hate, a wildly scornful hate for Clara's nimble lying, would come over my mind like the quivering red glare one sees for a time among thunderclouds, and pass again. It was not a very pointed and personal hate. I hated the situation and her share in it, but even then I knew that she was as much the victim of uncontrollable drives in her own nature as I was.

But what in this belated retrospect impresses me most

about the state of mind of this young Mr. William Clissold in Hyde Park one April afternoon in 1891 was the primary importance in it of wounded vanity and self-love. I realise again as I sit and think these things over and write about them here the profound mental effect a woman has upon the man to whom she gives herself. She becomes the sustainer of his self-esteem, she imposes her values upon his vanity; she secures an enormous power of humiliation over him. In every love affair there is a campaign of flattery and reassurance. It seemed of the first importance to me that evening that I should not be the rejected one, that I should, so to speak, shout it at her: "I don't want you. I never want to touch you again."

What an incredible thing that young man of twenty-three is to myself of fifty-nine! I am astonished as I look back into this little pit of memories at his narrowness and violence. Maybe I am self-righteously astonished and nearer to him still than I like to think myself. But how entirely self-centred he was! I suppose every young thing has to be self-centred if it is to get anywhere in a scrambling world. Youth and individuality are self-assertion; they have no other possible significance. Yet I cannot but feel that my self-protection was excessive.

I had a great desire to lie to Clara and tell her that I, too, had been unfaithful. It filled me with shame and anger that I had been steadfastly faithful to her and content with her. It would have been so much easier to have been able to write to her magnanimously: "Go your own way. I, too, love someone else." It appeared, indeed, as I walked about Hyde Park, fantastically important to me that I should balance Clara's infidelity with equally liberal behaviour of my own. Just to define Clara's place once for all and banish this " poor old Billy " business from the world.

I doubt if my behaviour was very abnormal by our present standards. Human society had passed beyond the phase of passionate possession between the sexes, when it was natural and proper for the husband to kill the wife for her treason and the lover for his robbery. That " Old Man " husband is buried deep now beneath whole mountains of suppression. But not so deeply as to be beyond danger of eruption. The mountains of suppression quake and move. I had trained my mind in the fashion of our time and held Clara to be a free person on an equality with myself. It remained to me, therefore, to solace my shattered vanity as well as I could, and above all to release myself as soon as possible from the ascendancy that Clara had gained over my senses. Because I knew quite clearly, even then, that if I did not do that, if I let myself dwell upon her relations with Weston, I ran the risk of an exasperation of mind that might fling me back again, in spite of all my civilisation, towards archaic violence.

And so for a time I thought very little either of my science, my teaching, or of the new position I was to take up in the autumn. I set out upon a search for sexual adventure, and, with the advantage of such knowledge as my marriage had given me, it was not long before I had distracted myself from the obsession

459

of my divorce proceedings with several intrigues. So long as one did not love and was not too scrupulous about the truth, making love was by no means a difficult art. I could be plausible and talkative, and had the instinct that restrains a caress until it is desired. I could soon count " successes " and had a healing reassurance that I could be desirable. For illicit love in London it is not so much charm and splendour that are needed as convenient premises and a certain leisure. There was hardly a particle of love, it seems to me now, in any of these businesses, and in the intervals of my various adventures I found myself wildly and terribly unhappy. Yet it may be, so queerly selective are our memories in all that touches sex, there was much tenderness, grati- tude, friendliness that I have forgotten. Yes—there was friendliness; of that I may tell later.

It was profoundly necessary to me that I should flaunt my freedom before the eyes of Clara, and since I had refused to play the part of " poor old Billy " in the drama it became almost as necessary to her to demonstrate her satisfaction with Weston. One among my three or four " affairs " had emerged to a sort of predominance. It was with a girl named Jones, who was a model, a sunny- haired, smiling, amoral creature whom everybody called Trilby. I had met her in some studio party. Du Maurier's *Trilby* had been the success of a publishing season, and the name itself was being splashed about the whole English-speaking world. She was blond and handsome and more effective than Clara; she knew her and had some obscure hostility to her, and so we contrived to be seen about together and

even to encounter Weston and Clara on one or two
occasions and go through the gestures of a liberal
amiability.

And Clara and I were sedulous to assure everyone in
our two little worlds that what we were doing was high
and calm and exactly what ought to be done, that we
had parted because we did not love each other as people
ought to do if they were to live together, but that we
maintained the highest esteem and the utmost affection
towards each other. Our marriage had been a mistake.
An agreeable mistake that had not lasted. She was
drawn to Weston by an old and natural passion. We
said little or nothing about the decisive intrusion of the
coming child or of any doubt that had ever troubled us
about its paternity. After all, very few people were
likely to check us back with a calendar. And in my
heart I hated Clara with a virulent hatred.

For the life of me I cannot now recall the exact
motives and intentions of these posturings and pretend-
ings. I know we were all set most resolutely upon
being emancipated, unconventional, free, and natural.
I think we all had a muddled sense of changing conditions, of the obsolescence of the standards of the past,
due to the altered population question and of the
necessity of readjustment; we young intellectuals were
among the first detached particles to fall into what is
now a great whirlpool of almost instinctive readjust-
ments.

Unhappily in all the proud and magnificent disen-
gagements and renunciations of our readjusting process
we took no account of an important legal functionary,

461

who was called in those Victorian days the Queen's Proctor. It was this gentleman's business to investigate the particulars of such divorces as the resources of his office brought within his scope, in the six months between the granting of the decree *nisi* and its being made absolute and final. To this day English law has no tolerance for divorce by consent. Its conception of marriage is the orthodox Christian one; its attitude towards divorce is punitive. There must be a party who is aggrieved and a party who is blameless, a party rolling and wallowing in " Sin " and a party of unspotted purity. The latter longs to continue the marriage, but the former has made it intolerable. The petitioner must to the climax live in a state of chaste grievance and hold out hands of reconciliation. It is the business of the Queen's Proctor to see that he or she does so. If the petitioner is rich, the petitioner goes abroad and, with a few expensive but simple precautions, is relieved of this obligation; the King's Proctor cannot, in the interests of national economy, pursue such a petitioner. But if the petitioner is poor, cheap, unpleasant persons of the minion type conduct their rude inquiries into his or her purity. They did into mine.

I petitioned. I got my decree *nisi,* and while Clara was in the amphibious state of a wife living in sin and under legal notice to quit, a daughter who is legally mine was born. Then the Queen's Proctor intervened, and I failed to get my decree made absolute. I was already at the laboratory at Downs-Peabody—I had been there two months—when I learnt by telegram that our iniquities were discovered and that since we had made it manifest that we *both* wanted a divorce, Clara was still, and was going to remain for the rest of our lives so far as I could see, my wife.

§ 6

NONE of us had reckoned with the Queen's Proctor. We had all been told of his legal possibilities, but we had answered airily that "they don't do that sort of thing now," and we really believed it. That was the *fin-de-siècle* assumption, that unfair or unpleasant laws did not work in the case of agreeable people, and it needed the startling trial and condemnation of Oscar Wilde that year to remind the world that even in the end of the most wonderful century old laws might still crush the wittiest, most impudent, and debonair of offenders. Elderly judges sat in the divorce courts delivering judgments that were none the less operative because all the clever people thought them half a century behind the times.

For my own part I was infuriated beyond measure by this smashing vindication of established institutions against our modernism. My hatred of Clara was overshadowed by a comprehensive rebellion against the world. It remained inconceivable to me that I was to have the burthen of her support and be barred against any decent remarriage, perhaps for all the rest of my days. I thought quite seriously for an hour or so one day of killing the Queen's Proctor to "ventilate" my grievance. I wonder what sort of dried-up old lawyer would have been swept out of existence if I had consummated that impulse. But that such a thought should have crossed my mind is a measure of my estimate of the situation. And I made a resolution, and kept it for three years, that whatever Weston decided to do about Clara, and however the law might stand in the matter, I would contribute nothing to the support of either her or her child.

She wrote a letter saying she wanted a good talk in private with me—"just to ourselves"—about "our daughter's prospects," but the latter phrase so irritated me that I did not answer. She wrote again twice. I was now getting deeply interested in the peculiar needs and conditions of Romer, Steinhart, but it happened that I had to come to London for a conference upon a more economical rearrangement of the refuse tilts at Downs-Peabody and that I had to visit the house in Edenbridge Square which I had at last let, in order to see a man and arrange for the forwarding of some of my books and the sale of the rest of the furniture. Accordingly I made an appointment with her there, and there it was we met for the last time.

(Except that once about fifteen years ago I saw her pursuing an omnibus in Trafalgar Square, I never set eyes upon her again. She died of influenza at Nice five years ago.)

She had arranged herself for my reconquest, very plainly but very prettily, and no one would have suspected her of a baby four months old. But I had determined to be insusceptible. I had hardened my heart and fortified myself. She asked me what I meant to do and what I thought she ought to do. Nothing,

I said. She could go on just as if she had been divorced. She could call herself Mrs. Weston. The press notices of the dismissal of our decree absolute had been very inconspicuous; even the notices of our brief trial had been rare and compact; we were too obscure for attention, and if she stuck to it stoutly that she and Weston were married, no one was likely to make any trouble in the matter.

She said that was reasonable, very reasonable, but there was something troubling her mind. She faltered for a moment and decided to be blunt.

"Philip," she said, "isn't sure about the child."

She eyed me. She seemed to be weighing my receptivity for some elaborate and circumstantial confidences. "Nor am I," she added meanwhile.

I shrugged my shoulders. "I don't feel an interested party," I said.

"*Billy!*" she cried. "You're pretty tough. . . . Legally anyhow—it's yours."

That stung me. I swore compactly.

"Well, we have to face facts," she said.

"Philip's your man."

"I shan't feel safe with Philip. I don't feel safe with myself. I was a fool, Billy."

"You were careless about yourself, Clara. And about me. Haphazard is the word. I've never thought of you as a fool."

"There's still the old tang in the things you say, Billy."

I had no defence against that. There was no one she had ever found so satisfactory to talk to as I was, she said. I put things so clearly and freshly. We had had some great times together. She glowed at her memories and sighed. "I suppose I've learnt too late," she said, "that everything one does has consequences. I've made a beastly mess of things." Life was like turning on taps that wouldn't turn off again. When one was a child one squalled and somebody came and slapped one and shut the tap off and put everything back. Then suddenly one was grown-up and nobody came. But the slaps came. "I've had some bad times, taking that in," said Clara.

I was touched. I relaxed a little in my manner. I said that what she needed in life was not a husband like myself, but a large sedulous male attendant of about fifty. Perhaps it was too late now to prescribe that. Old Crashaw for example. Where was he?

"He's married," she said, "and idiotic about her."

"So that's no good."

"No," she said, "I was a fool. I should have played the game by you."

I said that some day perhaps we should defer the age of moral responsibility until people were thirty or thirty-five. "As if I didn't know how I have spoilt things for you!" she exclaimed suddenly, the most successful thing she said in the whole conversation. It had never occurred to me before that she could recognise the damage I had suffered.

"I bit it off," I said, "and I had to chew it. You're not to blame for that."

"Poor old Billy! You've had a beastly time."

She was positively embracing my admission that the

affair had hurt me. The mule's ears went back again.

"Suppose now after all I come back to you," she threw out, so that it was doubtful whether it was an idle remark or a serious suggestion.

I forget the exact form of my reply. I considered the possibility for a moment. I told her that then, very carefully and deliberately, without causing her unnecessary pain, I should set about killing her. But if I forget my exact words I remember hers.

"That's the most attractive thing you've ever said to me!" she cried.

"All the same, you'd better stick to Philip," I said. "You can explain things to him so that he will believe. Unless you've muddled already with his confidence."

She was not quite convinced now of her power to humbug Philip, I could see. And once she had been so certain.

"I don't know what you're up to, Clara," I said, "but your one chance in life now is Philip. If you try any second string business with him he'll smell it, even if he doesn't know about it. Have you been shaking him already—by something? You pile your little all on him. I swear to you I'll go to gaol for ever rather than do anything to help you."

"I've never asked for that, Billy."

"What good would it be?"

But she still hovered undecided before the course she had to take.

"It gives Philip a frightful power over me. Whatever he does I shan't be able to divorce him."

" No doubt you'll contrive some consolation for your wounded pride," I said.

" You can sting.   You could always sting. . . ."

It was clear our talk was coming to nothing for her. Whatever vague intentions she had had, whether of a reconciliation, or an entangling afternoon's adventure, had failed.   I wonder to this day what she had wanted in that interview.

At the end we shook hands and then with my hand in hers her eyes scrutinised mine.   Mine told her nothing.   She hesitated.   She took her chance with me and flung her arms about me, and gave me the last of those wonderful kisses of hers that I was ever to receive.   Her first kiss had seemed to me to come straight out of heaven; this last, straight out of stock. I accepted the favour without excitement.   I held her in   my   arms — considerately,   even   appreciatively. " Ah!" she sighed, detaching herself and scrutinising my face again.

" You'd better play a straight game with Philip," I said, as though nothing had happened.   " You won't —but you'd better."

" Why didn't you *make* me play a straight game with you?"

I don't think I answered that.

" You could have done it so easily."

I shook my head.

" You had everything in your hands."

After she had gone I sat for a long time at the little table in the drawing-room at which I had worked so often, thinking.

I was extremely sorry for her. Suddenly having thus beaten her off from me, I was sorry for her, as I had never been sorry for her before. This futile attempt to raid back to my affections alleviated my hate for her by its very futility. I saw her flimsiness at last plainly, the poverty of her equipment, the adverse chances against her. Our separation had robbed her of her personal hold over me; I saw her now as a stranger, as detachedly. For the first time in my life I realised that pity for women which comes to all decent men sooner or later—in spite of our endless humiliations and subjugations and the way we spoil our lives through them. For it is not they who spoil men's lives, but the accidents of a bad time and a misdirection in ourselves that misuse them to our own hurt and belittlement.

But was I to blame? What else could I have done from first to last except the things I had been impelled to do? And now what was there to do? It was impossible for me to take her back even were she prepared for that. A little more kindness perhaps? But even that might prevent her from doing the one wise thing before her, which was to make herself Philip's only woman and he her only man.

I had a half-generous, half-insulting impulse, and I found a sheet of paper in my bureau and wrote her a note telling her to take all the furniture left in the house for herself. She had bought it with a certain avid interest; she was always a bright-eyed buyer, and suddenly I saw clearly that its poor little pieces and arrangements were personal to her and I had no right to deprive her of them. Fortunately the furniture man had made so poor an offer for the stuff that I had held it over to consider, or I could not have done even this petty act of decency. The real owner of the furniture I reflect now with a smile was Dickon. I had still to repay his brotherly loan. But I did not see it in that light then. Possibly because I knew certainly that I would repay.

I did everything I could to keep Clara out of my mind for some years and to heal the scar of her excision. But presently came a time when she was in dismay. She wrote to me pitifully and shamelessly. The ménage with Weston had broken down; I do not know how, the truth in these things is always obscure and complex and indescribable even to the principals in the quarrel. Her family had turned against her, and not one of her three sisters was well married. She was evidently as concerned for our daughter as for herself, and I have every reason to suppose she was by nature and intention a good mother. She was always cleverer and kinder with dogs and cats than I was; she had quick responses to all living things that came near her, and I have no doubt she was exceptionally attentive and kind to her own child. I decided to help her. But I helped her in such a way that even now I am not a little ashamed to write it down. The truth has to be told because it is an illuminating truth. It shows the make-up of the human male. I arranged she should be paid three hundred a year, and I saddled it with an ungracious condition that the money should be paid to her " while she remained chaste." She had to swallow that insult. My solicitor saw nothing objectionable in this ugly proviso, and would even have amplified it by a clause against "annoyance." But the law still keeps its moral ideas in cold storage in the vaults of the seventeenth century.

Two years later I made it an unconditional three hundred a year. What right had I to dictate her conduct of her life in this fashion? And when things were already going well with me and the sense of security and property was established in me, I heard that our daughter was being ill-taught in a National School in Hoxton, to the great distress of her mother, and suddenly I made a settlement of a thousand a year on Clara. My solicitor advised me to make it on the daughter with Clara as trustee, but I had as much confidence in Clara's maternal instincts as I had in her inevitable unchastity. It worked quite well, and she brought up her daughter as a very pleasant young lady, and married her off finally just after the war when the marriage market was good, to a prosperous doctor in Cardiff, who had met her first on war service. Then Clara travelled for a time, with first one woman friend and then another, visited Egypt and the Garden of Allah, and acquired a taste for roulette at Monte Carlo. Of her sisters I never heard anything more. I have been told she dressed young during this final phase, and was sometimes charming and sometimes rather haggard. She always had one or two very old men or very young men in attendance. Her death was due to the impatience that made her get up for a dance before she was well of her influenza. The fresh chill, and the casualness of the hotel where she was staying alone, killed her. She was about four hundred pounds in debt and overdrawn when she died, which sum seemed to me to be almost exactly like her—neither very scandalous nor quite solvent.

I made the acquaintance of our daughter as a schoolgirl at a vehemently healthy, manly girls' school at Brighton. I had learnt from Clara that she was a little worried in her mind, assisted by her schoolfellows, at the aloofness of her father, and so I went in state on several visiting days and showed myself with her and was introduced to her friends and found occasions to take her about in London. She was quite easy to be nice to. She did not resemble me in the least, but also she did not resemble Weston; I have sometimes fancied a resemblance to Billy Parker, but that may be a morbid fancy. She played and plays tennis very well, and is ridiculously grave and important in the art, practice, and politics of this epidemic.

I liked her, and I still like her, and I perceive that I loom large in her scheme of things, but I have never warmed to her; I do not feel and, to be plain about it, I do not believe, that she is bone of my bone and flesh of my flesh. I feel none of the instinctive harmony and intimacy that I do with my nephew William or even with his brother Richard. But I love William. I was temperately generous at her marriage, and I know that she has expectations that my will must not altogether disappoint. Sometimes I pay her a flying visit when my business takes me to Cardiff, and sometimes there will be a dinner and a theatre party in London. On occasion she sits on my knee, ruffles my

hair, and calls me " Daddy." But always a little tenta-
tively. I am gracefully responsive, and all the while I
feel as unreal as if I were acting a Charles Wyndham
part in a play by Sir Henry Arthur Jones, and she were
the celebrated and charming Miss So-and-So. The
doctor is good, solid stuff, though rather too prejudiced
against psycho-analysis, and the two children are
healthy, jolly little experimentalists with life, as amusing
to play with as puppies. If they are not exactly bone
of my bone and flesh of my flesh, I have no doubt they
would be quite willing to be so. It is not their fault
if they are not.

§ 7

I SAT for a long time in our empty house after Clara
had departed, with my note about the furniture on
the table before me. I sat there long after it was quite
dark. Then I found a candle and lit it and went about
the house musing over the things that had happened in
the various rooms, incredulous of its evaporated happiness. What a poor, stuffy little house it had become,
and how proud we had once been of it! I came down
to the drawing-room again and sat there.

It must have been half-past ten or even later before I
closed the door behind me, because when I went by
the Underground Railway to the Strand to get some
food I found the people streaming out of the theatres.
It was the narrow old Strand that is now being swept
away; it was lit then by a queer mixture of gas-lamps,
mantle-lamps, and fizzling arc-lights on trial that made

variegated glares and pallors on the bobbing heads of the crowd. The people jostled me because I was still half lost in thought, and when I sat down in Gatti's I remember the waiter annoyed me because he would not take " Oh, anything that's going " as a definite order, but insisted upon making suggestions.

That session with myself in that dusk-invaded room, in my first and last home, became for me a cardinal point in my life, the end of a chapter, the beginning of a new phase. It stands out in my conception of my life as our departure from Mowbray stands out, or the night when Dickon and I announced our secession from the Walpole-Stent household stands out. It marks the real beginning of the man I am now, the passing of a much more instinctive, passionate, and direct being. I have described my youthful self as a very detached scientific intellect in conflict with what seemed an alien and destructive sexuality. The two had fought a battle that was really an admixture. For a time sex had stormed along its own path with me, had seemed to carry all before it. It had made me aggressive and combative; it had turned me to acquisition and had made me aware of the need of power. My intelligence had not been so much defeated as hammered into new recognitions. The two had come now to a phase of balance and under-standing. I still thought that research, the clambering to new visions of reality beyond any limits of knowledge yet attained, was the best thing in life, but I knew that I could not go on with that toilsome ascent until the craving hungers that torment and distract unless they are satisfied were assuaged, until my personal pride was secure, until I could command beauty in my hours if I desired it.

I had realised at last the profound importance of the sexual motive in life. I could not live fully without that self-respect, that zest in my personal life that only woman could give me. I had to discover now how I could come to terms with womankind. I had to do this under the handicap of my entanglement. I had so to frame my life and to achieve such relationships that I should be safe from such another disaster as this empty house embodied. I had to gain a certain security and amplitude in the world, so that if presently I was able to build up some more than temporary liaison, it should be secure from the tension of wants and debts and safe against the attractions and distractions of a more prosperous Philip Weston. I had not realised before the *quid pro quo* in love. It was plain to me now and plainly reasonable. I saw why Clara with the thought of motherhood had been scared from the narrow bleakness of our little home, and I saw, too, the manifest connection of her attempted reconciliation with my new prosperity.

Can a creature made for motherhood be indifferent to a lair? I will not say coarsely that I learnt that women are to be bought, but I saw quite clearly that they have to be paid for. Well, I must be able to pay for them. I could not think now what it was I had expected from Clara. I had made vast assumptions. But though a man does research, so that new light and wonder such as no one has ever known before pour into the world, so that new things begin and all things are altered and

475

turned about, yet if that involves personal poverty, a certain preoccupation of mind, an inability to cherish and supply, no woman has any use for him.

I was not man enough, I saw, or perhaps I should say I was too much of a man, to accept the rôle of a scientific devotee, vowed for the best part of his life to celibacy and poverty. That would cripple me with a suppressed sense of inferiority and all the mental distortion that entails. I needed material success, embodied in its living symbol. I must have that living symbol. I had learnt now in terms of Clara and bitter experience what I had disregarded when Dickon told it to me in words that then had no meaning for me. " Research!" he had said. " Please yourself for a bit, Billykins, so long as you're let. But there's not even freedom of thought in the world for a man who isn't his own master. The show is a scramble, and it's going to be a scramble yet for centuries."

So I, too, would become predatory and set out to overtake Dickon in his scramble to possession and freedom and purchasing power. And, freedom and power assured, I must square my account with this craving that obsessed me. Then, as Dickon had said, for disinterested service, scientific research, or anything else, as the mood might take me.

Already I had learnt a great deal from the beginnings of my work with Romer, Steinhart. I had been able to measure myself against most of my directors and get some inkling of the scale and vast possibilities of their organisation. For those days it was a very great company, though it was a mere infant compared with the giant ramifications of annexed, subsidiary, dependent, and associated concerns into which we have since grown. We had practically no relations with America or Sweden at all then, and towards our German and other Continental homologues our attitude was still one of naïve rivalry. The authorised capital of the mother company is now thirty-two million pounds; in those days in was seven hundred and fifty thousand. The works at Downs-Peabody were still the largest part of our plant. But even then in the early nineties the firm's rate of growth was sufficient to foreshadow its present scale. Our ordinary shares of a pound were creeping up and round about thirty shillings. And it was clear to me that with my quite special knowledge and my peculiar aptitudes it would be extremely easy for me to secure a fair and handsome participation in the big things coming.

My directors had not yet made up their minds how I was to be handled. But I had already formed very clear ideas of how the firm was going to be handled. I had been brought in by Julian Romer, the younger son of old Romer and the brother of the great Roderick, the head of the firm. Julian was, perhaps, the best equipped technically of all the second generation of Romers. Roderick was a far better administrator, but of no account from the technical standpoint. Old Romer had been the business organiser of the concern; Steinhart had been the scientific spirit; but both the Romer sons—Steinhart had daughters only; Ralph Steinhart is a nephew—were sent abroad to learn something sound about modern chemistry and metallurgy before the intel-

lectual lassitude of the English public school could sub-
merge them. Julian had a real aptitude for scientific
work and also considerable business ability. He had
marked the drift of my early papers and leapt, long
before I had a suspicion of that side of the matter, at
the industrial applications foreshadowed. He had explained me to his co-directors and sought me out. He
was a high-coloured, black-haired, warm-blooded, bright-
eyed little man, very quick in his movements, very confidential in his manner, coming up very close to you,
insinuatingly. We were to work in the same laboratory
for a time. He was, if possible, to pick my brains; I
was to be the auriferous quartz, and he was to be the
extractor. His sedulous amiability, his pressing per-
suasiveness, were, however, just a little too warm and
eager for the metallic Clissold temperament. We ex-
changed. He learnt something of what I knew—
enough to realise the full value of what I could do for
the industry—and I learnt very rapidly of his business
and productive organisation.

I perceived I could be, that I was made to be, the
goose that could lay golden eggs for Romer, Steinhart,
Crest and Co. I did not intend, however, to lay them
in full sight of my employers. After a week I found
Julian's interest in my private thoughts so lively that I
took all my notebooks out of the laboratory back to my
lodgings and bought a safe to keep them in. I just
carried one notebook in my pocket. When Julian
embarked upon discussions with me I stressed the philosophical side. Julian showed a real feeling for pure
science, and I saw to it that he got it chemically pure.

I carried our talk at times, I believe, to a very close approximation to some of Einstein's subsequent work, but I doubt if Julian fully appreciated the high and novel matter I was giving him. One day he made a sort of quarrel because I didn't let him know what I was doing upon the crystallisation of alloys, and hinted quite plainly that I was paid to confide all my notions to him—at least all that occurred to me in business hours.

"Results," I corrected. "But I have to follow the laws of my being. I couldn't think if I thought I was watched while I was thinking. It would make me self-conscious and nervous. But when I have results I shall give them to you properly, ready for use. They're coming, rest assured."

"But I could help you so much more," said Julian, "if I could follow what you were up to."

"Couldn't bear you at my heels," I said. "It would paralyse me."

"I've got ideas."

"Don't I know it? But you will have to bear with my limitations."

He shrugged his shoulders and pouted and looked hurt and unhappy. "I had looked forward so to working with you, my dear fellow."

Quite at the outset I did some good work that proved my value to the firm. It was nothing out of the way; it was the natural consequence of bringing a fresh young mind to bear on an established routine. The system of the refuse tilts had grown up bit by bit, had been adapted several times to changes of method, had become a thing of use and wont to all the directors, and an increasing element of waste had crept in with each adaptation. Things had moved fast; there had been a lot of patching. No one had thought of standing the whole thing on its head, so to speak. I saw almost at once that that could be done at a very considerable profit, simply because I was not habituated to the old sequence. If I had been in the firm for ten years, I should have been just as blind to it as the others were. They saw my points and nodded to each other.

Julian behaved at the meeting as if he had begotten me, trained me, and taught me what to say. Also he prompted me. But this first golden egg established me with the firm and gave me time to work out my more primary and extensive problems in applied metallurgy and to devise a method of conceding them upon terms whereby the profit should be mutual.

My mind was already full of that possibility when I sat and thought in my empty house.

I remember very distinctly thinking over Julian, Clara quite forgotten for a while, and smiling to myself in the darkness. I was already very fond of him then, and my affection has grown with the years. He is one of the few men I can bear to play golf with. He knows so much, he puts his heart into every game, and he achieves even worse results than I do. With outcries, with something near tears. " What have I done?" he cries, to God and me, to the caddie and the earth and the sky and any casual birds or beasts that chance to be within earshot. " My God! But *look* at it!" He had left London directly after the meeting on the previous afternoon for Downs-Peabody, and he had been most solicitous that I should do all I had to do in London before I returned. I had thanked him warmly. I had expected something of the sort and prepared for it.

When I had unpacked at Downs-Peabody I had found, among other things in my boxes, two or three fragments of meteorites I had brought away from the Royal College. Just before leaving to come to London, I had fused these up together in a dark and intriguing lump. One side I cut and polished beautifully. I had marked this lump " B. in reserve. Final phase," packed it away in a little box, and left it, as if inadvertently, in the drawer of my laboratory table for Julian's benefit. I felt sure it would amuse him while I was away. He was probably busy with it now, missing his dinner to examine and perhaps analyse a scrap of it, and it was pleasant to calculate what he would make of it.

It *was* " in reserve " and " in its final phase." What else was there to be done with it?

No doubt my meditations wandered for a time to the characteristics of his people. I do not believe very much in all this modern fuss about races; everyone alive is, I am convinced, of mixed race, but still some of us are more white, some of us more negro, some of us more Chinese than others. Compared with me Julian was Mediterranean, South-Eastern, Jewish; compared with him I was Northern and Western and blond. And our minds worked with the most entertaining differences. In his presence I felt slow and stupid—but solid. His mind could dance round mine as it marched. It came into a question like a brisk young dog, which comes into a room, seems to see, hear, and smell everything, knows

481

what you feel about, wags its tail all the time, makes a remark or so almost absent-mindedly, and goes out again quite assured there is neither biscuit nor bone there. He thought so quickly that he never stopped to think. I had as little chance against him at chess as a gorilla. And yet I could get to things and do things that seemed impossible to him and that he knew were impossible to him. I could produce a path where he was convinced there was no path, and I could see, and make him see, things he had never seen. While he raced through the labyrinth of a question, learning its every turn, I seemed able to look over and reach over.

But the more one tries to state these differences, the more one realises how subtly they defy formulation. These brunette peoples, these dark-whites, made civilisation for us. I doubt if either we blonds or the yellows or the blacks could have done as much for ourselves. Then we came in upon an established system, we Northern and Atlantic peoples, migrants, invaders, sceptics, protestants, obstructive questioners, slow, recalcitrant learners, less brilliant but more original, rupturing conventions, releasing debtors, opening new ways, resuming the forward movement upon obscure new lines. . . .

Perhaps Julian and I represent a blend that may become very effective in human affairs. We two and Roderick have done quite a number of things together that none of us could have brought off in exclusive association with men of our own type.

But I see I am astray beyond my thoughts in my empty house in Edenbridge Square. From Julian my musing probably passed to my other associates at Downs-Peabody, and so came back to more intimate questions. For the first time in my life since I had begun to observe and think I had come into contact with rich people and with able people engaged in getting richer, and I was beginning to apprehend a number of points about human motives and my own possibilities that had hitherto escaped me. I had not properly understood before what there is in this process of getting and keeping rich; my estimate of motives had been too simple. I had regarded only the forms and habits of life. I was now getting a grasp upon the driving forces of life.

I can best put it by saying that in my younger view of the social order into which I had been born I had seen it mainly as a business of toil-shifting and a struggle for freedom. People were poor, limited, and oppressed because they had had too much of the necessary toil of the community thrust upon their shoulders, and my early socialism was a simple and reasonable scheme for the redistribution and economy of toil. Everybody might be relieved from any excess of toil and given leisure and a sufficiency of freedom. Then—seen from the angle of back streets and the common life of worry and insufficiency—it seemed reasonable to expect that everyone would be happy. But now I had begun to share the lives of these Romers and Steinharts and Crests and their womankind, and to realise the power of pride among their driving motives. I had come back into large houses and parks and gardens and into an atmosphere of many servants and abundance and display; a multitude of dormant memories of Mowbray were revived in me, and I was reminded that so soon as a human being is housed, fed, and made to feel secure, it proceeds at once to seek occasion to swagger over other human beings. It seeks reassurance.

That everyone should have a fair prosperity, no one toil, no one be enslaved, would not simply leave this overbearing and conquering craving unsatisfied; it would release it to unexampled activity. The Romers and Steinharts spent and swaggered like English county families out of the best novels, with touches of Oriental splendour they did their insufficient best to restrain. Roderick's dressing-gowns are indescribable, and I have always suspected Julian of secret cloth-of-gold pants. The Crests, an old English family born to coal and ore, were in comparison coldly and haughtily victorious over the common ruck of mankind. Crest was about as intelligent in our business as a horse, but his very incapacity increased his effect of being thoroughbred. He was silent in the board-room and very cunning; for generations the Crest family had grown richer and richer by being in the way and having to be bought out, and I think that both he and Lady Muriel, his wife, despised the Romers and Steinharts for actively creating wealth instead of passively insisting upon it. Julian in lapses from his habitual ingratiation had had occasion to remind me once or twice that I was a salaried employé, but the Crests made me feel it from the moment we were in sight of each other. They were going to walk on me. They were going to be aloof, condescending, unaware. Such ascendencies were what life was for.

I had been over to lunch with the Crests at Folingden,

and Lady Muriel had made it abundantly evident that I was unsuitable for sustained conversation. I had to be addressed with polite consideration, I had to answer when I was addressed, and then I had to lapse into respect. Having honoured me as one might pat a dog, she proceeded to talk across me with Mrs. Roderick Romer about the condition of the poor in their respective parishes. The cottagers in the Crest village were not providing sufficient girls for domestic service; the Romer village had plenty of girls, but our works at Downs-Peabody were too near and were beguiling them away.

"I want Roderick to close the works to Brampsheet girls," Mrs. Roderick had said.

"A girl who is not broken to service by fifteen," Lady Muriel had generalised, "will never make a good servant."

"I tell him he's destroying the breed. He's destroying all their standards."

Difficult stuff for the excluded middle to cut in upon.

A sad and handsome "Nordic" face with an expression of enigmatical aloofness had hovered behind Mrs. Roderick's Oriental opulence. It was the Crest's family butler, waiting with the peas. He might have been Crest's first cousin. He was exactly the same creature—minus the acres that had the coal and iron below. . . .

I sat in my empty house and I found my irritation against the Crests and my sense of the exuberant triumph of the Romers and Steinharts over the Oreshire domestics and poor, interweaving with my bitter realisation of the share that economic inferiority had played in my disaster with Clara. I philosophised widely. I was beginning to understand how the issues and ramifications of sex spread into the whole complex of social life. I had thought two years ago that sex was simply a sensuous craving, an appetite needing assuagement and trailing with it a sense of beauty. I knew now that that was not the tenth part of it; that was merely the red centre of a far ampler desire—a desire for possession, assurance, and predominance. I understand now how that spread out into the general competition of life. The desire of a woman to own and dominate a man, or the desire of a man to own and dominate a woman or women, is only the intense focus of a vastly greater nimbus of purpose, to dominate men and women at large. It spreads out into a craving for servants, for dependents, for wills that wait on our wills. It branches out into a desire for possessions of all sorts; it finds a grotesque specialisation in the accumulation of pets. This hunger for the sense of mastery over life accounts for the otherwise idiotic pleasure people take in the shooting of pheasants and suchlike poor, attractive creatures. The ultimate expression of dominance is to kill. The specifically sexual drive is merely the apex of a drive which at its broadest is a desire to own and dominate all life.

And I was, in fact, as sexual, as aggressive upon life as these Romers and Steinharts and Crests, as Dickon and all the rest of the world. Only I had failed to perceive it until Clara had developed me.

So I saw it in my empty house. I saw life stripped

bare and plain as a struggle from which there was no remission. One might have the freakish desire for scientific knowledge; it was no excuse. One had to fight for its gratification just as one would have to fight for any other fantasy that caught one's will. One had to fight or gratify the lust and the craving within one before one could serve it, just as one had to fight the conflicting purposes of one's fellow-men and the antagonism of nature. The service of mankind through science gave one no natural claim for help or consideration in the scramble of life. One had to struggle with one's enemy and beguiler, woman, just as much as one had to struggle against one's enemy and rival and would-be subjugator, man. That was the quality of life. Fight, establish yourself, or go under—go under even though your every wish was benevolent. And happily for me I had a weapon in my special gifts and in this metallurgical knowledge I had chanced to acquire.

I would fight. What else was there to do? The prospect of a frank struggle to get the better of the world bored me but did not dismay me. I was fairly sure of myself. I would somehow get to power and freedom round the reservations of Romer, Steinhart, and the Crests, as I would somehow get round the entanglement Clara had made for me to the gratification of my desires. And that was how the prospect of life spread itself out before me. To that I had come at that time. Such quasi-scientific, quasi-religious mysticism as I have now is all of later growth. In those days I had no intimation of that wilful reconstruction of human affairs which now dominates my activities. That came during and after the war. That was a result of the war. Simply I contemplated and nerved myself for struggle. If I contemplated anything at the end of that struggle it was a resumption of pure research, aloof from and disregardful of the common affairs of men. I was a hard young man, far more narrowly egotistical than I am now.

The memory of those hours is all dark loneliness and stern resolve. Clara was already at an infinite distance, clean out of my universe. I had parted from her and given her the furniture, and she was, I thought, handsomely disposed of.

The candle flared down to extinction at my elbow, and made the shadows dance about me. Outside a bleak gas-lamp lit the railings and black bushes of the unfrequented square.

§ 8

IT was not until nineteen seven or eight that I could feel I was accomplishing what I had set out to do and that the Romers had accepted me for good and all as a necessary part of their combination. By that time I could count myself a rich man as riches go now. It would be a long and tedious story to tell, full of petty manœuvres and cunning shifts and counter-shifts, before my group came to realise that they had to pay fairly for the science and initiative I could give them. Crest did his best to block my intrusion upon the board-room and even drove me to negotiations with a German-American group. He would not understand what I signified. His preponderant inheritances were against me. To this day he treats me with a sort of provisional equality, as though he had somehow mislaid his social ascendancy over me, but that at any moment his butler might find it in the hall or conservatory and restore it to him. But Lady Muriel, with the social flexibility of her sex, now consults me about the incipient love affairs of her grand-children.

Within four years I was a director of one of our subsidiaries, our queer little profitable Clissold Mineral Paint Company, but I did not become a director of the mother company until after ten years of steady work. It was interesting, this business; it was exasperating and it was boring; it was difficult at times to resist the temptation to smash the game and get out of it all, and the years between twenty-five and forty-five slipped away almost unperceived. Meanwhile I continued a respect-able scientific career with a steadily ebbing freshness and vitality of thought. I got my F.R.S. in 1902 chiefly on the strength of my papers upon intercrystalline stresses, but two young Germans, Stahl and Bütow, were already running away with my ideas and getting at things I had been too preoccupied to see. And so my purely scientific career petered out.

In 1907 I made an attempt to revive my scientific passions. I organised a private laboratory. It was beautifully equipped, but from the first it had an in-curable flavour of the amateur. Julian had just such another. His was as neat as a dressing-bag, as lavish and handy as the things on the toilet-table of a pro-fessional beauty. It had everything that heart could desire in a laboratory—except the heart to use it. Julian even had an assistant, a London B.Sc., a sort of intellectual valet who brushed and folded his researches and put them out for him when he wanted to resume them. I didn't go to that length. I did some reading, brought myself up to date. But the glory had departed.

I do not think I have spent three hundred hours in my private laboratory altogether since it was finished eighteen years ago. And half that time was given to special war stuff of no scientific value. I feel that such seclusion is now an affectation for me. I am no longer a leader anywhere upon the scientific front, and I lack the special energy to push up again. For the last year Siddons, not the astronomical Siddons but the Cambridge brother, E. A. P. Siddons, has been using the place and justifying its existence. Siddons, I think, will presently come in with us and take his place beside Trippman at the head of the firm's central research station. When I came into the firm we had exactly twenty-one men working in our laboratories, from myself to the bottle-washer and counting in Julian. Now we have four hundred and seven qualified men doing scientific work for us. It is all I can do to keep in touch with the new stuff they are opening up. Most of them are, of course, of the " trained " type and their research is routine inquiry, but ten or a dozen are fairly original men, and one or two of these are personalities of quality who promise well for our future.

Between 1908, when Sirrie Evans died, and the beginning of the war I passed through several phases of deep discontent and unhappiness; I shall say more about these experiences later. I was dissatisfied with life and restless. Whatever I did, I wanted presently to do something else; wherever I was I wanted to be somewhere else. I found business excuses for travel; I went into Russia, into further India and stayed for the better half of a year in Siberia. But nowhere was there any escape from this uneasiness of mind, this persuasion that in some essential respect my life was not right.

Then came the profound excitements of the war, and for a time it was possible to believe that real and fundamental things were happening. I have already written about that period in my account of Dickon. As I have told, disillusionment was harsh and speedy. Another phase of profound distress and unsettlement followed. It was complicated by a queer irrelevant passion that distracted me excessively. The need of a clear unifying purpose in my existence became imperative if I was not to go to pieces altogether. It rose to complete ascendancy over the confusion of my desires. It brought me at last to this tranquil sunny room in Provence and this pause for a final assembling of my purposes, before it is time for me to go altogether.

I have been working here at this book—with three brief intermissions in England—since last November. It is now June. Once more I note with gratitude the intimate and tranquillising beauty of this land. In April there was a great blaze of blossom; the big Judas-trees flowered magnificently, and a lot of little and medium sized Judas-trees I had hitherto not observed, its family, flowered in unison. There was also a great foam of lilac. All sorts of iris clamoured successfully for attention, and the roses, always more or less in flower here, suddenly took their task of beauty seriously and did wonderful things. That was our spring after a wet and windy March that flooded our kitchen. Now the days are baths of warm sunshine, and my common daily wear is pyjamas. The nights are nights of magic. They are scented nights. This week they are saturated in moonlight, and they abound in fireflies, fireflies that prick the darkness intermittently as they drift athwart the pallid roses and lilies and the black, still bushes and branches. In the depths of the ivy lurk green glow-worms. I find the nightingales too abundant and very tiresome with their vain repetitions, but Clementina does not agree; her mind has been poisoned by literature, and she does not really hear the tedious noises they make, she hears Keats. On the other hand, the carpet of sound made every evening by the frogs in the valley below is indescribably beautiful in itself. We disputed agreeably, and now she has gone and left me to my study table and my thoughts.

Here, tranquil before the still moonlight, serene as shining silver, defended from moth and mosquito by an invisible gauze, I can brood over my papers into the small hours. I have been sitting here not troubling to write since eleven. It is now nearly one. Here I can get all that Romer, Steinhart turmoil into something like its proper perspective against the world at large. I can look back upon it now across an interval of five-and-thirty years and make a companion picture to those still hours I spent in Edenbridge Square when my adventures with Romer, Steinhart lay all before me. Space, time, and the pressure of life are all altered in their values now. I can see our huge combine broadly, and my work for it as a quite typical item in that change of scale and material that is the essential fact of current history. I can see how extraordinarily representative we are of the general quality of contemporary life, both in its large wilfulness and its retarded consciousness of itself.

§ 9

HOW new and significant a thing we are! Of the various substances that we extract from crude matter and pour into the workshops of the modern world there is scarcely one that was even thought of a hundred years ago. Even the various steels we co-operate with White and Halbow in producing are new. Steel was a fudged, rule-of-thumb product in 1825; nobody knew what it was exactly; it was variable and uncertain, and to have produced a hundred-pound lump of it would have been thought a miracle. Now we can make steel play its tricks like a performing seal; we can make you steels as brittle as glass and steels almost as flexible as rubber, we can make crystalline steels as obdurate as carbon and malleable steels that at a temperature below red heat you can draw into wire and beat into leaves hardly less thin and ductile than gold. All you have to do is to pay the price. Some of these steels are still expensive toys, but to-morrow they will be staple needs. But that is only an overflow of our metallurgical activity. Steel is not our main interest. In ten years' time every other automobile body will be made of our light alloys, and in twenty there will be scarcely an aeroplane in the air that is not made of some stuff of ours. Again, for main roads, for all roads and streets where the wear is hard, Romer, Steinhart in twenty years' time will supply the only possible road metal, all over the world. There is hardly a modern contrivance from an incandescent lamp to a gramophone needle and from a toughened lamp chimney to the type that will print this book, that does not owe something to us—and pay it.

All this has grown from nothing in less than three-quarters of a century. In 1858, the original Steinhart, who was a Swedish chemist of Jewish extraction visiting England, met the original Romer, who was then travelling in mohair trimming for his uncle. They met in a train between Sheffield and London, and Steinhart talked about the slackness of the English and the peculiar opportunities that were, he thought, going to waste upon the coal and iron properties of the lordly Crests. Romer, who was a youth of nineteen at the time, and who detested mohair and his uncle, jumped at the possibilities of independent action these remarks opened out, and made himself so ingratiating to Steinhart and afterwards so importunate to Crest, our present Crest's father, that at last he brought together the first experimental company, the founder company of all our branching tree. This was the Crest Slag Works, and it was afterwards reconstructed as the Crest Bye-Products. Romer, who had a really vigorous intelligence, went off to Germany and studied metallurgical chemistry for two years to fit himself better to control this business he had made possible.

In 1879 he succeeded in shifting the central works from the Crest properties to Downs-Peabody so as to be in easy reach of the Brampsheet and Hinton-Peabody deposits, and the Crest Bye-Products Company was swallowed up in the bolder enterprise of Romer, Steinhart, Crest and Co. with a capital of fifty thousand pounds. The rearrangement of the names showed, among other things, that the Crests were no longer on the back of the concern but dragging along at its side. Where alas! they continue to drag.

But I do not see why I should write here the details of an industrial development which are easily accessible to the curious in a variety of forms. The external facts have always been stated very plainly and fully at our annual meetings; we are widely documented. What interests me now is the social and mental significance of this rapid and amazing growth. It spreads through the once formless worldwide commerce in metals and raw material for mechanical production, it sends out processes, it joins on to cognate bodies and bodies that become cognate in a way that is extraordinarily suggestive of the appearance of a vertebral column and its linking up to rudiments of rib and limb in the body of an embryo. And side by side with it and capable of either consuming or amalgamating with it are similar and rival organisations. Parallel with it are other great organising systems dealing in oil, great food trusts, cotton, shipping combinations. It is a new

economic structure where formerly there was fragmenta-
tion, open market, and crowd commerce. It is only
being recognised for what it is. We ourselves, Romers,
Steinharts, Crests, and myself, and all the other twenty-
odd outsiders who have come into the direction of our
main or openly associated concerns, are only beginning
to see what it is we are doing. Hardly any of us
realise the full extent of our tentacles; we expand as if
by instinct, and at times our right hand has scarcely a
suspicion of what the left is closing upon. It is still
more interesting to compare what we are, we creatures
inflated by expansive forces beyond our expectation,
with what we might be and what perhaps we ought
to be.

I do not believe that our primordial Steinhart dreamt
for a moment of the nature of the egg he was laying in
the nest of the conservative Crests. There was a bolder
imaginative touch about our ancestral Romer; he may
have had previsions of the things that are coming.
Not one of our present gang has ever seen what we are
doing as a whole. Or if anyone has, the vision has
vanished again instantly like the Holy Grail. Here am
I in Provence, the new Thebaid, living the life of a
hermit—with Clem installed within a mile as the
official temptation—in order to get a view of it. Possibly Roderick comes nearer than anyone to a comprehensive conception of our rôle in the world's affairs.
He is something of a statesman. He made a mistake
in taking a peerage. He is rather lost up there as Lord
Brampsheet. He has barred himself out of the House
of Commons by this splendour, and only discovered too

late that he can make quite good political speeches. It was some feeling between the wives about the Crest barony that added Brampsheet to the glorious roll of Lloyd George's peers. Crest wanted his caparison, Lady Romer saw an opportunity of drawing level with Lady Muriel, and manifestly it was impossible to honour the impassive Crest and leave the energetic and possibly malignant Sir Roderick untouched. And Sir Roderick at the time did not realise what he was doing for himself. Perhaps it is just as well, for him as for us. He likes to argue, and this vice of debate might have grown upon him until he gave to party what is meant for the business of the world.

He has imagination; he has ideas; he is aggressive; he is not content to fall into the moulds of preceding things. He will talk at times in quite revolutionary fashion. He respects Crest more than I do, but he hates him just as much. He respects Crest more than I do, because there is still a lingering instinct in the Romer blood, due to a thousand years of pogroms, that these hippoid types should be propitiated. He dare not believe as I do that modern science and mechanism have made cavalry and the landed gentry obsolete. Apart from this weakness my Lord Brampsheet is as progressive as myself and much more energetic. To him we owe the steady extension of our interests beyond industrial production to international finance. Through his tentacular instincts and the intervention of banking it is that we are in co-operation instead of cut-throat competition with our German and French and Swedish parallels, and allied and linked to mining and coal interests in all parts of the world, to cotton growing, and gold and diamond mining, which were once as remote from us as concerns in another planet.

Roderick is physically a bigger man than my Julian, and his methods of address are less insinuating and more familiar. Occasionally he seems to be trying, as the Americans put it, to "jolly" you. By an odd coincidence he resembles the Bolshevik leader Zinovieff so closely that when first I met the latter in Petersburg in 1920 I laughed aloud. They might be identical twins. Yet neither is pleased to hear of this resemblance.

The parallelism is more than physical. Their imaginations are similar, constructive and a little grandiose; they have an enormous amount of mental energy, and mental energy, I should think, of very much the same type and grade. In 1920, after the phase of extreme Communism, Bolshevism in Moscow was as intellectually bankrupt as any "capitalist" government. In spite of such purely comic efforts as Lenin's "electrification of Russia" and Trotsky's valiant splutterings, it plainly did not know what to do next. But Zinovieff had already hit upon the spacious idea of an appeal to Asia, and the evocation of a sort of godless Islam out of Russia and the Turk and Central Asia. So far as any politico-social idea has ever realised itself, Zinovieff's dream might realise itself. And so in this vastly richer Western muddle of ours, which has so much more time and stuff to waste before it gets down to bare realities, I find in Roderick an idea where other people seem to have no ideas; not, indeed, a clear idea, but an adumbration with something very like an outline, the idea of a sort of shelving or subordination of political forms and a reorganisation of economic and social life under the control of a union of big financial and industrial groups. The same idea looms up even more distinctly in some American circles. It foreshadows a statecraft of realities. Beside Roderick, our old Asquith seems to me as unreal and empty as one of those figures of Chinese porcelain that nod their heads and move their hands in country houses. I do not mean that Roderick has ever sat down and worked out his idea to even its broad implications. He has never detached himself enough from current activities for that. But he has it. Power has happened to him. In this present world he is one of a number of men who wake up in middle age to find power flowing past within their grasp. He has at least awakened. He blinked, he snorted and made startling sounds, he shut his eyes again, but he had awakened.

He knows as well as I do that the politics, the parties, the governments, and empires of the world to-day are all a swiftly passing show, masking, but growing at last dimly transparent, to reveal the real processes that are going on in human life.

But these things belong to a later part of this book. I am discussing now the motives and ideas that have made us what we are. Roderick interests me most of all our group, and I watch him as closely as anyone. What do these gleams, these phases of broad politico-social vision amount to altogether with him? Very little—yet. To me they amount to much more, but with me also they are conceptions that stir rather than conceptions that control. With him they have a quality almost of improper thoughts. When we talk of these things and I betray a belief that there is a vital reality in our talk he becomes manifestly a little shy, a little scared. "But to come back to business, my boy," he says. "To come back to business———"

He has not made himself. He has been made. His motives in building up this great system about Romer, Steinhart, Crest and Co. have been all of a piece with my motives. He wanted to live, to assert himself vigorously upon things and upon life, and he came in at a lucky angle. I believe, with the same differences that make him physically a contrast to myself, his mental and moral life is very parallel to mine.

And for the rest of our people I find no driving force at all commensurate with the great plant which nominally belongs to us, but to which we indeed belong. Men like Spink and Gedge came in by making themselves useful, young Brand by making himself agreeable. Trippmann is able and alive, but almost wholly a chemist. Siddons may develop; there is more in him than in the others, and he is still very young. The rest are wheels or links. Several do good research work and make excellent arrangements to exploit their results, but they do not seem to apprehend the business as a whole and in relation to the world as a whole. They run after fine houses and fine wives; they appreciate knighthoods and baronetcies; or they sniff after the imaginative excitements of the artistic and dramatic world, and the sands of their lives run out.

None of us are very great sportsmen; it is too heavy a call on our time. Lord Crest is still under the impression that he is a great English country gentleman a little distended by commerce, and so in need of a sort of moral tight-lacing. He is enormously respected in the Carlton Club, and both his sons have been through the Guards. Everard represents Offerton in the conservative interest and will some day succeed his father as the drag on our wheels. Sons and father are all associated with various attempts to create strike-breaking and quasi-Fascist organisations in England against the active Labour people. Gods! how that sort of prancing and threatening exasperates some of our men, some of our very best men! Crest has recently had his portrait painted in the Ruritanian style as Lord Lieutenant of Oreshire, scarlet and splendid. The background even is romantic. No chimneys are visible. There is a beautiful carriage with horses in London for Lady Crest, as well as several cars. Lady Muriel is a friend of the Family, of the most exalted Family.

"My boy," said Roderick, when I was letting myself go one day upon Crest's costliness and general ineffectiveness, "have you ever thought of his value as our shopwalker?"

"Mask," said I.

"Mask!" said Roderick with a sudden outbreak of racial self-derision. "You've said it, my boy! He can go and do our business where I can't show my nose. . . ."

I sit here and think over these things, I think of Roderick and Julian and the rest of our group, and the wives and houses and dinners and week-ends, I review the galaxy of our chief shareholders and dependents and profit-spending associates, not forgetting my little neighbour Lady Steinhart, whom I have already described; I recall what I can of the phases and moods, the cravings and pettiness of my own story, and then my mind wanders off to our works, to our wonderful plant with science and subtle ingenuity in every trough and tap and furnace and mould, to our staffs of skilled workers, to our collateral associations with mines of every type in every climate, to the great regions we search for ores, fluxes, solvents, to the cultivators whose output we buy by the countryside. When I think of this worldwide system, seeking, extracting, recovering, and sorting the crude substance of the earth, fusing, sublimating, condensing, fining, allaying, placing its finished substance at last in the hands of ten thousand sorts of manufacturer and returning its sifted by-products to fertilise a hundred lands, when I think of the myriads of workers whose lives we direct, the hundreds of myriads with which our work is associated, and the far greater multitudes whose employment we make possible, when I contemplate the totality of all this achievement threaded through the jostling human crowd, and then put the swift, incessant efficiency of this human process of ours, side by side even with the best of the motives that move us who are its nominal directors, it seems to me it is not so much we who have got all these things out of the earth as the things themselves that have called to us and compelled us to extract them.

They have compelled us as the soil of any place selects and determines the trees that shall grow there and stunts them or gives an extravagant vigour to their

growth. Romer, Steinhart, which began as a single
sapling, has become a great tree, that like a banyan,
the Indian market-tree, expands into a grove and joins
to other groves and shelters great mutitudes and may
at last coalesce into one single canopy of confederated
businesses to cover the economic life of the
world.

§ 10

OUR main plants, our essential companies, are
things of a new economic type. I doubt if
many people realise how new they are. Our
businesses are not only new in scale and correlation;
they are new in their internal constitution. There is
not the same necessary antagonism of employer and
employed in them, because they are not merely nor
mainly toil-shifting organisations. We employ hardly
any brute labour at all in our own concerns. Almost all
our labour is either skilled or semi-skilled. Over three
thousand of our people draw more than a thousand
pounds a year each from us, and that number increases
in a larger proportion than the increase in our general
employment. There is nobody at all with us on a flat
subsistence wage; not a soul. And since our plants have
been costly to construct and are destined to be superseded
by better plants within very definite limits of time, since
many of them would deteriorate rapidly with disuse, it
has always been the policy of the firm, from our early
Crest Bye-Products days onward, to keep its workers
content and interested in our common welfare, and so

never to have a break in production. We have never been held up by a strike in all our history, and we have never closed down a plant upon its staff because of trade fluctuations. We have kept our workers together and our plants going steadily—if only for the sake of the machine. Business shrewdness and a certain goodwill were both active in determining that policy; the original Steinhart was, we know, a student of Robert Owen, and regarded his employés with an amiable generosity of intention. His idea, and it is still a tradition of the firm, was that there is a sort of moral partnership of the business inherent in those who have been employed by it for some time. But I won't pretend that our virtue has had to struggle against our interests; old Steinhart's good intentions happen to have yielded the very best policy possible for us.

Wherever we have bodies of our own workers in sufficient numbers we subsidise the science teaching in the elementary and continuation schools in that locality as generously as possible, and at Downs-Peabody we run a big technical institute at which scholarships can be held, side by side with our research laboratories. We have nine professors with salaries far above the normal University scale. Spink and Gedge are both sons of men who worked in the Crest Bye-Products for weekly wages. We have a savings' bank organisation and an investment system; we have workers who, some of them, hold up to two thousand pounds' worth of our ordinary shares. We pay no day wages at all, and we are steadily changing our weekly wage-earners to a monthly and quarterly salariat. In alliance with our staffs we participate in subordinate housing companies, recreation grounds, cricket clubs, swimming-baths, two art museums, and a number of social clubs. We subsidise two weekly newspapers to explain what is going on in our business and what becomes of our products.

All this is just sound modern business. We cannot afford to use our premises as social battlefields. We do not discuss the right of this or that person to a greater or lesser share of the surplus profit of our activities, but we mean to keep our processes going on as largely, handsomely, healthily as possible, and this is the way it has to be done. And one must remember we are not demoralised by any vehement competition—which is the true cause of most sweating and commercial ugliness. The sweating system is only an economic expression of fear and greed, the economic bad manners of rush conditions. But we happier moderns are working often with patented processes, often with a monopoly of raw material, with a staff of workers that it has taken half a century to assemble, and always with a scientific and technical superiority that makes us unapproachable. Energetic new people do not seek to wrest things out of our hands; it would be hopeless; they come in and offer to work with us.

We do not spread our broad methods about the world without internal friction. The Crests have held lands in Oreshire since the thirteenth century; great grabbers and savers they have always been, a hard-fisted, firm-mannered race; they guessed right at the dissolution of the monasteries and grew mightily at their expense.

Galsworthy's Forsytes are mild stuff compared with our Crests. Crest seems to have kept the beastly economic medievalism of his ancestry intact. He is as hard and mean as a French peasant and a British duke rolled into one. In the unproductive disorder of the Middle Ages the only ways of getting rich were to oppress, compel, sweat, or rob outright. Usury was forbidden, and besides, usury required arithmetical gifts accorded only to the Jews. Trade was a rare occupation, and as a trader you monopolised naturally, even if you had to fight and murder to do so. There was no increase in values going on; what you gained someone else lost. What you got you held with a scowling, swaggering dignity tempered only by the showiest possible largess on holiday occasions. When some unasked improvement in our workers' condition is in contemplation, Crest will still come to our board meeting with the clatter of rusty armour in his voice and demand where all this sort of pauperisation is to end. Where is the money to come from? he asks.

Nothing will ever convince him that our dividends do not come out of the pockets of other people, nor that our profits are not abstracted from the wages of workers who have been held down while the abstraction is effected. He is equally persuaded that the object of foreign trade is to pauperise foreigners. He is not really an employer as we conceive it; he is a medieval robber baron who offers terms. He is always trying to force our people into rifle clubs and the Territorials because it would give them a sense of discipline, and once he wanted a man dismissed because he did not touch his hat to him outside the works. The man was, unfortunately, a humorist. "Hey, my man!" said Crest. "I don't think you know me!"

"Don't think I do," said the man. "Who might *you* be?"

"I'm Lord Crest."

"I'm Billy Watkins. What aba't it?" . . .

It took nearly half an hour of our time at the next board meeting to convince Crest that gestures of social abjection were not among the duties for which Billy Watkins drew his pay.

"We can't interfere with their manners, my boy," said Roderick, pawing Crest's shoulder with a familiarity that made Crest pale with anger, and infusing an unusually Eastern oiliness and the shadow of a lisp into his voice, "and that's all about it. Why! if we began on that sort of thing where should we end? I'm always speaking to Julian now as it is about tapping in the tops of his eggs. *Will* tap 'em in. It isn't done in the best families. It gives us away. All of us Romers. And Clissold went out of this very room before me only yesterday. He's equal to going out in front of *you*. No sense of precedence. You've got to put up with this sort of thing these Bolshevik days, Crest, and thank God if they do their work."

"If you *want* to see discipline go to the devil——!" flashed my Lord Crest, and dropped the subject. . . .

But as our tentacular connections have spread our interests from our original mineral and metallurgical operations, we have come into relations with labour and with organisations for production developed upon less fortunate lines than our own. There we find ourselves tangled in responsibilities of every grade of difficulty. That's the less pleasant side of our picture. In the early days, for example, we bought the whole Crest Collieries output upon a sliding-scale arrangement and left the treatment of the miners to the parental Crest, their Union and God, and afterwards we filled our increasing need for coal in the open market. Now we have the infernal Crest mines practically on our hands; we hold all their shares, we are bound in a Federation to this, that and the other line of action, and indirectly by various purchases, working agreements, and amalgamations we have become miners and sellers of coal as well as consumers, but we have no finger in the direction, nor in the labour organisation.

Mining is as ancient a business as the first Pharaohs; it has always been a form of mass labour, and, like all labour which draws its traditions from the ages before machinery, it is a very unpleasant, inhuman, and wasteful form. That side of our great machine remains excessively unsatisfactory to me. It runs along, jarring and occasionally jamming, wasteful in substance and wasteful of life. The typical British mine-owner still belongs very generally to the horse-headed class; the equestrian tradition still dominates mine-owning. Economically he is an antiquated nuisance. Since he gave nothing for his coal and ore he does not care how much of it is wasted so long as the royalties come in. Royalties to these landowners are a tax on every coal-consuming industry. Cheap coal is as necessary to the industrial life of Britain as good roads. Coal winning is a common interest that we industrialists are fools enough to treat as a private trade.

I am not on the Crest Collieries directorate, and it is difficult for me to do more than gibe and grumble at this equestrian inheritance. Our mining and mineral interests are dotted all over the world, and conditions in the mines that concern us, here and abroad, are determined by conditions in the others beyond our reach, and one set cannot be changed without the other. Before we can begin a fight with Vishnu we must be reasonably sure that Siva will not rise against us both. Much the same sort of thing applies to our transport interests also. We are big enough to be affected, but not big enough yet to exercise an effective control. I would like to see our tentacles grow and grow, bigger and stouter, until a single combine could take the whole mineral resources of the world into one problem. But that seems a long dream still, and before it can be realised and the creative Brahma can get to work, Siva, in other words the passionate destructiveness of labour awakening to its now needless limitations and privations, may make Brahma's task impossible. I would even favour nationalisation if I believed, which I don't, that there was even a sporting chance of the politicians sustaining a competent management.

I am afraid of the obstinate injustice of all these ancient forms of employment, mining, shipping, transport work—which still carry on the traditions of the gang slavery of the ancient world. There seems never a day when one can turn them round into a new path and animate them with a new spirit. Yet on their present lines they are accumulating wrath and disaster for the whole system. The wastage of life is frightful. There is no more reason now why coal should be picked out from the seam bit by bit by hunched-up men working in darkness and dirt and foul air than there is that steamship furnaces should be hand-fed by sweating stokers or the harvests of the world reaped by hand.

Some day I may begin to see more clearly than I do at present a way of extending our hard and scientific methods into these old industries that the needs of finance and the markets have obliged us to annex to our comparatively clean, original system of enterprises. I would like to tackle a whole coal district as one system, survey it and sound it, reassemble the housing and surface cultivation, burrow into it with passages and air tubes and pour out coal tar, carbonised road-metal, pipe-steam and electric power for the towns and houses and factories, and so let the whole countryside run happily until nothing more was left below to burn. That might not be for a century or so, and by that time our industrial people would be moving on quite cheerfully to some new district and some fresh phase in the exploitation of natural resources, and we should have the old Black Country coming back daily and beautifully to agriculture and horticulture again. And as for our miners I would have them on salaries instead of day wages, work them at most five days a week and ten months a year, pay them for two months' annual holidays, pension them comfortably when they had done thirty thousand hours' work, even if they hurried up and did it soon, and get tons of coal out of them where now we worry out hundredweights. This is no dream, but an entirely practicable possibility. Only Crest and his kind, and the general foolishness that tolerates and supports them, stand in the way.

§ 11

THIS book, however, is not to tell of my social and economic imaginations and desires, but about the conflict of motives that has gone on in me, beneath the surface of my very considerable business activities. I write about my motives not because I suppose they are at all remarkable, but just because they are not at all remarkable among my class. I try to lay bare in myself the soul of a successful business man. A considerable number of active men nowadays are in much the same case as myself. I am a fair sample of a new attitude of mind which is appearing here and there in the world and becoming more and more common.

I worked. I succeeded. I appeased myself with women. That is my history in brief. I followed out the programme I had planned in my empty house. But I was not satisfied. Always I was restless. And since mine is an intelligence which dresses itself up very little, this unrest of the spirit found its chief outlet for many years in fresh sexual activities. I suppose all the energy of life is sublimated from the sexual energy; the waters have a compelling tendency to return to the ocean from which they arose.

I have been what the eighteenth century called a rake. It is natural for me to find redeeming characteristics in a rake, to plead that he is at least obliged to be personally clean and fit and seemly, and that he must needs be of some imaginative activity and responsiveness. And also that no mere force of physical desire makes a rake. Grossness is no incentive to change and exploration; there is no need in modern life for a simply lascivious man to betray that quality to the world. The house of ill-fame is the natural resort of the man of good repute. But to me such conveniences, such imitations, have always been shameful and abominable. Bodily desire has been the lesser part of this business to me. Whatever else I have desired, invariably the leading thing I have desired has been personal response. And the next thing to that has been something hard to name, a kind of brightness, an elation, a material entanglement with beauty.

And still there was something more. I think now that I have been the victim of one of those exaggerations of promise that our restless, purblind old mother Nature never hesitates to put upon us. Always through my fuller years there was a feeling, a confidence I never had the power or will to analyse, that somewhere among womankind there was help and completion for me. How shall I express it? The other half of my androgynous self I had lost and had to find again. You remember the fable Aristophanes told in the Symposium.

I have never found that completion. For me, at any rate, it has been no more than a sustaining illusion. But I do not repent of my love experiences. I am glad old

Nature put that *ignis fatuus* into my wits and nerves to lead me the dance I have had. All these affairs have been touched by imagination and have revivified my imagination. I have nothing to reproach myself about in them. I have never prostituted a human being in any of them, I have never cheated, made dishonest promises, nor wilfully inflicted humiliation. If I have lied at times I have lied in small matters to mitigate or reassure; I have escaped from essential and fundamental lies. I am a rake unrepentant and unashamed.

I state these things here not by way of apology, but because they interest me as matters of fact. It is too often assumed that a rake is necessarily a seducer, a sort of area-sneak of the affections. He breaks down the sweet temple of virtue in spite of its pitiful pleadings and resistance; ransacks it, leaves it hideously and incurably defiled, departs with triumphant mockery. But that is pure romanticism. There are just as many women, in this modern world at least, as ready for love and as impenitent about it and as little desolated by it as men.

If I were seeking an exoneration for my life I suppose I could make great play with the fact that I was so tied to Clara that I could not marry again and live in a seemly, ordinary fashion. I am sorry for that fact because I would have liked to have sons and daughters; I envy Dickon his youngsters, those sympathetic, organically linked extensions of oneself; but if I am to be frank with the reader as with myself, I am not sure that if I had been married and tied to almost any one of the women I have known intimately, my life would have been essentially different from what it has been. I understand how deeply husband and wife may trust one another, but there must be excitement in love and a sort of magic and adventure. It must be difficult to sustain the excitement, magic, and adventure year after year, with anyone whose every gesture and intonation one knows by heart. A separation and then a homecoming to dear familiar things? That is a different story.

But then, as I have written already in my account of my own futile marriage, I think that the same forces that are breaking down the separations between small businesses, fusing production into concerns upon a world scale, and driving the peasant from his immemorial holding, are breaking down the walls of the home. The faithful, fruitful wife was a possessed and secluded woman. But now the home is a service flat, a lodging, a suite in some hotel, and the man who once tilled the soil his ancestors tilled before him wanders from job to job about a world that is almost as homeless for him as the high seas. Man, who settled down to plough and increase and multiply twelve or fifteen thousand years ago, is now getting adrift again in great streams and clouds; it is a sort of harvest of mankind from the fields into the great camps of the new towns, and the woman who was his helpmeet is becoming once more his camp-follower. Or is ceasing even to follow his camp and, against all nature and precedent, setting up one of her own. Or is simply at large in the streaming crowd and amazed.

My life has been spent where the disintegrative forces

are most at work. As a young man I was living rather exceptionally the sort of existence a great and increasing number of young people are living to-day. I indulged in great freedoms that are no longer freedoms but widespread practices. From the days of my separation from Clara until I was nearly thirty-two my opiate for that recurrent hunger in my heart was a series of intrigues that often overlapped and sometimes went on simultaneously two or even three together. The facts of these relationships are so flat and commonplace that it is hard to convey the glamour, the sense of depth and delight and reassurance they could afford.

Most of that satisfaction was the most patent illusion. I have to confess that, considered as a man, I am the least marvellous that can be imagined; the chief word in my description upon my passport is " normal," repeated several times; remarks, " none "; eyes grey, hair brown. A new hat makes me unrecognisable to most of my acquaintances. I suppose I am fairly alert and interested in people, and that is my most attractive quality. Yet my entire lack of personal splendour has not prevented my being the happy lover of a number of charming and interesting women. I can only suppose that they wanted to make love as much as or even more than I. I admired them, I was grateful, I delighted in them, and as a man I was good enough to pass muster. Of course, we called each other " wonderful " and " delicious," and so forth. We were so, I suppose, in that light—as any meadow may be wonderful at dawn. What I gave them was almost exactly what they gave me—an exquisite sense of personal reception, a vividness of being, a surcease of this pursuing hunger of the heart that overtakes us in leisure and security.

Women have gained great freedom even during my lifetime. A few generations ago a woman's work, as the proverb said, was never done. Now for many it is over before it has begun. It is not that they are better paid, but that they are wanted less. Much knowledge that was once hidden has come to them. Motherhood is no longer an oppression, nor even the fear of motherhood. For a great number this means a release of sexual imaginations. They have blank time, unexpended energy, and an inherent predisposition for the excitements and beauties of love.

I do not think these modern women want men very badly; they want love. Usually they are married women or women already possessing lovers. But their man is masterful and oppressive, or he is negligent or wandering in his attentions, or preoccupied and dull. Mr. Smith or Brown reminds our lady too plainly, too flatly, that she is just Mrs. Smith or Brown. He ceases to make her a goddess for his adorations. In a life of thin, unexacting routine love also becomes a routine. She has no sense of glorious giving, no sense of self-escape. But when she steals away to a lover all that is changed. You can hardly call her an unfaithful wife, for when she steals away she is no longer a wife. She ceases to be Mrs. Smith or Brown. That is the gist of the whole thing. As her lover ceases to be Mr. Jones. They both keep holiday from these commonplace verities. They go out of the world. She becomes as much a goddess as Diana visiting Endymion. As Mrs. Brown she would

no doubt be betraying Mr. Brown, but as Diana in a
secret cave remote from the things of everyday she
betrays nobody. Restored to her self-respect, to her
belief in her possible loveliness, she can return to her too
casual and negligent husband with a pleasant sense of
dignity preserved and equality restored.

It is a fundamental convention in the romantic version
of life that when a married woman takes a lover she
prefers him to her husband. In three-quarters of the
illicit love affairs in such a great centre as New York,
London, or Paris, this is not true. It is probably less true
even than the converse proposition about men. And the
mere suggestion to most of these modern women rakes
that they might go off and live in blissful union with the
lovers they have been adoring would, I believe, be quite
sufficient to end the affair for them. I cherish no
illusions about my relations to the goddesses for whom
I have been a worshipped and worshipping god, dear
friends though they have been to me. For only one of
them have I been the anti-husband. For most, I have
no doubt that if the husband's life or prosperity or pride
had been seriously threatened I should have been sacri-
ficed with about as much regret as, let us say, a once
worn dinner-dress that he had found too frank and dis-
creditable, or a pet dog he did not like.

And yet in the secret cave we would be very earnest
about our business and things would be very lovely
between us. In all these affairs there are not only
questions of more or less, but each one has its distinctive
elements that do not enter into the others. Athwart my
memories of these little opium doses of love there flits

the tall, slender figure of Sirrie Evans, with her fever-touched cheeks, her strong profile, and her burning, deep-set eyes. She came into my life like any other adventure, but perhaps a little more vividly and happily. There was nothing to tell me that she was destined to live with me for nearly seven years and die at last exhausted in my arms.

I met her first at a dinner party in London—I think at the Rudhams'; it was a large white dining-room with grey marble pillars—and she did not sit next me but across the table. We glanced at each other and liked each other. We were both being held rather tenaciously by dinner partners of the low-voiced, semi-confidential type, the sort that cut up dinner parties into horrid little cellules of viscid duologue. I seem to remember that my own lady was plying me with questions like the questions in an old Confession Album in a search for common ground, and I rather suspect that Sirrie was being subjected to arch and clinging compliments. Our eyes met in a common distress which changed to a mutual appeal. We recognized kindred. " Let's get out of this somehow," we telepathed.

The couple at the end of the table were talking rather loudly; the man was a challenger, the sort of man who makes controversial statements and looks about him. " The Russian moujik," he said, " will be the Saviour of Europe, simple, industrious, profoundly Christian, worshipping his Tzar as God's Vicegerent." They all said that before the war.

I let a question on my left fade out neglected. " I don't agree with you," I said. " Have you been there?"

"They have divine beards," said Sirrie, grasping the situation with decision and speaking directly to me.

"They are extremely kind to animals," said the lady at the end.

"I judge by the evidence of the Russian literature," said the man I had contradicted. "Dostoievsky in particular."

It was a large reply, but I took it up manfully.

The others fell helplessly into their proper places, and we kept the conversation at our end of the table general until the ladies departed. By that time we had discussed Russian literature and Russian characteristics, peasants, and primitive people generally, whether peasant art and peasant costumes were not everywhere very much the same in Europe and Eastern Asia, and whether the essentials of peasant life had altered very greatly since the Middle Ages, and so it was natural for me when presently we went upstairs to go across to Sirrie and pick up the threads again.

It was not so much a case of love-making between us as of mutual attraction. We arranged to meet next day to see what there was of peasant art in the Museum at South Kensington, as though that was the most natural thing in the world to do. Later I learnt her name—I had missed it before—and discovered that a sturdy, dark, thickset man with an expression of defensive self-satisfaction was her husband. I saw him watching us, and when he was aware that I observed him he turned away. She ignored him. Always she ignored him. And I ignored him too, as completely as I had ignored the Queen's Proctor in my separation from Clara.

It is impossible to convey by writing and telling the distinctive effect and charm of Sirrie as I knew her at that time. She was a brave thing—essentially brave. It was not the thing she said or the thing she did that seemed to matter so much as her style and carriage. She had a gallantry all her own, an alertness, very fine dark blue eyes, very fine brows; her cheeks were a little hollow and her voice very beautiful. But altogether she was beautiful. She had a lovely adventurous humour that seemed always seeking for the fun and quaintness and colour of life. She had a strong impulse to travel, to wander into fresh surroundings, to discover freshly different things. She was a born explorer.

The greater substance of our early escapades was altogether innocent. She loved to prowl in out-of-the-way parts of London, to peer into queer shops, to see contrasted sorts of life. She wanted a congenial man to go with her. We spent days exploring Whitechapel, Shoreditch, Clapham, the Crystal Palace. She would laugh with delight at the old and neglected exhibits at the latter place. Her sense of the absurdity of forgotten pretensions was very acute. "What were they up to here?" she would ask. "What did they think they were up to?" We never missed the stuffed animals; we traced the decay of the ethnological groups. The Picture Gallery was a great joy to us. And the "ante-diluvian animals." Seeing things with her was like looking through a telescope in the sunlight at familiar garden flowers. We stole a night or so from our outward for our inward lives and went for walks and boated together upon little flower-smothered Surrey and

Sussex rivers and canals. They were not so much passionate times as glad times that we spent together in
those days. Never before had I known so keen a
flavour of pure holiday.

It was only very gradually that I came to understand
that the underlying force in her life was an intense
hatred for her husband, and that beneath her keen
superficial interests and quick responses she hid the
wounds of some profound exasperation. She had been
one of four brilliantly pretty sisters, and he had married
her before she was eighteen. I do not know what
particular things had happened between her husband
and herself; she never talked to me about them and I
never questioned her; but they had so scarred her that
even her happiest moments at that time were touched
with the quality of something done in his despite. I
am by no means sure that she was altogether in the
right. Possibly her hatred of him was unjust and
freakish. She was quite capable of inexplicable animosi-
ties. She had neither justice nor morality in her apart
from her æsthetic standards. She never said an action
was wrong. She would condemn it as " not pretty."
A gallant act was good enough for her.

Even in those days Evans was rich and growing
richer in that slow, unproductive, creeping way that
adds nothing to the wealth of the world. To him a
wife also was no doubt an acquisition. From his point
of view he had bought her, but the four lovely sisters
thought they were a gift to the world. He had to beg
for her thrice; when he married her I imagine he was
already exasperated by the resistance to his wooing and

by her gay flirtations with other men. She on the other hand may have been exasperated by the fact that she had yielded. He was the sort of man who is filled with dull, deep anger at the idea that he is not the most attractive and irresistible male in all time and space. The Old Man of the primordial tribe must have been much the same. He seems to have tried to break and subjugate Sirrie so soon as she was legally his. She tried some " nonsense " with him, and he stood no nonsense from her.

But I do not know what happened. I do not know what happened and I do not care to know. Perhaps very little happened. Perhaps she merely discovered that Evans was Evans and that she was inseparably linked to him. She had sold something for too low a price, something of fundamental value, something without which life was spoilt for her. And she had sold to an ungracious purchaser. At any rate, within a few months of his marriage he had this slip of a schoolgirl fighting him bitterly and successfully for her freedom — for her quite excessive conception of freedom.

The weakness she seized upon at first was his inordinate tender vanity, his fear of appearances. She made him realise that at any moment she might appeal against him to friends, to servants, to passers-by. Her appeal might be startling and unjustifiable; he was not safe from her unless he let her go her own way. I know that quite early she ran away from him for two days and dealt with him from an unknown address by telephone. " Leave me alone," she said in effect, " and

I will still appear to be your wife. Otherwise, though it tears my world to pieces, I go."

But even though in a sort of way he left her alone, she would not respect his public honour. She despised and hated him too much for that. She broke the treaty, not he. I do not defend her. I set these things down. She came to me out of this ugly past, and it was not my concern to judge her.

Evans, blinded by his essential vanity to the fact that the most animated of women can still find many men entirely unattractive, sought to awaken her jealousy. She should be kept short of attention, kept short of money, left about and humiliated. She retorted by a scarcely ambiguous friendship for a young Guardsman, Lord Hadendower, about whom I know nothing. I never met him; he was killed at Soissons. Evans made his infidelities conspicuous and stopped her allowance altogether. She concluded rather rashly that the former action made a divorce impossible, so she, too, made her infidelities public and met her financial inconveniences by running up bills. All their world talked. He did not like advertising to restrain her credit and her allowance was turned on again. For a time she had the upper hand, and Evans was her suitor.

This bickering, dismal business developed. He shirked the rude publicity of a divorce for five or six years. She tired of Hadendower very soon and flung him away from her. But that meant no kindness to Evans. She was not a woman of strong passions, but an absence of passion is often associated with an absence of shameful emotion, and she was lively in her imagina-

tion and wild in her talk and letters, and quite reckless of appearances. Somewhere she had met a dangerous and folly-begetting word, the word Orgy. She
was much sought after socially, a brilliant talker, a
mimic, unfeelingly funny, capable of a calm indecorum
of speech that left people gasping but delighted, and
Evans was acutely aware of the powerful support she
would have in any open breach in which he was not
entirely in the right. So he waited until he was entirely
in the right. For a time he made no breach. He had
developed a consuming desire to recover her. He tried
to buy her back, threaten her back; at last even to win
her back. But nothing he could do now could touch
her detestation. Her life became more and more a
scoring of pleasures, social successes, stolen outrageous
adventures that had a subsequent publicity, defiant
freedoms, against him, the heavy thing to which she
had got herself chained. His love, such as it was,
became at last a deep vindictive hate. That was the
bristling situation into which my wanderings had
led me.

I just imagined I had had the good fortune of an
exceptionally refreshing passade.

I had known Sirrie scarcely four months when Evans
exploded his long-prepared mines under her feet and
commenced proceedings for divorce. It was his amiable
intention to make it as scandalous and dirty a divorce
as possible and ruin her completely. Since at last he
must come to complete publicity, he seems to have
decided, then the uglier it was the better. He wanted
to drive her into hiding and exile so that her visible

existence should no longer trouble him. She should know what poverty was. She should appreciate the rare and precious advantages she lost by despising him. Every possible or probable man was cited as a co-respondent so as to present her as entirely abominable, disgust her lovers with her and deprive her of any help in the world. It was a great case for the newspapers.

None of her lovers stood by her at the outset. Not one. I was as bad as the rest at first, jealous and ashamed. I had not known a third of the things thus dragged into the light. My first feeling was anger, because she had troubled so little about my being implicated. She must have known of the gathering storm.

So far as I was concerned we had been cleverly watched and documented. The other side got at me very neatly with a nasty little clerk who broke things to me. They were so quick at the crisis that Sirrie had no chance to tell me beforehand of what was coming. I managed to be out of London when the case came up. I read the first day's proceedings in the morning paper.

"Damn!" said I, over my breakfast things at Downs-Peabody.

"Damn!" became, so to speak, the password of the day.

I took my little car and started vaguely north before Julian could get at me.

The plain English of that is that I ran away. I ran away for the better part of a day at an average speed of about thirty-five miles an hour and left my reckless, shameless, brilliant fellow-sinner to face her consequences alone.

In the morning I was blindly angry with her, merely angry. I saw myself—I remember the phrase among my self-reproaches—as "one of a row of accursed fools." My views about the charming levity of promiscuity were badly shattered. It was only as the morning wore on that she became anything more in my mind than an object of anger. Slowly she came through the wrathful mist, no longer as a feminine mischance, Eve and be damned to her, but as herself.

I began to see her face and hear her voice. And— for all the circumstances—her form was still slender and her face still fine.

How was the business taking her? After all, it wasn't going to be such very great fun for her. She must be having a nasty time up there in London while I was motoring northward, a very nasty time. She would have to go into the box. That was the idea that stuck itself like a thorn to my mind and gradually changed its tone. I tried to think of her still as a shameless woman, exposed and exposing all her friends. But I could not do so. I ceased to think of what she had deserved by making me ridiculous and asked myself what she must be feeling and how she would be carrying it off.

I began to be obsessed by the figure of her as she would stand there, with the court staring at her and the clever ones sketching her, slender and flushed and holding her head up—I knew she would hold her head up. Whatever happened to Sirrie, she would certainly keep her head up. That, you see, was how it was set on her neck. And there would be no whimpering or being overcome. Once I had surprised her at a theatre with her eyes bright with tears and that memory supplied the high light of my picture. Tears were possible to her but not weeping. "If I did these things I did them," she would say. "But I didn't do them like that." And that would be true. The more illogical the distinctions she made, the sounder they always were.

They'd ask her filthily intimate things. The old judge and lawyers would gloat over her. The court would be crowded. At the back all the young lawyers would be packed, alert not to lose the chance of a juicy line. Evans would see his lawyers did the job properly and that the juicy lines were forthcoming. She had written some exaggerated letters. She had a trick of using improper words—almost as a child uses them to startle. She had done that in her letters to me, and I had no doubt she had done it to everybody. They wouldn't give such letters a chance, I knew; they would read bits out without the qualifying context. The pure-souled gentlemen in the wigs and gowns would boggle modestly at her worst expressions as they read them. The court would blush to its straining ears. "I'm afraid I must paraphrase this, me lud." She had been wild and fantastic. These comparatively passionless women can say and do the most outrageous things at times—through a kind of insensitiveness. "Why not?" is their formula.

"How old is she?" I asked, and did little sums. She had been married at seventeen. She was now four or five-and-twenty.

I can only recall dimly now what sort of see-saw went on in my mind. I have to guess at most of that as though it was something in the mind of a stranger. I must have felt a great disgust at the whole business, I must have been indignant with her and have condemned her or why should I have continued to travel north hour after hour?

But I must have dismissed all that indignation later. I cannot recover it. It is like trying to reconstruct the torn letters from the wastepaper basket of the day before yesterday. Perhaps it was a sort of inertia kept my foot upon the accelerator.

"If I go back to her," said I. . . . "It's a complete return."

My decision hung fire all day and then it exploded. Suddenly I knew what I was going to do. As if I had known all along. It was the last possible train to London I took that night. It was behind time, and I got to London in the small hours. She was all alone, I found, except for one sister, at Berridge's Hotel. I telephoned and was answered by the sister—she was in bed and asleep, tired out. The next morning I went to her.

"I've come to stand by you," I said.

"You'll learn a lot of new things about me," she answered, looking me squarely in the eyes. "Not very graceful things."

"I've read the morning papers."

"You could hardly help it. It isn't a pretty case, is it?"

"Unpleasant for both of us," I said. "I admit the surprises. Nevertheless, I'm going to stand by you."

"You know—the things—— They'll bring them up in the ugliest way—but substantially—they will be true."

"I don't expect to see you vindicated like a Drury Lane heroine. I've thought that out."

"What does this mean? What do you mean to do?"

"Stick by you."

She stood without betraying any emotion, rather like a woman who weighs a business proposition. Then she turned to me with the same air of entirely controlled reasonableness.

"But you didn't know of these other affairs. You came in late and innocent. I gave you no warning. I ought to have had the sense—— There is no earthly reason why *you* should come into this mess. It's *my* mess. My little affair with Jim. Silly to think so much of Jim—to hurt oneself annoying a thing like that! I drove Jim frantic and he's got me. I've . . . There's been some rotten men in this. I've been an utter fool at times. No one will blame you for standing out."

"No one will blame the other fellows either. I see that. But you want someone. In this business. After all, I'm the last on the list. Forgive me if I'm unsentimental; I won't even pretend to be in love just now—but I'd as soon see a little child drown under my eyes, a little child I knew, as let you go through this alone."

" But after?"

" I've thought of that."

" What do you mean?"

" I mean—I like you. More than I dreamt I did."

" What's that?"

" I stand by you—now and afterwards. I'm not a green youngster. I've told you—how things are with me. You won't be taking advantage of my innocence. I know a little about women. It's easy to love you. But somehow also in spite of all this—I respect you. I'm not shocked. I don't care what their evidence is. It can't alter the knowledge I have of you. You have— a crazy side. I don't know all you may have done, but I have some idea of what you are. For me you began when we met. Have I seen nothing of you? All the evidence in the world won't convince me that your soul—if I may say so—isn't as straight as your body."

She did not speak at once. She shrugged her shoulders at my last sentence. She seemed to be taking in the new situation.

" You'll come to the court?"

" Every day. Your brother. Your friend."

" Like someone holding my hand! Oh! . . . Billy! when you know the sort of thing——!"

She stopped short. The tears flashed for a moment in her eyes.

" Friendship," said I.

" Friendship," she echoed, and her eyes questioned me, and then slowly she smiled at what she saw in my face. " You old brick," she said, and for a moment her mouth was awry before she recovered her smile. She held out her hand. "All right."

We clasped on it, a hand-clasp that was better than any embraces.

"I've been playing rather a lone hand," she began. . . . "I've deserved what I've got. . . ."

She bit her lip and looked helpless.

"Put a hat on," said I with my spirits rising unaccountably. "Run! The court won't wait."

And in that way in the lounge of Berridge's Hotel I married myself for all practical purposes to the scandalous Mrs. Sirrie Evans and faced for the first and last time the legal consequences of my adultery. For two days I sat in court, to the great interest of the smart women who crowded it, and was conspicuously assiduous to the needs and comfort of the respondent. And when it was all over I carried her off and put her in a flat and for all possible purposes treated her as my wife.

It was an irrelevant accident, an extraordinary digression in my life. I went to her and I went to the court primarily because of a sense of obligation. I was bound to stand by the consequences of my own misconduct. But insensibly and very quickly my attitude changed to one of what was I now admit unreasonable championship. It was unreasonable, it was instinctive. I felt that Sirrie was essentially as honest as, and finer spirited than I, that her sex put her at a frightful disadvantage and threatened to penalise her horribly for acts no more immoral than many I had committed with impunity. I took up the cause of laxity in general, in my appearance at her side. I defended the whole series of my paramours in her. We were fellows in the common business of erratic and forbidden adventure and desire. But from championship and fellowship I passed very rapidly to a keen affection and pity for a creature misused by herself and by the world that had produced her.

And the affair opened a new phase in my own life. I had been hitherto an exceptionally lone animal. Now I found myself carried completely out of myself by care for another human being. I did my ineffectual best to reinstate Sirrie socially, to mitigate the penalties of those sins of hers that I could understand so well. I enabled her to take a pretty little house, secured her good servants, and would not dine nor associate outside my business with any people who did not treat her as my wife. We travelled and visited together. We were faithful to each other, and every moment that my very active business occasions permitted we spent together.

Weighing this phase over now, I am most struck by the fact that our living together was not the result of any passionate crisis, not the outcome of any grand passion. There was no tremendous declaration, no irresistible elopement. I do not remember any strong desire to possess her or be with her before we lived together. There was no such urgency. Our union was forced upon us by Evans' malevolence. I am not sure that I should have gone to her if I had not been cited in the case. Before the divorce we had liked each other greatly, been pleasant to each other, made love lightly. My dominant mood at the trial I can best describe as a sort of indignant tenderness. That so fine a thing should be treated so scurvily! So fine a thing!

It was only after we had kept house together for some time that we developed very deep personal feelings for each other. We grew into one another by imperceptible degrees.

I have never been able to make up my mind whether my early life was one of exceptionally starved affections or not. I know of no quantitative standard by which one can measure oneself against others in these matters. I have never been able to determine whether young people are as capable of love as their elders, whether disinterested love is not necessarily a concomitant only of the fully adult state. My own youth was certainly a very loveless time. I had an imaginative love for my father, and a brotherly affection for Dickon was always present, but beyond that there was very little. There were no passionate boyish friendships, or if there were they have faded out of my mind. Even before our mother estranged us by her second marriage I did not care very greatly for her. Either I never loved Clara or that love is effaced. I was on good terms with many men and women, but none seemed necessary to me, and for none was I prepared to sacrifice myself in any way.

My impulse to defend and vindicate Sirrie surprised myself. It also surprised Sirrie. She had liked me greatly from the first, but after her divorce she became acutely interested in me and curious about me. There was a phase in our life when she seemed always asking me questions about myself—questions that were excessively difficult to answer. I had not been in the habit of answering questions about myself. I was something new and unexpected in life for her, and, as it appeared to her, something unexpectedly good. She had had bad luck with her men. She threw over her idea of being a wicked woman, a sort of defiant insistence upon it as her *métier,* without another thought. I heard no more of it.

She set herself to understand my motives and the way I worked. Her social outlook had never included a laboratory, a railway, or a smoking chimney, and she thought that the lower classes were all either cottagers or servants. Trade unions were as much outside her world as totem groups. She thought that when you wanted anything you went to the best West-End shop that sold it, and I doubt if she realised completely that the first step to getting it was to wring or wrench its substance out of the soil or out of the rocks. How far she ever came to understand my ideas I do not know. She accepted my urgent preoccupations with business as a strange but forgivable thing in my composition. Since it mattered to me, it mattered to her, but it might just as well have been the Turf or a preoccupation with big game.

But if she did not understand my ideas, she came to understand many things in my character that are still hidden from me. She controlled me for my own happiness, invisibly, imperceptibly. She gave me a dis-interested friendship, which is so much greater a thing to give than sexual love. While she lived my discontent with life was greatly allayed. I never worked so well as I did during those years.

When I had made a home for her I had had a streak of warm self-approval in my mind. I had thought I was doing something rather handsome and generous. Instead, for the first time I was getting the most precious things in life, love, faith, understanding, fellowship, and the reality of home. I was getting all that was good in marriage except children. But plainly she was tuberculous; we knew from the outset that her lungs were "wrong," and we did not dare to have children.

It was a friendship, it was a fellowship; it was these things first and foremost. We made love; we had spells of intense happiness of that kind, but our reality was our friendship, based on our unfaltering belief in each other's soundness and goodwill and our common repudiation of the current moral verdict upon us. I do not think we would have been very jealous of each other if there had been any real occasion for it, but there was not. I was too busy in those days to follow up any competing interest, and she was too tired of men to experiment with them further. Jealousy is an active reaction to a sense of insecurity, and we were both very secure with each other.

Our first home was a little pinched-in house on Richmond Hill with an iron balcony in front and a wedge-shaped walled garden behind. There Sirrie could be ingenious and decorative and house-proud. But later we had to move to Bournemouth because of her health; I was growing in wealth, I could give her a fine new house there, gracefully designed, and she made a pretty garden amidst rocks and pine-trees on a slope that looked towards the sea. I would run down by the afternoon express like the most orderly and moral of business men, and she would meet me in her car. How well I remember her erect figure and her fine thin bright face, brightening still more at the sight of me. And every time I settled down in the car beside her to be driven home, to my home, I would have the same thought pass through my head—the wish that she was really my wife and that this pleasant security against passion and unrest could last for ever.

But I had the best of these two homes. While I was there we had each other, and she was very skilful in making me happy. What did she do when I was away? The " nice " people kept away from her both at Richmond and Bournemouth—which did not prevent them from being endlessly curious about her doings; and the incorrect people who did call were for the most part rude or dull or humiliating with their freedoms and confidences and assumptions. She took my name of Clissold; she was my wife in the sight of the butcher-boy, but everyone who mattered knew about us and remembered about her. She was wonderful stuff for the imaginative anecdotalist *sotto voce*.

She read enormously. The house was always full of new novels. She was acutely critical of the problems in conduct they raised. We had great discussions. She made me a reader of contemporary novelists—a thing unusual among business men. She also played with her garden endlessly. But she was an impatient gardener. She suffered a few acquaintances. She must have spent endless hours staving off the talk and tedium of their limitations with the new game of bridge, that presently developed into auction bridge. She became a great bridge player—when I was out of the way, and if these callers and associates bored her at the time, she got a certain compensation in preserving their choicer fatuities for my entertainment. She could be extraordinarily funny, but at times more than a touch of bitterness was mixed with her derision. She developed an acute perceptiveness for furtive tentatives to gallantry on the part of timid, vain, mean, and unsubstantial men and for the elements of pose and falsehood in the romantic confidences of the women.

Those years we spent together seem to me now in the retrospect to have passed very quickly. They were broken up by long journeys I had to make through the Urals, into Siberia and into the Canadian Rockies. It was impossible to take her on these expeditions. But wherever I could I took her, for her passion for travel was insatiable. She went to the Argentine with me and to Sweden. It was only very slowly and too late that I realised how rapidly she was dying. The last three winters of her life were spent, one in North Italy and two in Switzerland, and it was in a sanatorium in Switzerland that she died.

I do not remember when her cough began, but it is an essential part of my memory of her. She grew thinner, her cheeks more hollow and more flushed, and her eyes intenser. As she grew weaker she grew more daring. A craving, a great love for speed grew upon her. Motoring was developing, and I got a big Italian car that could jump up to eighty miles an hour on a straight. She would crouch together by my side, wrapped in her furs, her eyes gleaming over the grey stole that covered her mouth, silent, ecstatic. "Faster!" she would whisper.

Once or twice she drove—and these were memorable experiences for me. I held myself still beside her, controlling an impulse to snatch the wheel from her poor wasted hands.

As I realised her weakness and her sufferings, insensibly companionship gave way to protection. For the last four years her movements were more and more restricted, rain and sundown drove her indoors; she had to live in rooms at a measured temperature; she could no longer face exertion. Her restlessness increased perpetually; she did not like any place she was in because she did not feel well there; she wanted to go on, where the sun was still kindlier and the air easier to breathe. She had phases of acute unhappiness, but her hopefulness always rescued her. She felt the shadow of social isolation that lay upon us as though it was a chill, and that, too, drove her on. She fretted, she had a vague, shamefaced ambition for some social demonstration, some vindication, some recognition imposed upon people. I cannot imagine her troubling about anything of the sort if it had been freely available. But she felt and imagined exclusion. The further one is abroad, the less evident is that exclusion. At an infinite distance from London all English people meet. She wanted to be met. It was childish, no doubt, to feel desire for a worthless thing simply because it was denied, but are we not all children when it comes to such social uneasiness?

538

When she died we were planning a journey to the South Sea Islands and afterwards a tour right round the world. I could contrive it without breaking up my own activities too much, for everywhere now there are minerals and possibilities for Romer Steinhart. She would sit with a soft green and blue and crimson Spanish shawl about her, the most fragile and ethereal of creatures, with a dozen travel books upon her couch and one or two on a table close at hand. "I must see Easter Island," she would say. "It cannot be far out of our way to see Easter Island."

I would bring the Atlas and sit down on the couch beside her. "Let us see where it is. Yes. . . . Yes, I think we can bring in Easter Island."

Her hand would stroke my head.

"Billy Cook, the dear World Tourist Organiser. You can really spare me all this time?"

"I want to see these places," said I.

"I'm rather a lump to take about. But down there I shall recover. Last week—unless that machine is wrong—I gained two ounces. And we will swim in the warm, warm sea."

"And I will guard your toes from the sharks with a cutlass between my teeth."

"Brave Billy! Of course you will! Kiss me, Billy dear."

She hoped and longed for the south seas to the very day of her death. She hoped to the end. On the morning of the day when she died, she explained how favourable a thing hæmoptysis was.

"I believe that was the last of that stuff," she whispered. "One coughs away . . . all the diseased tissue . . . all the tainted blood . . . and then, of course, one heals . . . heals."

"Be quiet, my dear," I said. "Talking isn't good for you. You will have to heal quickly if we are to start next month."

She was very tired that afternoon. She had had a spell of coughing so violent that it had alarmed me; she had nearly choked with blood. The flow ceased at last; the doctor gave her a sedative and she went to sleep in my arms. "Stay with her," said the doctor. "You had better stay with her. If she wakes she may cough again. She is very weak now."

But she did not cough again. A tired, flimsy, pitiful frame she had become, something that one just took care of and treated very gently; her motionless eyelashes touched my cheek, and she passed away so softly that until, with a start, I noted her coldness, I did not suspect that she was dead.

§ 12

SHE died in 1905, and I was just forty. Her death left a very great gap in my life. While our relations lasted my life had an effect of being filled and my hunger of the heart was assuaged. I was needed, I was necessary. If I was not fully satisfied I was at least fully occupied. Since then I have never quite lost the sense of loneliness as a thing painful in itself. I had acquired a habit of looking to someone else for kindness. I wanted someone to smile a welcome to me and be glad when I came home. It was a new need.

During my years with her I had parted from an earlier, harsher self and become the more tolerant and less intense self I am to-day. My earlier self seems to me to have been tacit, whereas now I am explicit; it was, in comparison with what I am, compact of self-reliance tempered by lust. Only through desire did I ever trouble myself in those younger days to propitiate my fellow-creatures. For it seemed I could get everything else without propitiation. But that had now been changed. In part that change may have been a natural change as one ripens, but far more I think it was the effect of my relationship to Sirrie. With her friendship, her charm, and at last her weakness, her involuntary appeal for kindness and service, she gave me in a few brief years all that is given to most men by marriage and parentage. I had acquired the habit of referring myself to the needs and standards of a life that was not my own. From her at least I did not take. From her I had learnt the fear for something one desires to protect and cannot always protect. Her death, moreover, coincided very nearly with the close of a phase in my relations with Romer Steinhart. The fun of winning my way to the inner fastnesses was at an end. My position was acknowledged and my share established; I was Roderick's most trusted colleague; I was becoming free to do something, if I would, with our great businesses.

I remember myself during that decade of copious low-grade living that passed at last into the Great War, as empty with the deprivation of my lost solicitude for Sirrie, consciously lonely, and with my old dissatisfaction with the disconnected multitudinousness of my impressions greatly deepened and broadened. The world as it ceased to be a battlefield became a riddle. The struggle for existence being won, came the less natural question of what to do with existence, to which question—except for reproduction—nature offers no instinctive reply. So we fiddle about with reproduction and do not even reproduce. I will not say that such moods of discontent possessed me, but they were always in waiting for me when I was not vividly active. They did not hinder me from continuing to play a leading part in the aggressive extension of Romer, Steinhart, Crest and Co. throughout the world.

Copious, low-grade living seems to me to express the quality of that time very exactly. The automobile was becoming prevalent, and prosperous people were using it more and more in headlong attempts to escape from their tedious and uneventful selves. The vacuous face of our collective life grimaced with the pretence of a solemn grief at the death of plump old Edward the Seventh, and then went through expressions of grave expectation at the accession of his worthy, conscientious, entirely unmeaning and uninteresting son. Save for some irreverent verses by Max Beerbohm that solemn front was scarcely broken. The parading attention to the immense passings and comings of our intrinsically insignificant royal personalities, blocking the traffic, filling the papers, delaying business and legislation, caught my mood of disillusionment, and accentuated for me the extraordinary triviality of human association. These pervading unavoidable royal personages stole dignity from knowledge, mocked progress, and dishonoured all life for me. When they went in public procession to thank the God of Earth and Heaven for an averted illness or a fresh addition to their respectable family, or to open something or come back from somewhere abroad whither they had expensively, ridiculously, emptily gone, I found the closed streets, the oafish spectators, incredibly exasperating.

This stuff was the formal crown of my existence. This was the Empire, the legal purport of my world. For this, I reflected, our great organisation was supposed to work, for this we won our beautiful metals from the obdurate earth, and fought nature and human indiscipline. To this end we increased the wealth and power of mankind. The German cousins, the Russian cousins, in their still more gaudy uniforms, came and went; envious rich American women crowded to London, bowed down and worshipped.

It seemed to me that this sort of thing might go on indefinitely. Life was not even tragic in those days; it was neither tragic nor comic; it was elaborately silly and vaguely dangerous. Flags, armies, national anthems, stuck upon my world like straws and paper gewgaws on the head of an idiot. But I did not conceive this idiot could blunder into actual war.

The result of maintaining political forms that are beneath human dignity and religious pretensions that are beneath human belief is to impose a derisive cynicism upon great multitudes of people who would otherwise live full and vigorous lives. I link the feverish playing of games, the onset of rowdy dancing, the development of night-clubs in every city in the world, the hunt for immediate pleasures that was already in full tide before the war, with this dominance of outworn loyalties and faiths that block out any living vision and sustaining hope from the general mind. Amidst the rhythms of jazz and the heavy blare of national anthems, what other voices could be heard? Industrial recriminations there were—strikes. The mere shadows then of our present considerable discontents. They brought no hope to me.

My unhappiness in those pre-war years, you may say, was essentially grief for Sirrie. And the personal lone-liness to which she had left me. But that is not exact. The loss of my preoccupation with Sirrie exposed me much more than I should otherwise have been exposed to the clamorous futility of the times. But it was the times that distressed me, the times and a certain growth of my mind, my powers and my sense of responsibility. I wanted not simply a better life for myself, but a better life altogether. Thousands of people were as con-sciously bored and distressed as I was, by the resonant emptiness of those years. Millions were bored and feverish without any clear apprehension of their trouble.

It is one of the most respected conventions of the contemporary literary man that people's lives and actions are never determined by political and social con-ditions, but only by personal reactions. That prepos-terous limitation may be the reason why so few fully adult people read modern novels. Life is more coloured by the morning paper than the literary man will admit. I know, for example, that the enormous preoccupation of the community with the fuss of the king's coronation and with the posturings of the German Emperor, irritated and depressed me far more than the actions of any individual with whom I came in contact during that foolish period. I was a unit in a half-witted social body quite as much as an individual, and I suffered acutely from the mental degradation of the half-wit who included me.

For a little while I was interested in the new invention of flying. I worked upon a group of light alloys with special reference to the elimination of wood from the framework, and I was a good deal at Eastchurch in 1911-1912. Those were primitive times in the air. I used to have joy rides in aeroplanes of 35 h.p. and less, and Shortt was considered a bold pioneer when he put 80 h.p. engines into his machines. But after a few flights I lost any sense of wonder when we ceased to bump along the earth and roared up over the cows in the meadows and worked our laborious spiral way up and up until we were over the Medway and looking down on the Thames and Essex coast. There we hovered, churning the sweet air, rather conscious that we were holding ourselves up and that it was undignified to come down too soon. It would have been a fascinating method of travel if there had been anywhere to go, but the only really long journey aviators made in those days was a sudden, unexpected nose-dive out of the world. They were only discussing air-pockets in those days; no one was ever strapped in, and every landing was an adventure. But the essential things were done.

"This we can make," said I to myself, high and swaying unstably above the Thames estuary. "This we can improve. This is only the beginning. . . ."

And then: "What will be the good of it?"

It was this pointless achievement of flying that first forced upon me the realisation how largely inventions were being wasted on mankind. That foolish gift-giving uncle, Science, was crowding up the children with too many mechanical toys. The children I half discerned could only misuse them and hurt each other. Or fail to use them at all. I recall that thought, and with it I associate a downward vision, washed with bluish haze, of little fields, a pale yellow thread of road along which a slow-moving black dot was a motor-car, and a group of farm buildings seen in plan, all roof and hayrick.

"What will be the good of it all?" said my private devil in my ear. "Why bring the duffers sailing up here? Leave them to grow turnips and swap diseases till the crack of doom."

I suppose I did quite a lot of promiscuous love-making in those vacuous days. It is nothing to boast of and nothing to conceal. For a long time I found no one I could love very much, and I began to prefer women who plainly did not care for me very greatly to women who brought a personal passion, or the pretence of one, into the game. I was ready enough to admit they were charming and delightful creatures, but not that they were personally indispensable, and that I was tormented by yearnings, uncertainties and monstrous fidelities on their account. I began to feel a tolerance for meretricious love which I had once thought revolting. But I rarely came to absolutely meretricious love. If I had been a poor man and manifestly ungenerous I should have failed in some of these love affairs in which I did not fail, so much of paying was there in it, but that is not quite the same thing as meretriciousness.

Such was the quality of my life in the middle forties. Cut down in this fashion to its heart, it was friendless, loveless and aimless. But that is not to say that there was not steady, extensive, interesting toil, much fellowship and kindly commerce with pleasant men and women, æsthetic gratifications, fun, excitements, a great deal of incidental happiness in it. But always there was dissatisfaction waiting for me in the shadows and the quiet moments. It was not good enough. Life was passing by. I was not being used to the full. By all the common standards I was a winner at the game of life—and I was doing nothing with my winnings. Romer Steinhart was a big thing to be in, but I was not taking Romer Steinhart anywhere; it was taking me nowhere in particular. If I had been a less successful man I might never have discovered my unhappiness. But then I should have had no story to tell. I should have lived, suffered, spun my hurried time about the whirlpool and vanished according to precedent.

Came the huge, thronging, deafening excitements of the war, the stresses and fatigues of the war, the headlong hopes of that period of Reconstruction that I shared

547

with Dickon, and our rapid and immense disillusion-ment. That disillusionment, I see, was necessary and had to arise from vast and tragic events. If it did not seem ungracious to the valiant dead and to those who still suffer in body and memory from that tremendous catastrophe, I could find it in my heart to say the war was a good thing for the world. Not in what it destroyed nor in what it achieved, but in what it released. I have told of our reactions to the war in my account of Dickon. I have told of our realisation of our own haste and superficiality and how at length we subdued our minds to the real nature of world recon-struction, which that period of frothy projects had only caricatured. Of my ill-conceived attempts to enter politics I will tell nothing here; they were tiresome, humiliating, expensive and absurd. We had, we realised, to brace ourselves to serve in a cause for which we might never see even the beginnings of a triumph, but an imperative and unavoidable cause, a cause identi-fiable with the main process of life.

That needed a great effort in me, all my mind, a re-examination, a reorientation of my ideas. Without that effort I should fall back into the dissatisfied cynicism of the pre-war period. But my efforts to pull myself together, for what I have already termed the last lap of living, were complicated and impeded by an emotional entanglement into which I had drifted without any appreciation of its possible power. I was deeply in love, in love in a fashion that was new to me, and I was in love with a woman who had no knowledge of nor interest in these vital troubles.

Once more, just as in that early passion which led to my marriage, I found my double nature tormenting me. I had vowed in my empty house in Edenbridge Square that no woman should ever again turn my life about. I would take my freedoms and have the better of women. And for all my incidental adventures and digressions I had, in the main, kept my course. Suddenly now I found myself in the toils again. I had a mistress without whom, it seemed, I could not live. And, equally, I could not live with her and continue myself.

This story I have to tell about myself and Helen is, I perceive, an experience different in kind from any other love affair in which I was ever involved. It is too recent for me to write about yet with complete detachment. In a sense Helen has been exorcised here in Provence; I can hardly trace how; but the scars are fresh and plain. The essence of every great passion is by its nature a thing untellable. We do not tell our love experiences; at best we tell things about them. Only the reader who was in love with Helen could see her as I saw her. For other people she was a strong, clever, ambitious actress with a charming smile, an adorable voice, a reputation for a hot temper, and an ungracious way with obtrusive admirers. Many people found her beautiful, but no one called her pretty. She was a mistress to be proud of, but only a brave man would attempt to steal her.

For me she was wonderful and mystical; she was beautiful and lovely for me as no human being has ever been; she had in my perception of her a distinctive personal splendour that was as entirely and inseparably her own as the line of her neck or the timbre of her voice. There was a sideways glance over her shoulder full of challenge; there were certain intonations, there was a peculiar softness of her profile when it was three-quarters turned away, that gave me an unanalysable delight. My passion was made up of such things. If that explains nothing, then there is nothing that can be explained.

We met before the end of the war, and then she was a comparatively unknown young woman, very fearless, and quite prepared to be interested and excited by a man of my standing and reputation. She fell in love with me and I with her, and I ceased to trouble myself about any other woman. We loved romantically, ostentatiously. Hitherto she had despised her suitors. We became lovers, friends, allies and companions. For a time I was very happy again. I immersed myself in the reconstruction movement, and I spent all the time I could spare and refreshed myself greatly with her. She, too, was busy with her profession; she was doing fine work and becoming well-known, and almost from the first we had to fit our times rather carefully to get together as we did. But to begin with we did not mind that trouble.

How easily can we fling one common name over different things and believe they are the same! I suppose everyone would say that with Clara, with Sirrie, with Helen, just as with the chance love affairs that have happened to me, I was a lover and the business was love. So far as the chance love affairs go, they had many things in common—the furtive elation, the gratified senses and vanity; but all these three relationships, these relationships that signified, were unique in root and branch and substance. With Clara I was animated by the sexual egotism of the young man, with Sirrie by a profoundly tender protectiveness, with Helen by the glamour of a beautiful personality. Only when we began to be estranged did I realise the hold her quality had taken upon me and the depth of my feeling, my utterly irrational feeling, for her.

What a lovely thing Helen was—and is! She not only evoked and satisfied my sense of beauty in herself, but she had the faculty of creating a kind of victorious beauty in the scene about her. She had a vision that transformed things, annexed them, and made them tributary to her magic ensemble. It was our custom to snatch a day or so and go off together from my business and her career, and I do not remember a single place we ever went to that did not reveal, through her, the most happy and wonderful qualities. It was as if the countryside turned out to salute her.

We frequented the Thames Valley, and I shall never go there again for fear of finding the soft morning mists over the brown mirror of the water, the deep shadows of the trees, the tall attendance of the still poplars, and the brightness of the little inns all disenchanted. There is a small, squat hotel under the shadow of Corfe Castle. Is its sunlit garden of flowers among the grey stones the loveliest in the world? I remember that it was. I will never risk a disillusionment. I will never drive my car again through old Wareham's streets and along that white causeway beyond the prehistoric earthworks and so to the Swanage Road. That was the way to Corfe and to a walk over the grassy hills above, commanding vast distances of marsh and woodland and inlet, that touched the heavens of loveliness. Thrice we went there. There is a great park near Tunbridge Wells and an inn with some quaint armorial decorations of gates and chains; is it the Marquis of Abergavenny? I think it is the Marquis of Abergavenny. That also is an enchanted pavilion. A tall, broad-browed, smiling woman will haunt that place for me to the end of time.

I remember, too, an inn that cannot really exist, but I remember it as out beyond Staines and Egham—the inn at Virginia Water. One goes southward along a broad tarred road, bearing red omnibuses and charabancs and tradesmen's vans and tooting motor-cars and motor-bicycles and bicycles, a dusty din of traffic hurrying to no end of places. That stream flows on into the twilight and presently, with an outbreak of headlamps, far into the night. It is as modern and prosaic an improved and enlarged motoring road as can be. One comes upon this inn I write of at a dip in the road; comely enough it is and busy all the day with excursionists and trippers, but apt to become empty and quiet after sundown. At night the passing headlights flare upon its face, and its face is very still.

One descends to be welcomed by an easy, accustomed waiter. It seems no different from a score of such good wayside inns. You do not see at first what it and the tall trees about it are hiding. But there is a great winding artificial lake there, a queer freak of George the Fourth's. It stretches away with wooded islands and a further shore of woods for six or seven miles into the Windsor Great Park. This is the Virginia Water. It is not without some daylight vulgarities. There is a cascade of the utmost artificiality close by the inn, and further away some quasi-classical ruins, made of polished pillars and marble capitals that were stolen from Greece in the great days of Lord Elgin and intercepted royally on the way to the British Museum. These are unimportant accidents. By day the trippers swarm about them and gape and go away, and more trippers come. In the evening all that is changed. The black knots of trippers vanish before the gloaming. Sounds of the road become quite remote and negligible. The stolen ruins are wrapped up in a deep blue veil and disappear. Perhaps they are carried away. Perhaps they go back to haunt their proper place in Greece. Imperceptibly beauty prevails and is presently discovered enthroned. The still water reflecting the slumbering trees and a hemisphere of afterglow becomes a magic mere in a world of infinite peace.

" Death will be like this," said Helen, standing white and shadowy beside me. " With the high-road we have left—near and yet—suddenly—quite away from us. Perhaps we shall come to a place like this some day, my dear, and we shall scarcely realise we are dead."

" The high-road matters no longer," I said, and believed it as I said it.

I had a new and interesting car in the garage behind us, and some faint memory of its presence may have passed by me and faded into the shading tranquillity about us.

Our hands touched.

" We have done with the high-road to-night," I said.
' I wish we had done with it for ever."

How vividly I remember that quiet moment side by
side, and how passionately I longed later to recall its
quality! And yet it was as unreal as a picture painted
on glass. It was a picture we had found to buy and hang
up and presently forgot. It was the loveliest shamming.

We stood in silence.

" What a scene this would make!" said Helen in a
voice that was almost a sigh. . . .

How vividly, too, do I still remember her shadowed
face as she watched the reflections from the wavelets
dance upon the brickwork of a bridge across the
Thames.

She had discovered that there was a definite pattern
at play in them.

" Like thoughts—with a sort of order, a sort of logic,"
she said, and it seemed the wisest thing I had ever
heard said.

How was it that at times she could say such things?
She did say them.

I thrust an oar into the reasoning liquid and turned
its argument to quivering ecstasy. The reflection danced
upon her face. And I, too, was all a-quiver with love
for her. . . .

But such memories as these will mean little to the
reader. It is only for me that they are charged with
beauty. They have the intense, irrational significance of some of my childish memories. There were
moments, many such moments, with Helen that seemed

to be worth all the rest of life put together. Inexplicably and incommunicably.

And we quarrelled and parted. We quarrelled and parted because neither of us, when we were put to the test, would consent to regard these moments as worth any interference with our work and the things we wanted to do. We did not really apprehend them as real. We could feel together, but we could make no sacrifices for our feelings. Ours was an intensely sympathetic and an intensely selfish fellowship. We were exacting with each other and grudging.

I confess I had little respect for her work, and she regarded mine as coldly. What was this making that I found worth while? What was this business of producing strange and untried materials from which ten thousand beautiful devices and creations could be wrung? She could not and would not understand. She thought one did such things to make money. And then when one had made money one sought the proud and magnificent Queen who satisfied pride and dispensed happiness. Her imagination lived in a world of brave men and beautiful women, and would have no other.

I could as little understand her ambitions. The exploitation of a personality in public was a thing incomprehensible to me. She, on the other hand, was the conscious priestess of her own divine qualities, her grace and dignity, her wonderful voice, her power to evoke the lurking emotions of her audience. She could not see what better rôle there was for me than to be her champion and supporter in this lovely self-absorption.

I put our antagonism plainly here, but it was not apparent in our earlier relations. It came into them by little degrees, and surprised and amazed us as we discovered it. At first we were greatly in love with each other in the sense that we felt an extreme need for each other. It was from my side that the first revelation of dissevering motives came. But when I had been with her a little time, and when I was fully assured of her, then aglow with happiness and fit and energetic, I would hear the call of my business operations and of my political interests as a call to self-completion. All the other women I had ever had to deal with since I became an actively prosperous man had accepted these inattentions and disappearances as things in the course of nature. I had been used to go away to my real life. But my going away, becoming customary, must have impressed Helen as the supreme outrage. Because, you see, it was not that I went away to see to tiresome, necessary things; that might have been forgiven. But I went away to things because they were more important to me. She was incidental and they were essential! It was incredible. Could anything be more important in life than the service of personality and the mood of love?

I knew I was costing her tears, but I could not suspect how much I hurt and stung her. She was not jealous; she was too magnificently sure of herself to be jealous; but she was superbly angry. I threw her back, amazed and wounded, upon her own proper work. She had loved me, she had made me her lover, and I was only half a lover. She had sailed into life very bravely and confidently, and a perfect lover had seemed one of her elementary rights. I had failed to be the perfect lover.

I am telling all this with the utmost simplification, but to tell it in any other way, to relate comings and goings, moods hidden and betrayed, insensible changes of attitude, would mean an inordinately long and complicated story. It would need the intricate faithfulness of a Henry James. I doubt if I could retrace my steps through that maze. At first I was stronger than Helen, and I was overbearing with her and thoughtless and cruel. But she was younger than I was and with greater powers of variation and recuperation, and a time soon came when she was stronger than I.

The life of any actress is a life of uncertainties. Now everything falls away, the sense of frustration and failure is overpowering, and the poor lady is beyond measure miserable. This is the lover's moment, to console and sustain, to make life worth living. Then, quite irrationally, things conspire to make the actress queen of the world. She blazes into success, her personality is illuminated and admired from every point of view, she is talked about, sought after, she blossoms gloriously. The lover must run in the shadow then, carrying the cloak, ready for the moment when she will have to go out of the warmth and light again into the chill.

I perceive that always it was impossible for me to have been a worthy lover of Helen. In Paris—or, at any rate, upon the Parisian stage—there is the sort of lover I ought to have been. And there are such men—indubitably. But there was something in me, whether it was innate or the result of my upbringing I cannot tell, which declared that though I found Helen almost intolerably lovely and necessary to me, I would be damned if I waited about for her in the shadows with a cloak. And there was something equally powerful in her which insisted that, although she was intensely fond of me and fond of my company, she would not bother her head for a moment about me while she was actively warming her hands at the great blaze of applause and adulation she had lit. Meanwhile there were quite a lot of arms ready to hold the cloak in the shadows, and many intimations of consolation for me during these periods of neglect.

I had seen very little of the world of theatrical folk before my relations with Helen took me into it. I found it saturated with an excessive self-consciousness, with a craving for strong unsound effects; its lack of intellectual conscience continually amazed me. It was pervaded by sly and hovering young men and by habitually self-explanatory women who made up their personalities as they made up their faces. It never seemed sure whether it was smart or Bohemian. It affected a sort of universal friendship and great liberties of endearment. It sat about at unusual hours and gossiped and talked about itself, endlessly, emptily. And collectively it was up to nothing at all.

At first I could not believe it was up to nothing at all. For me the theatre hitherto had been something to which one went occasionally and contemptuously, preferably to see something laughable. I was prepared to concede there was a serious drama, outside my range of attention, but I did not really believe in its existence, I merely avoided dispute and inquiry. I liked and admired Shakespeare, though I did not find anything fundamental in him; I regarded—and I still regard—most of the popular fuss about him exactly as I regard the popular fuss about the smile of the Prince of Wales. I mean, there is about the same amount of original judgment in both these cases. The rest of the Elizabethans I thought to be highly artificial or rather drunken or delirious stuff. I liked a good many English and French comedies from Congreve and Gay down to Barrie and Noel Coward. I lumped Ibsen—except for *Peer Gynt*—with Pinero and Jones and all the other " serious " dramatic shams of the Victorian time. I knew that such people as Granville Barker read lectures about a National Theatre and produced intricate and industrious plays to substantiate their talk; but that mattered as little to me as the Turf. Shaw alone I read with interest, a perverse but entertaining Manichean, an elusive wit, who took refuge from solid, sober expression on the platform or behind the glare of the footlights, and then repented and came back in a preface to say plainly all he had not said plainly—a preface that itself became forthwith as tricky as a platform speech. But always in the clearest, easiest English prose that was itself a delight to me.

Now with the advent of Helen I did my best to modify these views and believe that behind the " Drama " was some reality that could be correlated with my general vision of life, just as I assumed that within her was something fine and immortal that also could be correlated with that general vision. I tried to impose a grave attentiveness to things theatrical upon my unformulated sub-conscious conviction that a show is a show and the stage of the very slightest importance in serious human activities. I went about as far as possible with the air of a man who regards the Theatre as a great human institution.

I became more and more like a playwright soliciting the great actress with an inappropriate and unattractive play. My play, which I had been working out all my life, was the drama of our whole universe, the soul of man growing conscious and wilful out of nothingness under the silent stars. I wanted Helen, with her grave beauty, her air of tender wisdom, to be a heroine in that eternal play. But Helen had no suspicion of the existence of that drama, could apprehend no hint of it. Her idea of a play was one with a sustained series of emotional states and a crowning situation that would do justice to her fine voice, her lifted face, and the inimitable gestures of her arms and hands.

Absurd that two people so incompatible should have clung together, with conflicts and quarrels and partings and reunions, for nearly six years! My own obsession I can understand, but I have no inkling of hers. Perhaps she realised her peculiar hold upon me, and knew that such a power might never be given her again over any other man.

My love for her and my jealousy of her deepened together. I was jealous of her, not on account of any rival, but on account of the world of display that was taking her away from me. From indifference I passed to an irritated detestation of most of the people who gathered about her, the serviceable young men, assiduous dear Bobby This or dear Freddy That, who were always free to fetch and carry for dear Helen because they were doing nothing that mattered, the over-familiar journalists who intimated by a sort of cringing patronage how necessary they were to her publicity, the little agent fellows entangling her in vexatious agreements, the galaxy of women intimates who consumed dear Helen's time with lunches and confidences, the large, idle, rich men exuding vague suggestions of taking a theatre for her, the men of letters about town who lifted her reputation to the higher levels of culture, the hostesses with an air of helpfulness in their stupendous exactions, the intrusive Americans coming frankly and blankly to admire, loudly, interminably, unprofitably— a lengthening, inexhaustible queue of them. I had to wade, ankle-deep, knee-deep, and at last waist-deep in this swamp of people to have any time with her at all. I performed incredible gymnastics of civility.

Year by year and month by month I saw her subdued to the likeness of this crowd, becoming more insolently assured of its incense and attendance, less and less free for any privacy and depth of living. If at first I had gone away from her overmuch, she, as her successes grew, became more and more deeply embedded against me. And yet we retained an obstinate attraction for each other. I had long days of anger and frustration, and then an hour or so together would silence every discord. By act and letter we could slight each other unendurably, but we could not continue to quarrel face to face. Her smile enchanted me, and she had a habit of affection for me.

Yet we had some sharp encounters.

"Damn that telephone!" said I, in her flat.

"Oh!—*you* want a slave in a harem. . . ."

"You ought to make your private secretary your mistress," she said, coming back from her conversation. "Then she'd be always at your disposal."

"You will end by marrying your impresario."

"Well, I may have to. If I can't manage him without it."

Anger.

"He'd know his place. He wouldn't make me cry. Why do I stand you? Why on earth do I stand you? Why do I let you bully me? Nobody has ever made me cry but you."

It was a ridiculous and pitiful situation. Our several careers, our several conceptions of what was good in life, a deep obstinacy in both of us, tore us apart inexorably, and yet we had a primitive and essential affection for each other. For the reader this can be nothing but comedy, but that does not alter the fact that these things wrenched me abominably and hurt her very greatly. We were not only hurt but perplexed by ourselves. That quarrel in her flat recalls another preposterous occasion. We had gone to an inn near Petworth for two or three days, and she brought down a new play by Lawrence Lath with her, an utterly empty play, twenty thousand words of smartness, called *The Golden Woman*. She was learning her part; she was full of little ridiculous problems; how to treat this foolish line and what action was best to bring out the flavour of that. Consultation was imposed upon me. An exegesis of Lawrence Lath!

" I can't stand this rubbish," I protested. " It is cheap, knowing, vulgar—Rue de Rivoli. Why have you got yourself mixed up with it?"

" How can I learn my part when you talk like that?"

" Why are you in the position of having to learn such a part?"

" It's a part. My dear, what does it matter? I shall come right through it."

" And what do you come to when you come right through?"

" Is this to begin all over again?" . . .

" And meanwhile have I no existence? Is there nothing in me, no obligation to call me away from this—this vacant pleasantness?"

Helen became an indignant queen and the manuscript part of *The Golden Woman* a sceptre. " Go back to your money-grubbing!" she cried.

" I'll go!"

" Go!"

A sudden appeal to high heaven for justice against me. " And I have to be ready with this for rehearsal to-morrow afternoon! How can I *think*? How can I do any decent work?"

We broke off with each other and repented and came back together again with tears and tenderness. We renewed our conflicts. There loomed up a tour in South Africa for her, a tour which might extend to the United States and become indeed a conquest of the Anglo-Saxon globe. She would cease to be an ordinary human being; she would become as universally visible as some celestial body. I protested selfishly and savagely at this vast separation.

"Your wife is dead now," she said suddenly. "You could marry me."

"What difference would that make?"

"We could go about quite openly. We could travel together."

"You mean you would give up the stage?"

She appealed: "What would be left of me if I did?"

"You mean I am to marry myself to the theatrical profession and follow you about?"

"You put everything in such ugly fashion. I am asking you to marry me. . . ."

She became obsessed by the idea that I must marry her, and then "everything would be different."

It was only too plain to me that nothing would be different. We parted again with some heat and bitterness and had a second inconclusive reconciliation. I had never before begged for mercy from a woman, but I confess I did from her. What did I beg of her? That she would be in some profound and fundamental way different, that she should not be herself in fact, in order that I should be myself. What did I really want of her?

There were times when I behaved like a thwarted child. She had become a habit of mind with me. I beat myself against her. I stopped thinking about things in general. I neglected business. She had got my imagination so entangled with her that for a while it would not serve me for any end of my own. I came near to a complete surrender and to giving her a marriage that would have done nothing at all for either of us. And then, filled with wrath, not so much with her as with myself, I set myself, sullenly and steadily, to break those humiliating and intolerable bonds.

I told her that now at last we had come to the end of our relationship.

We parted in a phase of grim anger—and she started out upon the subjugation of South Africa.

How completely had this hard, ambitious young woman changed from the dark, tall girl I had loved! And how swiftly so soon as she departed did she become again the dark, tall girl I had found so splendidly lovable! How I longed to hear her voice once more and see her again with my eyes! Directly she had gone I was asking myself why I had let her go. I forgot that for three years she had been going away from me far more than I had been going away from her, and it seemed to me simply that I had let her go. The love alone was remembered; the quarrels all forgotten. Why had I let her go?

And at the same time, cold and clear in me, disregardful of my general tumult and dominant over all, was my decision that we had to part.

§ 13

I WAS left in England with my nerves, my personal pride, and my imagination jangling unendurably. Gusts and eddies of unreasonable anger whirled about in a vast loneliness of spirit. I did my utmost to pull myself together, and for a time I could not do so.

This phase of distress is still very present in my memory. It seems the worst phase I have ever been through, and perhaps it was the worst phase. The perennial conflict in my nature between sensuous eroticism and creative passion had come to its ultimate crisis. I had made my last attempt to reconcile them, and it had failed. I had decided for creation and broken my servitude to this romantic love, but at a price. My will went about now with a white face and no power to do anything further.

The universe said to me in effect : " You are founded on sex. All you call life is founded on sex. You have been given the woman who is the loveliest woman in the world so far as you are concerned, and you have refused to give your life in return. Very well, you suffer. You have some gimcrack idea of getting the best of me, me who made you yesterday, me who need not trouble to destroy you because of your own self you die to-morrow. Success is yours and the beauty of that woman might still be yours. And yet you cannot be content until this gimcrack idea of service rules it all. You have a sense of obligation! What sense of obligation? To whom? You insult my gifts. Victory and possessions, women and spending-power are all the gifts there are for men, and all these have come to you. Not good enough for you! Then somewhere beyond sex and hunger you must find the thing you need. I cannot give it you. Go your way, but I doubt you will end your life on a pillar like St. Simon Stylites, cut off from earth and not much nearer heaven!"

For a while it seemed to me that I had at last brought my life, outwardly so successful, to a revealed defeat. My will was crippled by the strength of this desire for Helen that I had still in me; it had exhausted itself in the effort to break free from her, and I was left incapable of any vigorous initiative, neurasthenic and suffering.

I thought of making a tour of the world to get away from the thought of her, but I knew that flight would accomplish nothing real. It would mean at best the stupefaction of fatigue. The other end of the world had no secrets and no releases for me that were not also in London and Paris. Excitements were mere temporary refuges; I might as well take to drink or drugs. Flight was not to be thought of, therefore; I had to sit down in front of this desolation and dig myself in and fight and beat it. I had to set my scattered thoughts in order and arrange my work for the last years of my life.

I had become so used to the delight of Helen's company, her voice, her careless close affectionateness, that all the world seemed haunted by her. For five years I had never been outside the beaten track of business except to go with her. I had been moved neither to happiness nor anger except through her. I had referred my pride to her; she had been my sufficient satisfaction. In England I was quite unable to escape from my memories. I went abroad. I wanted something which might excite and revivify my imagination. I thought I would go to the meeting of the Assembly of the League of Nations in Geneva and interest myself in such hopes of world peace as that gathering could afford. I flew thither on a private plane from London through a great storm of wind and rain that fell from us like a cloak as we crossed the Jura; and that at least was entertaining.

It was the year when that queer, vain, simulacrum of a statesman, Ramsay MacDonald, was posturing with poor Herriot as his rather abashed protagonist. Mac-Donald played to an imaginary audience, a Victorian audience that had been dead five-and-twenty years. Herriot and he, he intimated, were two great, noble, and righteous men in an otherwise wicked and foolish world. He made dramatic scenes with Herriot, holding out his arms to him from the rostrum and almost embracing him. Mighty things were to be done against " the powers of darkness." Beyond that he was vague. His second in command, Lord Parmoor, amazed the gathering by a display of simple evangelical piety unusual in European statesmen. I sat with cramped knees in the stuffy gallery of the Assembly and listened to the slow unfolding of these discussions that discussed nothing, in which there were no exchanges, in which every prepared and inconsecutive speech was duplicated by an interpreter's rendering. I listened. I laughed bitterly at some of the phrases my representatives used.

I could not even be indignant. These political men seemed now all flibber-gibbers and phantoms, who could do nothing but recall the forms and gestures of a life that has passed out of reality. What substance, what nearness was there in all this stuff compared with the substance and nearness of a remembered face?

I went about Geneva in a state ripe for disillusion-ment, and I was abundantly disillusioned. The gather-ing was enormously polyglot and various, and there was a tremendous lot of lunching, dining, meeting and talk-ing, plotting and intrigue going on beside and beyond the formalities of the Assembly. It was too crowded for me altogether. There were deputations of all kinds of odd people seeking all sorts of queer ends. I remember a charming Red Indian from Canada with a wonderful belt of wampum; it was a treaty all done in beads; by it the British Government gave sovereign dominion for ever and ever to the remnants of the Five Nations over a long strip of country running right through Canadian territories, territories in which prohibition and all sorts of bizarre modern practices now prevail. The Canadians were infringing the freedoms of that ribbon of liberty by sending in excisemen and the like. So the Five Nations, with a grave copper face, wampum treaty very carefully wrapped in tissue paper, were appealing from the British Empire to mankind.

Another figure that stands out in these recent memories of Geneva is Dr. Nansen, tall, white-headed, with the big black slouch hat of an artist. I do not know him, but I saw him about everywhere. He was tremendously set, I was told, upon the inclusion of the

Germans in the League of Nations. They refused to come in prettily, and he was spending considerable sums in cables of exhortation to Berlin. There was also a little group of German socialists, sadly, endlessly explanatory of the obduracy of their Government. There was a score or so of shock-headed, bright-eyed boys and girls from some Maori school in New Zealand; they all wore hat ribbons of red, white and blue, and what they were doing in Geneva I cannot imagine. They exercised Swiss curiosity considerably but not sufficiently. I was told by my hotel porter that they were Siamese, and by a policeman that they came from Madagascar, while a cabman said Mexicans without hesitation. After a day or so I never set eyes on any of these Maoris without at once seeking a new point of view from the nearest Swiss, and I never failed to get one. It was the most cheerful item in my Geneva pilgrimage.

There were unofficial as well as official Chinese about. There were Druses with grievances against the French, and Turks and Kurds with grave charges against the British. There was a strong contingent of representatives from the various societies, unions and so forth formed to sustain the League by propaganda. They were there, I suppose, to administer first-aid if it showed any signs of distress. And there was a vast concourse of Americans. One was always coming upon them having large luncheons and dinners and meetings or going for excursions on the lake, in the interests of this League their country had put upon us Europeans and then declined to support. I met scores of them. Brilliant rich girls in enormous automobiles; small, grey, rich men with great retinues of stenographers and secretaries. They were prepared to champion the League of Nations against all comers. They took enthusiasm in enormous volume into the Assembly galleries, ready to endorse whatever happened. A little gentleman named Filene— they told me he was the Selfridge of Boston—had been offering some huge number of dollars for a solution of the problem of peace, and a considerable proportion of the less attractive American men appeared to be candidates for this reward and would at the slightest provocation draw duplicated manuscripts from their hip pockets upon totally inoffensive strangers.

It was sunny and close and dusty in Geneva all the time; there was no air that did not seem to have been breathed several times by every nationality on earth; to respire properly one took a motor-boat out upon the lake or an automobile far up into the mountains. My central memory in the scene is that long bridge which spans the Rhone from the principal hotels to the Assembly. Everybody seemed to be always going or coming over it. There anyone could be waylaid. Heaven knows how many times I myself did not tramp to and fro across it trying to get away from myself to something that would hold my interest.

In any other state of mind I should have found much to watch and think about in that astonishing gathering, but my mind was heart-sick. The Labour Bureau of Albert Thomas was something escaping from the initial foolishness of that polyglot sham Parliament of Mankind, and men like Salter and Maderiaga, whom I met, might have told me, had I been tuned to listen, of many less conspicuous and more important activities that were arising in this meeting-place, out of the mere fact that it was a meeting-place. Some day soon I must go back to Geneva and look at it again from the angle of these things. In a hotel lounge one afternoon I saw Lamont, of J. P. Morgan and Co., and Lubbock, of the Bank of England, sitting together with an air of having met by chance and fallen talking about nothing in particular. Yet these two, while Ramsay MacDonald and Parmoor waved arms and bombinated in the Assembly, were doing things of fundamental importance to human life. And I saw my friend Loucheur, who is now taking his turn—a transitory turn, I fear—at saving the franc in Paris, very busy eating in the Restaurant du Parc, and wondered for a moment what schemes he might have brought with him and why he had brought them.

But I could not induce my distracted mind to penetrate below the most superficial aspects of Geneva at that time. Wherever I was I fretted to be somewhere else, and there was no peace in me. Everything irritated me. This is all, said I, that humanity can muster to make a world order. This is, perhaps, as near as it may ever come to establishing a world state. Compared with the size of the world and the immensity of the problems the League pretends to face, this is a small city and a small multitude of debaters and workers, and yet nine-tenths even of those who are here are trivial, frivolous, dishonest or absurd!

And then in this phase of discontent Helen suddenly came back bodily and took possession of Geneva.

Of course she was away in South Africa, but it

chanced there was a woman about in the town sufficiently like her to play the part of her double. I was lunching with Edwin Mansard at a restaurant on the lake when I became aware of this woman sitting with a man at a table a little way off; she was talking to him, and as she talked her very pretty hand, exactly like Helen's hand, was playing with her roll and the things upon the table exactly as Helen was wont to do. My imagination was so out of control that I could hardly keep my talk with Mansard going for watching her.

My intelligence, my eyes, told me that it was impossible that this could be Helen; nevertheless, the resemblance released a storm of pent-up longing.

"I'm not boring you with all this?" said Mansard, pulling up in the account he was giving me of the International Labour Bureau. I suppose I had answered him vaguely.

"Not in the least," said I. "Not in the least. Go on, my dear fellow." But I spoke with my eyes still on this double of Helen's.

Then with a wrench I turned myself to Mansard's offended face. "You were saying?" said I.

Presently the couple got up to go. She held herself like Helen. She walked like Helen.

With a renewed effort I returned to Mansard.

Afterwards I saw her, high up above me on the balcony of some hotel looking on to the lake. She was wearing a blue dress of a shade that became Helen extremely. Helen had just such another dress, and would lean on a balcony rail and look at a sunset in just that fashion. I stood gaping. I was filled with the fantastic idea of seeking out this woman and getting into talk with her. But this was madness. I pulled myself together, packed up, and fled to Paris.

As I pitched about in the *wagon-lit* through a sleepless night I argued with myself. In some way I must get back my control over my mind and drive my thoughts away from this obsession. I was persuaded that the best thing to exorcise one woman from one's mind is to invoke another, but so far I had not been able to get up sufficient interest in another woman to make love that was in the least degree convincing either to myself or to her.

I found myself envying the good Catholics for whom there were cloisters and retreats, cool, quiet places in which one could escape from galling suggestions and inflammatory reminders, and settle one's business with one's soul, deliberately and definitively. A time may come when we who have parted from the old religions long ago shall also have our retreats.

As the train tossed about, tearing along too fast on the bad French permanent way, with a clumping rhythm of the wheels and strange roarings and echoings as we passed over bridges or through tunnels and cuttings, I found myself wishing there could come a conclusive smash, a wild clatter, blows and crushing impacts, fire perhaps, and one last ecstasy of pain that would take me out of all my perplexities. I have a strong conscience against suicide, but latterly I had been flying a good deal and with a preference for a defective engine in an overworked service in bad weather, and I now realised how this smothered desire for a release was at work in me. It was impatience. It was cowardice and indolence. I knew in my heart of hearts that I was not beaten, that at last I should come out of these distresses of desire and be my own master again and serene; nevertheless, they did so weigh upon me that the chance of death had become a temptation.

I talked aloud to myself in the swaying, jangling, creaking compartment. "Now what are you going to do with yourself?" I said. "What are you going to do?"

Whump, bump, went the train over some points, one was tossed up and jolted sideways, a receding diminuendo of bumps.

There was a beastly contrivance in the compartment so that you could not turn out the light completely. When I turned off the full light a nasty little mauve lamp came on and threw a ghastly pallid illumination on racks and curtains and the greasy shining panelling, and there was no way of extinguishing this.

"What are you going to do? Since there are no monasteries for you, you must go into retreat by yourself. Be a hermit. There were hermits before monasteries. . . .

"What you have to do is to get it plain—write it down. . . . Get it plain. Write it down. Get it plain. Write it down."

I argued the thing out with that accursed railway playing cup-and-ball with me and shaking the teeth in my jaws, roaring and chanting my thoughts into rhythms.

What was wrong with Geneva? What was the good

of turning my back on that attempt unless I had something better in mind? It missed its object, but what was the object it had missed? It didn't deal with realities. Very well, think how men were to deal with realities. That wasn't clear. Then get it clear. No one had got it clear. Then someone had to begin.

If only the train would run smoothly for a moment I felt I should have everything right.

The vile uproar of this train was only an intensification of life. One never had time to assemble one's ideas. Never. One was always being hurried on, always being forced to think in rhythms and refrains because of the beating oscillations of the vehicle. Through it all quivered that idea of a retreat, a hermitage. It must not be a place with a lot of other people. It must be a little house alone. My mind insisted, for some obscure reason, on a little white house, very low and long. It was to stand in sunshine and air. Plenty of air—not like Geneva. And isolated. Far away from people with arguments and irrelevant grievances, wampum treaties and telegrams to Germany; and, above all, far away from anyone who looked like Helen. There I could live very simply for a time. I might look after myself and walk to an inn for a meal.

And there I could have a table—I saw the table, too, very stout and plain—and at it I could jot down all the heads of my difficulties, and balance this against that and *think*. There would be no hurry; day would stretch beyond day. Then I could decide what I meant to do with this universe, which hitherto, it seemed to me, had done what it liked with me.

And there must be no more women in it—no more women.

The engine, as if I had amused it, set up a whooping, derisive scream, blundered clumsily over points, and rushed through a station, and a flicker, flicker, flicker of lights in fives and fives glared and swept and vanished one after another, athwart the walls of the compartment.

I felt that I should never sleep again and that for all the rest of my life my head would ache. My throat was dry, I was excessively thirsty, and my mouth had the evil taste of sulphurous coal fumes.

Nevertheless, it had suddenly come into my mind that I was fighting my last battle with my universe and that I was going to win. Perhaps the metallic uproar of the train had suggested the metallic uproar of a battlefield and stirred some slumbering imagined wilfulness the wartime had left in me. I became militant. I swayed and vibrated through that noisy night, but now, within an infinitude of vain repetitions, I was making definite plans.

Where was I? There were to be no more women at all—no more women. That was it. I was losing all purpose in my life because I had never faced and fought my essential weakness. I must do without women. Henceforth I must do without women. Henceforth I must do without women. Henceforth I must do without women. That is what I ought to have decided in Edenbridge Square a third of a century ago.

I talked aloud against the loud mockery of the train. "This is the end of women. Overdue that! Long overdue! I have wasted time and strength and influence upon them. I deserted science. I deserted science."

My mind held to that. Clara became mysteriously identified with Helen, and Helen with Clara. They were my enemies, my wasters, Alpha and Omega, the chiefs of a great array of adverse women.

" But what are women for?"

I thought for an interval and then raved.

" Never mind. Leave them alone, my boy. Get on with your job, damn you. Get on. Do it, as you *can* do it, alone. Tackle these half-condensed ideas and get them clear. Think it out. Work it out. What else is there to do? What else is there to do?"

The train accompaniment changed into a genial, obstinate, confidential " Get on with your work, *alone*. Get on with your work, *alone*." And then burst into a clatter that was like the laughter of a giant gear-box in hysterics.

" The little white house, anyhow," said I. " And if the worst comes to the worst and the old craving must be drowned again—the brothel in the valley."

For a while I held myself still and stared that mauve light in the eye. Hell will be lit by such little, insufficient, unquenchable lamps. I do not know if hell is hot or cold, or what sort of place hell may be, but this I surely know, that if there is any hell at all it will be badly lit. And it will taste like a train.

I must have slept. I found myself standing up in the swaying compartment, raising the blinds. Trees and fields were visible, hurrying past me. The dawn had come, the sky was flushed and clear. There were exquisite bands of cloud, band beyond band, like luminous rose-coloured knife-blades.

Nothing lasts for ever, I reflected. Presently I would breathe fresh air in Paris, I would hold my head under cold water for a bit, and then for a bath and that cottage, and we would see.

§ 14

I PUT up in some rooms I had had before at the top of the Hotel Meurice and looking on the gardens, and I recall it as a quite extraordinary thing that this fancy of a little white house high up in the hills, where the ordinary passions of life are allayed or forgotten, so comforted me that for a day or so I was almost at peace. And then I began to be troubled by the problem of where I was to find this house and how I was to obtain possession of it. And in the lounge I turned over a back number of the *Bystander* and came upon a portrait of Helen that I had not seen before, and that also ruffled me. It was not Helen as I loved her, but it was Helen looking very magnificent and successful and triumphant, Helen more of a banner and a challenge than ever.

It is queer what limitations there are to everyone's ability. People call me a fairly competent man; I have planned great works and carried through great business operations, but I found myself now quite incapable of discovering any such house as this I dreamt of. I have not that delicacy of touch. I could not imagine how to set about looking for it; I did not know even whether I should look for it in Italy or Greece or Austria or

France, and I felt I could neither secure it nor furnish it and organise its service if I found it. I saw all this as an impossibly complex and laborious task. Largely this was due to my neurasthenia, which deprived me for a time of any power of effort, but it was also due in part to the fact that I had never done any of these things; always before I had got someone to do them for me. I thought vaguely of sending over and borrowing old Deland from Dickon.

I stayed two or three days at the Meurice doing absolutely nothing, and then came a warm, serene and illuminated day, a quintessentially October day that would have lifted the heaviest heart a little, and in the afternoon, as the sun was setting, I turned out for a walk, and I crossed the Place de la Concorde and set my face towards the Arc de Triomphe.

Far away the outline of the great bluish arch stood up without a feature visible against a sky of intense pale gold. The upper lines of the remote, tall houses on either side of it were faint yet clear, the nearer trees very bright and hard and black against their softness. A few lights were appearing in the distant shops and windows; some of the hurrying traffic in the roadway had already lit its lamps. Nearer to me was the space and dignity of the gardens that set back the exhibition palaces from the broad main avenue. What a gracious and splendid vista is that of the Champs Elysées, the finest, I think, in the world! Even the late afternoon loungers seemed tall and dignified as they strolled past.

For a time I was filled with the golden beauty of the scene, and then the faint sadness that lies so close to all purely æsthetic pleasure took possession of me. I reflected again that I was solitary and now not very far from being old, and that I had made myself solitary all to no purpose, with such a waste of will-power that I seemed unable to do anything now to justify my revolt against Helen. I had worked all my days to make myself one of the leading slaves of a great industrial machine that was as will-less as myself. And that was all I had been able to make of life.

It is a habit with me, and I suppose it is with most men, to note the women I pass. It is an almost unconscious habit of observation. Only now and then one notes what one's mind is taking in about them. Then one not only notes but notices. My life has had little occasion for casual encounters, but in some parts of Paris and London at certain hours one is aware that one is walking through gossamer filaments of adventurous invitation, faint elusive provocations, delicate strokes of not too critical approval. These gossamer threads become more perceptible the blanker one's thoughts. " Turn your back on your problems," they insinuate. " And if the problems return to-morrow you may find something else to amuse you."

So in the Champs Elysées I became interested in a graceful woman with a slender neck and a wisp of hair that was darkly ruddy against the light, who was going in the same direction as myself. She was promenading so nearly at my pace that only presently by quickening my steps did I overtake her. She walked easily. But there was that indefinable quality in her gait, a faint aimlessness, I think it must be, and something a little careless in her smart-spirited costume, that told me she was one of those who wait upon the accident of an encounter. She had not put on her clothes for herself or for anyone in particular. When she was still far off I saw her twice turn towards men with the unmistakable forced invitation of her kind and turn away. Then she ceased to heed the passers-by.

Her brows and cheek and chin I discovered as I came nearer to her were prettily drawn. A vague curiosity, the absurd and instinctive curiosity of the wandering male, brought me up alongside of her to see her profile.

So it was I first discovered Clem's abstracted countenance, elfin and pensive, infantile and sage. The uniform amber light revealed her professionally undisguised make-up and robbed it of personal significance. Those dabs of paint and powder were nothing essentially hers; it was as if her face had been ill-treated by some alien thing. Beneath these addenda she was perceptibly pale. She was looking at the great arch and the shining sky, forgetful for a moment of the hungry business that had brought her out, oblivious of the awakening interest of the quite possible Monsieur who was walking beside her.

I do not see why one should intrude upon a woman because, roughly speaking, it is her calling to be intruded upon. She paid no heed to me. I walked past her and went on before her. But her quality remained in my mind.

Old Nature—I sometimes suspect the old harridan of a visible body and a mocking mind—must have been cheered by this new interest of her rebel son's.

He had with immense exertion cast himself off from Woman, and here he was back at the old lure.

Clementina had seemed rapt in the beauty about us. That marched with my mood. And there had been something sad and tired in her abstracted face. That, too, appealed to me. And she was very graceful. Here was an extraordinarily interesting young woman, I said to myself.

"But hadn't I perhaps just imagined things?" said the Vieux Marcheur in me.

So often I have imagined things. I did not want to stare round at her. I dropped back to see if I should still find her off her guard.

She was, and then she woke up to my presence. Instantly her expression changed and her face became a mask, defensive but seductive. She was the woman of her class at the moment of invasion. And her personality and privacy hustled away out of sight. "Ware man!" What sort of loose, detached, occasional male was it this time? Was he of the impossible kind instantly to be got rid of? Or was he to be considered, attracted, dealt with? Two very intelligent hazel eyes met mine, businesslike and scrutinising, under long slanting brows.

I passed muster, I perceived, by such standards as she could maintain. She decided to smile interrogatively, but her eyes remained guarded.

I made up my immediate mind forthwith. For an hour or so I would forget my ache.

"I am all alone in Paris this evening," I said. "Would you care to dine with me?"

"This is very sudden," she answered in English, with a faint accent that for a moment I could not place.

"But will you?" I said, also in English.

"It is early for dinner yet."

"We could walk on to the Arc de Triomphe and then come back."

"Why not?" she said, with no pretence of pleasure.

"There is a comfortable restaurant at the Rond Point, the Franco-Italian. We could dine there."

She aroused herself to appear interested.

"That would be charming," she said.

"I want only companionship," I said, and she looked at me to read the significance of that. "Let me be pleasant to you for an evening."

"As you will," said she, and braced herself, I fancied, for the task of being pleased. Had she been free, I felt, that evening would have been her own.

"You like walking?" she asked.

"And you? You walk too easily and gracefully not to like it."

She smiled with a little less effort. "I could walk for miles. . . . Often I prowl about Paris—for no purpose."

"It is the most amusing city to prowl about in the world."

"There is a cheerfulness. Until the winter comes."

"Even in the winter."

"Even in the winter. If one is warm."

"There is a hard, clear animation on the coldest days."

"When it does not rain. But sometimes in the winter there are days—— When the gutters swill and the river is swollen and watery and Paris is wet and disgusting. Now, at any time, such days may come. And, anyhow, I feel the cold."

I had jumped into the encounter on a momentary impulse, and I had no intention of inflicting myself upon her to any extent that she might find disagreeable. I was buying her company for an evening; that was my conception of the affair. I had to treat her like any other pretty lady I might happen to know except that I must not press my attentions upon her as I might have done upon anyone who was quite free of me. I had no compunction about being seen about with her; that sort of thing has never troubled me. I began to talk of Paris to her and praise the place, its gay urbanity, its spacious grace, its light and freedoms, its brilliant kindness to the stranger. I supposed she was a Parisienne, and that this would flatter her.

But she made it appear that she was not a lover of Paris. "It is crowded. It is full of noises. They talk of the roar of London; it cannot be worse than this. London may roar; Paris—barks. Everything thinks only of itself, and yet everything clamours for attention. And nobody attends. They push against you. Everything pushes against you. I am always just missing being killed by taxi-autos and automobiles."

She spoke like one who was tired and at an ebb.

"But you were thinking Paris beautiful to-night."

"When?"

"Just now when I overtook you."

"No. The sunset made me long for the south. I was dreaming of the warm sunshine down in Provence. Where I spent a holiday—it seems ages ago."

I made her talk; I was surprised by my own interest in her. It was good anyhow to stop thinking about myself—and Helen, even for a little while. In some way I didn't clearly understand at the time this red-haired, pale young woman was also a disappointed and perplexed person.

I have learnt more since. Nowadays I am almost a specialist upon the subject of Clementina. She was the daughter of a Scotch engineer who had worked upon tramways in Athens and Asia Minor, her mother was Greek, and she had had a chequered and polyglot upbringing. She had grown up strongly patriotic both towards Britain and Greece, and she had had the unusual advantage of two sound religious trainings, Greek and Presbyterian. Her social experiences were jagged and distorted by the gradual lapse of the Scotch father from honourable employment into continuous but still dignified drunkenness. In the absence of an income the family, I have gathered, subsisted by the economies effected by the mother. In the distressful years at the end of the war Clementina, who was then one-and-twenty and fatherless, fell in love with an amorous, romantic, carefully beautiful but quite orthodox French subaltern in Athens, followed him to Paris, transferred all her patriotic emotion to France, and all her waning but still considerable gift of faith to the Roman Catholic Church. There was a ménage in Paris which went on rather happily until it

was time for the orthodox French subaltern to marry
the featureless but entirely eligible wife selected for him
by his aristocratic family. The parting was upon the
correctest pattern. He wept very freely and frequently
over Clementina, he contemplated suicide from a safe
distance and found it inconsistent with Catholic principles, he declared he would never love any woman but
her, he promised always to seek her advice and help in
moments of difficulty, and he gave her a ring of no
great intrinsic value that had belonged to his mother
and a quite surprisingly small present of money. He
declared that he would not insist upon her subsequent
chastity, and that he had abandoned any right to do
so, but the bare thought of his being supplanted evoked
passions of such splendour and violence in him, such
tearing of hair, such clenching and waving of virile
fists, that he broke two ornaments in her flat, pawnable
ornaments that under the circumstances she could ill
spare, and departed to his own aristocratic milieu in a
mood of the utmost nobility before she had time to
estimate the dimensions of his parting present. The
Greek mother had already died and left her daughter
a small, untraceable, and possibly imaginary house in
Smyrna. So equipped Clementina had to face the
world on her own account.

In quite a few years she had become a woman of
considerable experience, experience rather than wisdom.
Scotch heredity and Greek heredity do not mix; they
make a sort of human Macedonia, a mélange of hostile
and incompatible districts in the soul. Clementina is
in streaks beautifully logical and clear-headed, and in

streaks incoherently but all too expressively passionate; she is acutely artistic and rigidly Philistine. Flung across this piebald basis are the three great religious cultures of Christendom, not so much following as traversing the racial boundaries. There are chunks of intense Catholic, Greek Orthodox, and Calvinistic feeling in Clementina, pervaded latterly by a broad disillusionment and scepticism.

Her social ideas are also of very confused origin, drawn on the one side from the home life of a high-minded and influential Scotch engineer, whose austere respectability increased rather than diminished in his drunken phases, and from the excellent if extremely snobbish English school in Athens to which he sent his daughter, and on the other from the abundant voluble family of the Greek mother, aunts, cousins, uncles, hangers-on, which infested the sinking home, critically and voraciously, up to the very moment when it went right under water and ceased to be a home at all. She has the defensive disposition due to the mixed and uncertain social status of her childhood; she is alert to detect and resent imaginary slights and insults and to magnify negligencies into cruelties.

Imposed upon her heterogeneous traditions are the impressions and suggestions of two or three European literatures, for Clementina is a swift responsive reader. And then just at a susceptible age had come the dignified and dishonest conventions of Catholic France, which has sanctioned and codified even the fornication of its tenderly fostered but otherwise gallant young men. One must know only the right people; one must behave

with an icy loftiness in the nastiest situations; one must
keep one's wife and one's mistress apart; the meaner
the act the finer the gesture, and so on. So constituted
there was and alas! there still is a very considerable
amount of jangling in Clementina. Through it all, I
declare, runs a thread of gold, which I discovered at the
outset and select as the real Clementina. She is
delightful in that phase and for its sake I am prepared
to accept or forgive all her other phases.

I will not venture to guess what rôle in life Clementina was originally best fitted to fill. She was certainly
not fitted to become, at the age of three-and-twenty, a
brilliant adventuress with no social position in Paris.
There may have been something meretricious in the
Greek heredity, but whenever she was involved in a
love affair that was not an earnest business of body and
soul, the Scotch engineer arose staggering but resolute
and damned it root and branch. She had learnt to
dance beautifully from the charming young aristocrat;
his name, by-the-by, was René, but she always called
him Dou-Dou; and she did her best to make something
more than a sexual liaison out of her affairs with a
series of the kind of men detached young women meet
in dancing places. I am carefully incurious about all
this part of her life; it has nothing to do with me; she
was, I believe, given an establishment and put among
her furniture once or twice, and each time her Presbyterian father or her Catholic puritanism or her fundamental veracity made a shipwreck of the business. Her
native pluck was very great, but there must have been
times when she looked at this amazing universe with

considerable dismay. Where was this sort of thing going to end? And how long would it take before it ended?

There had been some great row just before I happened upon her. Neither Clementina nor I have any disposition to gossip about it, but I am inclined to believe that it was with a rich and agreeable gentleman from the Argentine who had carried his confidence in his personal charm and his general right to do what he liked with his own so far that it had become suddenly necessary to smack his face, throw the more suitable of his presents at him, say a selection of unforgettable things, and depart from the flat he had taken. It was a mess, and there was no going back on it.

Clementina had reverted to a single room in an obscure street and to perplexity about herself and God's intentions. She experienced a great longing for Provence. She had gone thither in the Dou-Dou days. It had not been really smart enough for Dou-Dou, but he had laughed and shown his beautiful teeth; it had been inexpensive, at any rate, and they were able to descend once or twice upon the Riviera coast, where he could display her quality to his similarly provided friends. There had been mistress-parades no doubt in Cannes and Monte Carlo, and everybody had shown off tremendously. All that she had largely forgotten. But the warm and gentle quality of friendliness in this land among the hills had sunken deeply into her spirit.

The better I know Clementina, the better I understand how hopelessly she was caught in a net from the very moment she was conceived. She feels and understands beauty exquisitely; she has the finest sense of intellectual and moral values, and a fire of disorder burns within her that will not let her rest. And also she has a passion for writing poetry in languages whose finer shades of sound she misses or misconceives.

Now in a mood of extreme disillusionment with Paris and all that Paris concentrated for her she was idealising this Provençal countryside and longing to be back there. She was under the charm of a dream of living in some extraordinarily cheap pension, walking, brooding, possessing herself. Then she could think over her life and its riddles; then she could make decisions. In Paris one was hustled from day to day. Things happened to one; one did nothing to determine them. She talked of this dream of getting away as we sat at dinner together with an admirable frankness and freshness of feeling. It fell in very aptly with my own desire to get away.

She might have gone to Provence a month or so ago; she had had money then, a few thousand francs, but she was not the sort of person who could make simple, quick decisions. She had lingered and her money had run out.

She talked easily and unaffectedly in her Scotch-English, a little Frenchified, helped out with French words and phrases. There was nothing common in her voice or gesture or the quality of her thought. Her thought was fine-spun silk, and in that at least there was very little mixture. She was open and wholesome in her mind, very outspoken, but never indecent. She was instinctive enough to know that I had a directness of mind to match her own. She talked of the inevitableness of prostitution in some form for women like herself. She had had no training of any sort, she explained; she was not capable even of hard physical work. She fell into no place. She had no race, no nation, no people, no class. She was the sort of bird that other birds peck at. Her manners were samples, and her social code a patchwork. She had tried dactylography, but she could not spell; she was bored, and ceased to attend to a task at once difficult for her and inane. She was not steady and continuous enough for a workroom. She had been rejected as a governess and as a companion. She was too distinguished for the one and too disrespectful for the other. Marriage of any sufferable sort was hopeless for her. The stage was beyond her. She couldn't act. What else was there to do but trade on her sex? She might be " rescued," but for what? Rescue in France meant a sham penitence, a surrender to the subtle Catholicism that had smiled on her relations with her first lover; it meant a subjugation to narrow and authoritative nuns, scrubbing, meticulous needlework, and being driven and sweated in those close, inevitable economies that underlie all Latin benevolent institutions. She would come out of that worse than she went in— and with her pretty wardrobe scattered and her hands rough and spoilt.

" Nothing for it but the streets of Paris."

" Thank your stars they are not the streets of London," said I. " But aren't there girls in shops?"

"Vendeuse? I'd rather sell myself straightly and simply than give myself in as a tip to my employers. . . .

"There are too many women in the world," said Clementina.

"Too many pretty women," said I.

"I see no advertisements for the plain ones."

I reflected. "Tell me more about this Provence of yours. I am interested. Are there little houses, little isolated white houses that look in the face of the sun and are simple and quiet?"

"White?" said Clementina. "No. They paint their houses pink or yellow. But there are many pleasant little houses among the grey olives, rather *austère,* but always with a *terrasse* in front of them with flowers and trees—where the peasants dine and sit. A Provençal *mas* can be very delightful in its plain way."

"I want a little house," I said. "Let me tell you something about myself. You are bored with Paris, but I am bored with the whole world. I want to get away from it and think. I want a respite for thinking. Every now and then—for I am still a very busy man. I have thought of a little white house in the sun, very quiet and simple. A little white house where I can think things out and recover my will. But I do not know where to go to find it; France, Spain, Italy, Greece? I do not know where to turn for it."

"You might find it in Provence," she considered. "I remember a little place where we had lunch one day, named Châteauneuf, the most adorable of villages. Perhaps one could be quiet and happy there."

593

I had had an idea germinating in my mind for some minutes. It shot up suddenly now, complete.

I broached it. " I think," I said, " I could give you a rest from the streets of Paris. I think I could find you a job that would take you back to your Provence for a time."

She scrutinised my face and waited.

" Suppose," said I, " I made you my house-hunter and sent you to find a little white house down there in Provence."

" Pink is more probable," she said.

" A pretty house, anyhow, tucked away out of sight. With a quiet white room and a table to write upon. To which I could come and go. And if you found me also a discreet servant who could cook and look after me, and if generally you established me there. Could you do a job like that? Can you be practical enough for that?"

" I'd try," she said. " Why not?"

" I have to go back to England in a day or so for some business. I shall have to be there a fortnight or three weeks. But I could give you my address, and you could pack off to Provence at once and begin looking, and when you had looked for a bit write and tell me all about it. Eh?"

" Why are *you* tired of things?" she asked. " You don't have to prowl about accosting people."

" One gets tired. I can't tell you my history now. And it would be unnecessary. And too complicated. But I want that job done for me, and you could do it."

She had dined, and she was warmed by my friendliness. The face that had seemed jaded was now ten years younger and very animated and pretty. " I think I would like to do a job for you," she said.

" Well, do it."

" You would be a pleasant employer."

" For once you need not sell yourself. This is straight employment."

Our eyes fenced. I could not see the Scotsman any-where. " Tell me more about the sort of house you want," she said.

I sketched a house for her briefly, as I desired it.

" I am to find it and arrange it for you?"

" So that I can come and go."

" How could we do it?"

" I shall give you ten thousand francs for the job right away—I will give them to you at my hotel to-morrow—and afterwards you will tell me what your out-of-pocket expenses are, and I shall pay those."

" You mean to give me all that money right away?"

" Why not?"

" But shan't I vanish into Paris with it and never appear again? Shan't I go off and spend it with my *maquereau*? What sort of woman do you take me for?"

" I don't think you will," I said. " For example, you don't keep a *maquereau*. You've no use for that sort of pet. If you do vanish there is nothing to prevent you, of course. I shall have guessed wrong, that is all. I shall have lost my stake. I shan't set the police after you, I promise you. You'll be perfectly free to steal the whole lot of it. I shall have to try some other way of finding a house."

"I will take that job," said Clementina. "You are not the sort of man one wants to vanish away from."

She came to a delicate question with the aid of a liqueur. "I am to live in that house?" she tried and blushed under her paint. She could blush, for all her *savoir-faire*.

"No," I said. "That is exactly what you are not to do. I shall live in that house alone. I want you to take this job as a business job. Forgive me if I am plain with you. I am tired of love affairs, grave or gay. I am near to being old. I am not making love to you. I . . . I have recently had my heart completely and finally broken. I don't see why I shouldn't tell you as much. You had better understand now. When it's mended I mean to keep the vestiges locked up out of harm's way. You said yourself you were tired of that sort of thing. You are going to be my house-hunting, servant-finding secretary. It's a purely business arrangement."

"I wonder," said Clementina.

"This is plain business," I said, "and you will be free."

"Still—I wonder."

"No," I said very firmly, and we smiled at one another. "Does it seem too good to be true?"

"I'll get you the house you want if I have to build it myself," said Clementina in an agreeable burst of approval.

She rested her chin upon her hands and looked at me. It was still all east and south in her eyes, and they were very charming eyes. There might have been no Scotland in the world.

" It can't stay like that," she said.

" I mean it to."

She fiddled with a grape upon her plate. " As you will," she said modestly. " I will try to be a good secretary."

We were now feeling very friendly towards each other. Friendly and rather amused at our strictly defined relationship. It seemed to me that she was disposed to linger, but at last I carried her off in a taxi-auto and dropped her at her obscure address. We did not loiter at her door. I made my parting salutations with a respectful decisiveness and returned to the taxi. To-morrow she was to come and lunch with me at the Meurice and receive her ten thousand francs. She came, very resolute and businesslike. There was just a little more of that tentative lingering, but not very much of it, and then, after a warm handshake, off she went with her money.

But the affair still seemed, I suppose, unsettled and incredible to Clementina. And in a sense wrong. Her father had been Scotch and conscientious, her mother Mediterranean and very feminine. For once the two strains worked together. She had not been gone two hours and I was writing some letters in my sitting-room when there came a *petit bleu* from her.

" You have left me humiliated," it said. " Please come to see me for a little hour before I go south. There is something important I really must say to you."

It proved to be of no importance to this history. She went south, and I returned to England.

The amazing part of the story is that within a week

she had found this delightful Villa Jasmin for me and she had discovered my excellent Jeanne, which are all and more than I could have desired. At times I am tempted to believe that after all there must be a Providence, but one more lax and sympathetic than the nineteenth century supposed. She wrote me several long, charming letters, in a sort of Scotch-French-English, describing her success and asking for instructions, and I astonished her by sending more money to get the garden and furniture in order before I came. So soon as I could get my hands clear I followed her and installed myself amidst her simple and clever arrangements.

But now began a serious trouble that still clouds our tranquillity here. Deep in Clementina's nature is an exorbitant desire to love, a possessive, protective, active and caressing love. She had done her best to lavish it upon the Catholic young officer and experimentally upon a diminishing series of unworthy successors. It was like a beautiful gift garment for which she could find no suitable wearer and not even a peg to hang it upon. This robe of passionate abandon had not been apparent in Paris; it had been packed up and put away, but now it became extravagantly evident in Provence. She declared with plainness and fulness and inflexible resolution that I was the Heaven-sent recipient of that delightful, soft and clinging cloak. She demanded the right to protect and cherish me for the rest of her days.

My own mind was fixed in the idea that I had done with love and love stories. I was kind but hard with Clementina. I insisted, and still insist, upon my inviolate study and my inviolate hours. I do not object to her being the official salaried guardian of my garden and my household, but I make her go on living in the little pension on the main road up the hill, in which, with that small, muff-shaped dog of hers dating from the Dou-Dou days, she had taken up her quarters. After all, it is not ten minutes away, and when it is dark I go with her up through the olives. We lunch and dine together, we go for long walks and keep holiday together, but my life as a whole remains my own. To these terms Clementina agreed with a feminine insincerity that never ceases to encroach.

So we go on. She has stayed on here, and in spite of some dangerous struggles I have been able to sustain my tyranny. We are intimate friends, and for the most part I keep her at arm's length from my personal freedom.

It is not always harmony here. Clementina can display some astonishing moods. The Scotch engineer must have had the devil of a temper, and the Greek mother transmitted a pagan streak straight from primordial times. I feel, too, that there must have been unrecorded odd elements on the side of the Scotch engineer's mother. She was, I guess, an extremely argumentative person. Rhetorically argumentative. Swift and fierce in her opinions. But all the Clementinas are swift and fierce in their opinions, whichever constituent opinionates. Sometimes everything is judged from the standpoint of a château in a backward part of France (Dou-Dou), sometimes from a Parisian parterre (various other authorities), sometimes from the Piræus (mother and the relations), and sometimes from the Longer Catechism. This complexity is perplexing, but by no means repulsive to a scientific intelligence. And in the end Clementina herself adjudicates. Through all these moods and confusions flows—sometimes in the sunlight and sometimes underground—a stream of affectionateness and whim and generosity that is all the Clementina that matters. It makes the final decisions.

There are occasions when I wish she would not ask quite so many questions about this book I am writing or that she would ponder some of the answers more profoundly. And generally that she would construct more of her conversation in some other form than the interrogative. But that is a minor trouble.

I know too vividly how Clementina in a stubborn or a storming mood can disturb and upset this philosophical tranquillity, but I doubt if I begin to estimate how much I prey upon her, what a stroke of luck this freak of devotion is for me, and how entirely she makes things possible here. Here I can come and go, working out the last phase of my life. Here at last I seem to find complete unity and peace of mind. I lead a full man's life here, and yet I exist also in London and at Downs-Peabody quite as fully and competently.

My life has, in fact, been doubled. If my mind stales in Provence, I go to the stir of England again, but I am glad to come back. Always a little more pleased to find Clementina still besieging me. I can appreciate my contentment with this place more easily than I can explain it. There is a novel and peculiar liberty in this seclusion. I am able to think in it without haste or disturbance. One came into the world to think. I am astonished to consider how little I have thought consecutively before I came here. Now I can live for days together without restlessness or urgencies, without invasions or distractions, apart from the world and yet still in the sunshine of life.

This house, this room, give exactly the aloofness and the detachment I was seeking—a detachment so animated and qualified by Clementina that it neither bores nor distresses me. I am never lonely spirited here.

With some hope of results now I can review my world as a whole, balance alien considerations, work out the form of the great revolution that is happening in human affairs and in the human mind. Here I can define at last the Open Conspiracy that arises in the human will to meet and wrestle with the moulding forces of the universe, that Open Conspiracy to which in the end I believe I shall succeed in correlating all my conscious being.

END OF VOL. II.

PRINTED BY BILLING AND SONS, LTD., GUILDFORD AND ESHER